For Rosanne

Life in Harmony

B.K. BERGMAN

Pangloss Sea Books
Los Angeles, California
a Division of VERVETIDE Media
www.vervetide.com

LIFE IN HARMONY
By B.K. Bergman

www.harmonynovel.com

Visit the author website: www.bkbergman.com

ISBN-10: 0615818633
ISBN-13: 978-0615818634

Cover design by the author in collaboration with VERVETIDE Studio

Anne Morrow Lindbergh
"Gift from the Sea"

Simplicity of living, as much as possible, to retain a true awareness of life. Balance of physical, intellectual, and spiritual life. Work without pressure. Space for significance and beauty. Time for solitude and sharing. Closeness to nature to strengthen understanding and faith in the intermittency of life: life of the spirit, creative life, and the life of human relationship

CHAPTER 1

Nothing Michael did made Kate happy. Not that it was his job to make her happy. All her life she had been able to do things herself. What was different about this time? She consoled herself that this time was different because wherever she was so was Michael. Kate knew Michael was a fixer when she married him. When he was only fifteen years old, he carried his mother through her grief after his father walked out on both of them. It was something she always admired about him. Yet Kate didn't need Michael to fix her. She wasn't the helpless victim her mother-in-law had been.

Kate had suffered miscarriages before, but it had never taken her this long to bounce back. The loss of this baby was so final. She was certain the *in vitro* hormones were the cause of the incredible wave of depression that swallowed her up so completely this time around.

From underneath the mound of pillows on their bed, Kate heard something smash against the outside of the bedroom door. Likely another wedding gift relic seized from the hall table was bearing the brunt of Michael's anger. Even with the pillows pulled over her head, the crash was loud. The sound echoed throughout the cavernous modern room that had been her fortress for the past several weeks.

Michael pounded and yelled, but nothing was going to break down her locked door. Kate didn't want to hear any more that he had to say. Why was he yelling? Didn't he know this was the last thing she needed right now? Her mom would have understood.

With thoughts of her mother, Kate's tears flowed freely again. *Where are you, mommy? I need you.*

Kate sucked in a huge breath and screamed into the mattress.

Forced to emerge from beneath her comforting sanctuary for air, she threw back her armor and surveyed the empty, stale room. The blank, pale walls of their undecorated bedroom were cold and gray; colorless reminders of her recent losses.

Michael pounded again and Kate was drawn back to the door.

"Kate, I'm sorry," he said. His voice cracked.

She knew he was disappointed in himself for losing his temper again.

"I don't want to see you," she called out. She readied herself with the bed pillows, prepared for his response.

"Kate! Open the door! We need to talk."

She stayed silent and listened, watching the space between the door and the carpeting for the patterns of light his feet left. Parallel shadows told her he was still there. She heard the door creak as he leaned against it.

"Come on, Kate," he said quietly. "Open up."

She didn't move. She waited on those two shadows and wondered if they would leave. She loved Michael. He had been kind, compassionate, and everything Kate wanted in a husband. Now look at what she had made of him. She wrestled with pushing him away and not wanting to hurt him at the same time.

Following the long silence, he shouted at the door, "Fine! You don't want to talk? I'm out of here."

As the two shadows retreated from the door, Kate panicked. Realizing she'd be alone, she reached out for them.

"Don't go! Don't walk out on me," she said as she opened the door.

Michael was already at the banister when the door flew open. She could hear the car keys in his pocket being tussled about. He was leaving.

Kate walked toward him and he stopped. She noticed the fatigue on his handsome face.

Approaching him with tears in her eyes, snot in her nose and in the same pajamas she had been wearing for the past three days, she grabbed him around the neck and held onto him, sobbing, "Don't leave me."

Putting his arms around her, he said, "We can't go on like this."

"I know," she answered, putting her head on his chest.

When they had met, Kate was working full-time and going to school to get her Masters. She was a strong and confident woman. She was her own person and that was important to both of them. Back then, the two of them could spar and still find their way toward a peaceful resolution.

When Michael proposed, he told Kate she was the most autonomous person he knew. He went on about how his mother had been a slave to her husband even after the divorce. He told her he didn't want a woman whose own self-worth depended solely on her husband. He wanted nothing like that in his marriage. It seemed a perfect match.

There at the top of the stairs, Kate said, "I'm sorry. Just be patient. I don't want to be like this but I can't seem to make it stop.

"But Kate, you've been like this for weeks now. You're not getting better."

"We aren't going to have a baby," she interrupted him and pulled away. "There isn't going to be another round of *in vitro*. Am I not allowed to grieve about that?"

"Yes, I know," Michael answered. "I lost the baby, too. I just can't see what us going on like this is helping. We've got to move forward. I can't do this anymore."

Kate stood back from him. "I think it's great you're moving forward. It's not that easy for me. Can't you be supportive?"

"Supportive? I've been nothing but!" The tone in his voice lowered. "You don't think I've been supportive? I don't have anything else to give and I don't know what you want."

Kate answered quietly, "How about giving me some time? Let me work things out in my own way."

"How much more time can we survive like this?"

Kate didn't know. The immediate response in her head was that there was no fixing anything they had together. But part of her loved Michael and wasn't willing to let him go.

"Michael, I don't know how long it'll take. But every day you're there waiting, hoping for me to be better and I just can't get there. That doesn't help. You can't always be the one to fix me and make me happy. Sometimes things can't be fixed."

"The difference is I can't stay here and wallow in what has happened. I've got to move on. Otherwise…"

"Otherwise what?" she asked him.

"Otherwise, where do we go from here? You and me? I can't go on like this and you need space to be you."

Kate let his words just sit there in the midst of their silence and thought about them herself. Maybe there was nothing to be done. Maybe this was the end. A tear formed in her eye as she thought about how much she had failed. How she'd failed everyone in her life.

There was her father, who had run out on her and her mom when she was still a baby. Her mother, who had wanted more for her daughter than being just a Consolidated Data Manager at some unoriginal company. Then there was Michael. She had taken him from the confident and loving man that he was and turned him into this man who was ready to walk out on her.

As the pace of her tears increased, Michael stepped toward her.

She interrupted him, "Can you please let me be? Please give me some space."

"You want space?" Michael said shaking his head. "I'll give you plenty of space." He turned to walk away.

"Go ahead," she told him as he took a step down the stairs. "Walk out, just like your dad did."

He turned back toward her and shouted, "I'm not my father!"

His volume startled her. Clumsily, she added, "Well, if you walk out then you're just like him, aren't you?"

He shook his head at her. "I don't understand you. What do you want from me?"

"I don't know," Kate said. "I don't want to be like this but I can't make it stop."

Lowering himself, Michael sat down at the top of the stairs. As he did, he put his head in his hands. Kate approached and knelt beside him.

Kate told him, "I'm sorry. Please don't be so disgusted with me that you can't take being around me anymore." She reached for his hand and put it in her own. He looked over at her. Her face was pale, her eyes and nostrils red and her lips puffy, the way they always got when she had been crying.

He let go of her hand and began to stroke her back and long hair. As he did, she took out a well-used tissue and blew her nose. "Sorry," she said, embarrassed by the practicality of the situation. He continued rubbing her back as the two sat there on the top step of the stairs unsure what to do next.

Kate blew her nose again.

"You alright?" Michael asked.

Wiping her nose, she said, "Dr. Roth said it could be weeks before the hormones are completely out of my system."

"I know," he said. "It's okay."

"No, it isn't okay. I want to get better. I do. I just can't seem to move beyond any of this."

It had been over a month since the latest miscarriage. Following the D&C to remove the deceased baby, Kate was told she could stop the once-necessary hormone shots. She was also told that the effects of the hormones would likely linger. Kate was certain this was beyond any reasonable time frame for it to be solely hormonal.

"Maybe you just need to get out of the house," Michael reasoned with her. "You've been cooped up in here for over a month now. Maybe you need to get away from everything that's happening here."

"Michael, look at me. I don't want to go anywhere. I'm a mess." Kate watched as Michael gazed down the stairs at the front door. She knew he was itching to run. She hoped it was with her and not away from her.

"Come on, Kate," Michael said. "We complain we never have the time to go anywhere and right now, we've got nothing but time. You're not expected back to work until Tuesday and I'm sort of between jobs at the moment. What do we have to lose? Nothing we're doing here is working."

Kate felt Michael's hand continue to rub that spot she loved just between her shoulder blades in a circular motion. As he tended to her, Kate watched the stream of light from the window above the front door hit the wall and carpeted stairs below them.

Kate knew he needed the escape. It hadn't been an easy year for either of them. First, it was her mom's cancer and the battle that ended shortly thereafter. Then came the revelation that Kate couldn't have children and the expensive scientific gamble for a baby that wasn't paying off. On top of that was the bankruptcy of Michael's graphics company. His unwavering attempt to make her happy stifled his own happiness.

Kate looked over at his well-worn and handsome face. "Where would we go?" she asked.

"I don't know. I don't care. Let's throw some bags in the car and let the road take us. You know, the way we did back when we were first married. Weren't those the best weekends?"

She listened and watched him. His eyes steady on the door but his hand constantly on her back.

"Okay. Let's do it," she said. "Let's just get in the car and go."

CHAPTER 2

Conversation was kept at a minimum as Michael fought through traffic on the 101 freeway heading out of town. They left with no plan. No map. No destination other than to get out of LA.

Kate only agreed to come out of guilt for putting Michael through so much. She felt she owed it to him. At the same time, she hoped for a sign to help her see a future for herself. With the constant starts and stops of the valley's bumper-to-bumper traffic, nothing felt right. Was this trip just a huge waste of time? Had she made a huge mistake? Perhaps it would have been better for them to go their separate ways. She contemplated life on her own. After all, her mother had lived all those years alone. She was even sure her own grandmother had lived her life alone. The thought of becoming her own woman and gaining strength from independence was inviting.

Hitting Ventura, with the traffic behind them, the sun overhead and the Pacific Ocean in view, some of the tension started to melt away. Kate hated the dance that played out in her head about what should come next. What she thought should have come easily hadn't, and the effects of the disappointment felt more grounded at home. But now on the road with the sun in full effect what seemed certain then no longer did.

From the 101, they traveled farther and farther up the coast, their car swaying with the coastline to the west. Instinctively, they turned north onto Highway 1 in San Luis Obispo, with plans of continuing their coastal skip.

Highway 1 headed straight for the sea before it continued winding north, hugging the coast like a ribbon coming off a spindle. The late afternoon sun shone into their eyes, blinding them until the visor concealed its gaze. Only then was the true beauty of the landscape revealed. Waves crashed against the rocky shore, and pristine vanilla beaches mixed with the greens of California's agricultural empire. Michael rolled down his window to take it all in.

"Ah, that's what fresh air smells like," Michael said.

Kate replied, "I don't smell anything."

"Exactly!"

They both laughed. Misting water from the Pacific blew in the wind like a sheet on a sun-soaked clothes line. There wasn't a house in sight for miles – just the natural surroundings of the great, God-given marriage of land and sea.

"It feels like we're millions of miles away, doesn't it?" Michael asked.

"It does," Kate said.

Kate took a deep breath of the salted sea air with its crisp and clean cooling effect. She closed her eyes. The warmth of the sun united with the wind and sea was intoxicating. Her mind wandered meditatively. She remembered their wedding that June day on a beach in Laguna. She recalled her mom fixing her departed grandmother's antique combs in her hair before the ceremony. Her mom wore her pride in her smile that day. Then there was that tear in Michael's eye that only she saw. She couldn't have imagined a more ideal man. It was the perfect day.

"Thank you, Michael."

"For what?" he asked as he smiled back at her.

"For wanting to get out. For loving me this much. For everything."

He didn't know how to respond. He hadn't done anything to deserve such affection. He allowed the moment Kate was feeling to color his mood and he placed his hand on her knee, knowing this was just an escape. Reality waited for them back at home. This was only a temporary solution to their sadness.

Over the crest of a hill was a grove of eucalyptus trees and sparingly dotted oaks. Dairy cows grazed in grassy fields and turkey vultures circled overhead. At the decline of the hill in a small valley between the rolling hills was a sign: "Harmony 1 Mile."

Kate said, "Look out…harmony is just ahead."

Michael laughed.

Kate watched as the tiny row of buildings, white clusters against the emerald of the surrounding grassy fields, came into view. The insignificant town reminded her of tiny bird eggs huddled together in a nest against the elements.

"I have to use the bathroom. Let's stop," she said.

"You got it," he said.

Barely a dot on a map, Harmony was by far the smallest town either of them had ever seen. With only a single road in town, no signal lights, no gas station, no fast food or hotel, there were just over a half dozen buildings in a valley between the verdant rolling hills and crystal blue sea. Coming into town there was a small green road sign with white lettering that read: "Harmony, Population 18, Elevation 175." Harmony was a blink of an eye along the highway, especially at speeds of over 65 miles an hour. If you missed the one exit, you missed the entire town.

As Michael made the turn-off into town, there wasn't much traffic except for the two cats that sat in the middle of the road. Michael navigated around them slowly. The single road in town ended at a fenced-in pasture, so Michael turned the car around to find a place to park. As he did, Kate noticed a tiny shop at the end of a larger white building which was identified as the "Harmony Valley Creamery Ass'n." The tiny shop, which had been hidden coming into town, had a hand-painted sign that read Gifts from the Sea. In the window were assorted trinkets made from seashells. One of them, an angel with huge white shells as its wings, stood out among the items in the cluttered window.

"Hey, let's go in there. I want to take a look," Kate insisted.

Kate opened the diminutive door to the shop and the delicate sound of bells filled the small space. Inside were two women at a counter. Kate looked over at them and immediately smiled. The woman behind the counter was a petite, frail woman with porcelain-colored skin and short gray hair that she held back with a pearled headband. The other woman seated at a stool in front of the counter smiled as well. With flaming red hair, gaudy jewelry and free flowing caftan, she looked like an older throwback to the sixties. The two were strikingly different but seemed sincerely chummy as Kate spied them enjoying some tea and conversation.

Kate quickly scanned the small shop. It sold mostly tacky ocean-related gift items like seashells glued together to resemble lighthouses, along with the typical tourist fare of candles, wind chimes and, strangely, some religious items. A cryptic quote from Anne Morrow Lindbergh about gifts from the sea was painted on the wall behind the counter. The shop and its artifacts looked as if they had been there for decades, just sitting there waiting for someone to stop in and rescue them.

The older woman behind the counter offered, "Let me know if you have any questions."

Kate smiled and said, "We will." Kate wore a playful smile as she looked around the humorous collection of tasteless giftware.

The woman seated at the counter asked, "Where you two from?" She caught Michael's eye and he answered her, "LA."

She nodded her head as if she knew just by looking at the couple where they were from. She said something to the woman behind the counter in a quiet voice. Kate noticed and assumed the woman was saying something in jest about them being from LA. Hastily, Kate picked up a candle and asked, "How much is this? I don't see a price on it."

The woman behind the counter squinted her timeworn eyes at the object Kate was referring to. Unable to see exactly what Kate was holding, she came around the counter for a closer look. Her shoulders arched forward over her tiny frame, her each step deliberate. She approached Kate and reached out for the item, her hand shaky from old age. "Oh, the unity candle, it's twelve dollars, I believe."

"A unity candle?" Kate asked.

"Yes, for couples getting married in the chapel. I keep them on hand."

The other woman asked, "Are you two getting married?"

Michael answered, "Oh, no. We're already married."

Kate put the candle down and continued looking around. The shop was not as interesting as she had hoped. The older woman stood by waiting to answer another of Kate's questions but there wasn't anything left to ask.

"Where you two headed?" the woman seated at the counter asked.

Michael, bored by the shop himself, answered, "We aren't really sure. We just needed to get away for a while. Can you recommend a place for us to stay?"

The woman answered, "Well, there's no place in town here. You can go on up to San Simeon like most people do or back down to Morro Bay. Doubt you'd make it all the way to Monterey before dark at this hour."

Still unsure, Michael asked, "Anything off the beaten path?"

"Like this place?" the woman asked with a lighthearted smile.

"Yeah, sure."

The woman seemed to come alive. She stood with the clatter of her plentiful jewelry. "Well, down the road, there's an inn. It's real quaint. The couple that owns it lives there too. It's just outside of Harmony Township. Nice enough, though. Quiet. You looking for quiet?"

"That would be nice," Michael answered. He was now leaning against the other end of the counter on his elbow waiting for Kate to say the word.

"Well, you're in the right place. Harmony is very quiet. You rent or own?"

"Pardon?" Michael questioned.

"Oh, I'm sorry. Force of habit, I'm the real estate agent in town."

Kate laughed and everyone looked at her.

"I'm sorry," Kate said, gaining her composure. "It's just, how many houses do you sell here?"

Insulted, the woman answered, "One or two."

"A month?" Michael asked.

"A year," she answered.

The older woman chimed in. "It's a special community here. We all take care of each other. And Raye here finds us just the right fit for our town. She doesn't sell to just anyone. It takes a special lady to do that."

Under her breath, Kate said, "I'm sure it does."

Michael changed the subject. "This inn, where is it from here?"

Raye responded, "This here is Old Creamery Road and the road you came in on is Harmony Valley. Take Harmony Valley until it becomes a dirt road heading east. Go all the way until it ends. There at the end is a residence with a sign that says Acadia Inn – Guests Welcome. Tell Lucy that Raye sent you. She'll make up a room for you."

"Great," Michael said. "What about places to eat?"

"In Harmony there is only one. Hope you like Mexican. Just on the other side of the Creamery building is Juanita's. She's only open 'til about six so you gotta hurry. If you need something open later, being from LA and all, you will have to drive up the highway a ways."

Michael checked his watch. "I'm sure Juanita's will be fine."

The older woman added, "She's got some wonderful dishes there. You won't be disappointed."

Michael nodded and walked over to Kate. He whispered, "We'd better get going. I'm getting hungry. You going to get anything here?"

"I don't know."

"I think we should. Just to be polite," Michael insisted.

Kate went back and picked up the unity candle. "We'll just take this."

Raye looked over at the other woman. The older woman came back behind the counter and wrapped up the candle in rose-scented tissue.

"I don't suppose you have a bathroom I could use," Kate asked.

"No, I'm sorry there isn't one here," the old woman offered.

"Oh, okay," Kate answered. "No worries. I guess I can wait."

Michael added, "Let's head over to that inn, then."

Handing Kate the wrapped candle, the old woman said with a heartfelt smile, "Thanks for shopping with us today. See you soon."

Kate thanked her and turned to head out.

Michael said, "Thank you, ladies, for all the help."

Raye said, "No problem. You sure you have the directions to the inn?"

Michael responded, "I believe so. Just take Harmony Valley all the way…"

Kate added, "…until it ends."

"You got it," Raye assured with a wink.

Michael thanked her again and they turned to walk out. As the door opened, Raye added, "If you're interested, I have a house for sale down the road on your way to the inn. It's on the left side. You'll see the sign, 'Raye's Realty.' Take a look."

Michael turned back and politely nodded. He had no interest in the house.

Kate raised her eyebrows at Michael as they left the shop. They both laughed a bit on the walk back to the car. The street remained deserted with only the same cats still sitting on the pale asphalt.

"Let's go check this place out, the Acadia Inn," Michael said.

Kate rolled her eyes. "You're kidding, right?"

"I think it might be best if we go check in for the night. I don't feel much like driving any farther today. Besides, don't you need a bathroom?" Michael said.

Kate agreed.

Their car inched past the motionless cats in the street. As it did, a dog jumped out from behind the bushes that guarded the town from the highway.

"A dog, watch out!" Kate shouted.

"I see him," he replied.

The dog walked slowly around the car at a leisurely pace. Michael checked his rearview mirror and noticed the cats were completely unfazed by the dog, and he paid no attention to them. The dog went on his way sniffing through a courtyard on the other side of the street.

"Can you believe this place? There's more pet traffic here than cars," Michael said. Kate looked around as they drove past the short row of buildings. "It's like a ghost town," she said. "Not another person in sight."

CHAPTER 3

Michael turned left at the end of the Old Creamery Road and headed east just as instructed. The paved road quickly turned to dirt but the grade on the road was smooth. Stoic oaks with low hanging branches dotted the edges of the meandering road that paralleled a creek. Veiled views of an occasional farmhouse could be seen as they continued on their path. Finally around a bend, the dirt road ended at a chocolate-box house painted bright white and trimmed in deep blue. Surrounding the house like a moat was a fence that had long been overgrown with wild vines of trumpeting blue morning glories. So uninhibited were the vines that they continued north up an adjacent telephone pole and all along the natural channels of the dirt road. The overgrown vines broke only at an opening where a gate had likely once stood on a concrete footpath that connected the house with the rest of the world.

To the right of the two-story house with its spacious covered veranda stood a miniaturized rust-colored barn with its doors opened as it looked to be swallowing a bloodshot Ford pickup in front of it. A hand-painted sign that read "Acadia Inn, Guests Welcome" stood nearby just as Raye had promised.

Michael made a U-turn at the end of the road and pulled in front of the house for a second look. There wasn't another car in sight.

"What do you think?" he asked.

Kate said, "I don't know. This looks like maybe someone's house."

Michael put the car in park and turned off the engine. "Come on. Let's just take a look." He opened his door and got out. Kate followed suit.

Together they walked up the front walkway to the house. Kate spied dozens of bees hovering around the delicate flowers of the vines, their humming chorus the only sound in the afternoon glow.

Just as they got beyond the opening in the fence, a dog made itself known by barking from behind a tall juniper tree on the left side of the yard. The lanky German Shepherd slowly rose from a dusty sleep position, as Michael stopped to assess the situation.

Michael put his hand in front of Kate, preventing her from going forward. The dog's bark quickly turned into a growl.

"Michael, I don't like this."

Michael looked up at the front of the house and noticed the door was wide open with only the wood-framed screen door closed. He called out, "Hello!"

The dog, staying in its place, continued to bark, only now more fiercely. Michael called out again, "Hello?"

The dog took a short step forward and Michael backed up in front of Kate. She whispered, "Let's get out of here."

A motion in the house distracted the dog. It ran to the screen door, looked in and then turned around to bark at the couple from its post at the porch as a woman emerged. She filled the doorway in a housecoat and curlers.

The portly, slightly senior woman opened the wood screen door and said, "Well hello, my goodness, Raye told me you were stopping by Juanita's first for something to eat. I thought I had time to set my hair. What a sight I must be." She pulled on the curlers and put them one by one in her pocket.

The dog stood in front of the woman and barked again. "Baby, you stop that. These are our guests." The woman swatted the dog on his head and tugged at his collar for him to back up.

With the woman's hand on the dog's collar, Michael took a step forward. Visibly, any escape at this point was futile. "Baby?" Michael asked.

"Yeah, he's nothing but a big baby so the name fits. Baby, go see daddy. Go see daddy. He's out back, you big mutt!" She spanked the dog on his hindquarters and the dog ran around to the back of the house toward the barn.

"Don't pay any attention to Baby. He's spoiled beyond any reason. Been that way since Ben died. Beck and me just spoil him rotten. Anyway, welcome to the Acadia Inn. I'm Lucy." She came down from the porch to shake Michael and Kate's hands, still pulling at her curlers.

"Sorry about how I look. Like I said, I thought I had more time. Don't you worry, though. I have the room all made up. I always do. We never really know when someone will need a place to stay, so I keep it made up for guests all the time."

Kate apologized, "Sorry we're earlier than expected."

"Oh no...no...it's no trouble, really. Raye told me about you. Ain't she the nicest lady? Been a real asset around here." Lucy looked around the couple. "Luggage? Do you have any luggage?" she asked with a frown.

"Uh yes, it's in the car," Michael answered.

Interrupting, Kate continued, "You see, we weren't sure if we'd be staying. We had no idea you'd be expecting us."

"Why not?" Lucy questioned with a puckered brow. "Raye told me you were coming. You did talk to her about a place to stay. Didn't you?"

Kate again, "We did. We just weren't sure where we would be staying. We don't want to put anyone out or be any trouble."

"It's no trouble. You see, Raye called me as soon as you left Ruth's shop and told me you'd be on your way. She doesn't send everyone our way, you know. And we don't advertise."

Michael interjected, "So you have rooms available?"

Lucy replied, "Of course. We always have room."

"Okay, then let me grab our bags from the car."

"Michael?" Kate asked as she looked back at him. She wasn't really sure she wanted to stay the night in a room in a stranger's house.

"I think it'll be alright," he said. "Besides, you need a bathroom."

Lucy added, "Sure, got flushing toilets and everything. Beck just put in new commodes last month. Darndest things though, they're low flow, so depending on your needs you may have to give it a couple of flushes. And besides, there really isn't anything anywhere near here as hospitable as the Acadia."

Michael touched Kate's arm to reassure her.

"Shall I call for my husband, Beck, to help with the bags?"

"No, I've got it," Michael assured her.

"Well, then," Lucy motioned to Kate. "Why don't you come into the house, give the toilet a whirl and I'll get you signed in."

Kate reluctantly followed. She looked cautiously at the house. The house looked well-tended, so it seemed safe enough. They certainly were out in the middle of nowhere. Kate reached into her purse to check her cell phone. It figured – no reception. Lucy told Kate, "Oh, those darn things don't work out here. No worries, though. You can use the phone in the house."

Inside, as the two women were standing over a writing desk, Michael appeared with the luggage. He was breathing heavily from the sprint he made to the door in order to avoid the dog. Lucy looked over at Michael bemusedly and said to Kate, "Here's the key to your room. It's the one at the top of the stairs. No numbers. You'll know it. It's the one with the blue heart on the door. Oh, I'm sure you'll find it lovely. It's our best room."

Kate said, "I'm sure it's fine, more than fine, lovely." She took the key from Lucy and noticed the key chain also had a blue heart on it. *Charming.*

Michael said, "Let's get settled. I want to get to dinner before it's too late." His breathing began to resume a normal pace.

"The stairs are back toward the front door and down that hall. Be sure to let me know if you need anything else," Lucy said.

Silently, Michael led Kate down the narrow hallway. At the foot of the stairs, he came face-to-face with a leathery older man wearing jean overalls and a red cap. His sudden appearance startled the couple. The man smiled and said, "You must be Michael and Kate. I'm Beck, Lucy's husband." The man reached out his stiff, rugged hand and grabbed Michael's, shaking it with both of his own, nearly knocking Michael and the luggage to the ground.

"Glad to have you here. Need any help with those bags?" Beck asked.

"Oh no, I've got it," Michael answered, regaining control of the bags.

"Say, how long you two staying? Could I barbecue something for ya?"

Kate explained, "Well, we're actually planning to hit Juanita's. Heard it was the best place in town."

"It's the only place in town," Beck said. "I can't eat there myself. Mexican food doesn't sit right with my old digestive system. Sometimes it's so bad Lucy makes me sleep out on the back porch with Baby," the old man said with a laugh.

Michael looked around for the aggressive dog. "Where is Baby, by the way?"

"Oh, he's around here some place. Don't worry about him, he's harmless. Say, what brings you two to town?"

Kate answered, "We don't exactly have any plans. Just wanted a quiet getaway."

"You know, let the road take you where she wants to go," Michael added with a smile.

Beck looked a little curious. "Why is it you city folk always have to get away? I don't understand it. Lucy and I have lived in the same place all these years. We never needed a getaway. We are where we want to be. I don't understand why you would live in the city if you need to get away from it so often."

Kate answered, "Well, you know how it is. You go where the work is."

"My dear lady, I think you have that backwards. I think you go where your heart takes you and the work follows."

Michael felt the need to interrupt, feeling any such argument Kate made at this point would be fruitless. "Well, anyway. I suppose you're right. Who has to get away from the getaway?" Michael said. No one laughed. "Well, we'd better get moving, since Juanita's closes soon. Nice meeting you...Beck."

Michael moved his left shoulder forward and pushed passed the man on the stairs. He grabbed Kate by the hand before she could say another thing.

Michael pulled her up the stairs. She tried haphazardly to stay on her two feet at this pace. "Michael, slow down."

He paid her no mind. As they reached the top of the stairs, he let go of her hand. "Come on. Come on," he said. Kate stared at him with a puzzled look on her face as she fumbled for the key.

"What was that all about?"

Michael panted, "Just trying to avoid...the dog."

"You've got to be kidding! The dog?"

"I don't know. I'm hungry and, frankly, I didn't really want you to encourage him. He seemed like the type that would have kept us here all night, and before we know it, we're eating chipped beef on crackers at the kitchen sink."

Kate laughed as she opened the door to their room.

The room was decorated in tasteful pale blue with white accents. The bed was made up with a cottony soft, handmade quilt with patterns of rings on it. The room itself looked to be the master and had an adjoining bathroom. It was clean and very simple; tasteful, and not tacky, as Kate had expected. The room had a view out to the front and Kate could see their car and the bend in the road down to the creek. It was as rural a setting as she had ever seen and like nothing she'd ever pictured for a getaway. It was surprisingly peaceful and not as creepy as she had imagined. Plus, Lucy seemed nice enough. Her hospitality reminded Kate of her mom.

"This isn't bad. It's actually quite nice," Michael said, plopping himself on the bed. "Comfy."

Kate nodded as she looked around in subtle agreement.

"What?" he asked.

"Nothing."

"What do you mean, 'nothing?' I know you. There's something."

"No," Kate said as she looked for a place to sit down. Noticing an easy chair next to the front window, she sat down in it.

Michael sat up on the bed, "Kate, I know you. What is it? Don't make me have to pull it out of you. Tell me what you're thinking." His frustration showed in the lines of his face.

She was silent for a moment. "It's just....it's just not what I was expecting."

"What were you expecting?"

"I don't know. Maybe something different, you know, more coastal. Something near the water."

Michael leaned over to the window. "There's a creek down there somewhere. We have water." He said it with a smile.

Kate shook her head at him.

Michael continued, "I know. I wasn't expecting this either, but what were we supposed to do? It was as if we were trapped. She seemed so excited to see us."

Kate knew he was right. Once they got out of the car, there was no way around it. Things just seemed to move on their own.

"It's nice and clean at least, right?"

It is," she said, assessing the room again. "It's charming."

"It's definitely unexpected. Isn't that what we wanted, to just take off and let the road lead us?"

"It is. It really is," she was convincing herself.

Michael got up from the bed and walked over to Kate in the big easy chair. He got down on his knees and kissed her lips softly. They kissed for a minute or two before Kate turned her head. She was uneasy with his advances. Michael knew she didn't want the kissing to lead to anything more. But, he wasn't expecting anything. He just wanted to kiss her.

It had been months since they had been together. The last time they had sex was the night before the *in vitro* procedure took place. It was more of a ceremonial session because Kate had wanted it to seem as if they had made the baby themselves. She'd wanted it to be as close to the real thing as possible. That had been the last time.

After that, the medication Kate was taking made her sick and she was never in the mood. Then after losing the baby, she felt uncomfortable in her own body. Her ability to produce a child was the most basic function of her body, she reasoned, and she couldn't even do that.

Michael had given her the space she'd needed. His attempt to kiss her was not because all had been forgotten. He was kissing her now because he was taken by the setting, and by Kate's beauty. Michael pulled back without saying a word. He didn't apologize this time.

Kate got up from the chair and began rifling through her suitcase. "That restaurant closes at six. We'd better get going."

Michael crawled over to the bed from the floor and leaned against it. "Sure," he answered. Without another word, Kate took her makeup case into the bathroom and closed the door.

CHAPTER 4

Finding Juanita's wasn't as easy as one would assume in such a small town. The restaurant sat behind the Creamery building and not next to it as it had been suggested. The undersized restaurant itself hid in the shadow of the monumental anchor of the town in front of it. It was nothing more than a rustic lean-to against the Creamery's solid walls and foundation.

Michael opened the door for Kate and she walked in first. The café was small by all visible standards. On the right were three small stools at a counter. Opposite of that were two small tables.

Inside, Kate immediately noticed another couple at the table farthest from the door. The man, facing the door, made quick eye contact with Kate. He was purposely bald, tattooed, and he wore several piercings. The woman with him had hot pink hair that had been shaved around the bottom half of her head but she had her back to the door. They were the type of couple Kate would associate with Melrose Avenue but not small town nowhere.

The man's attention toward Kate waned. It appeared the couple was engulfed in a heavy conversation. The man became visibly animated even though their voices at the table were still inaudible. The commotion between the two was enough to keep Kate's interest.

A clean-cut short Hispanic teenager came through a backroom door and smiled at Michael. He was carrying two plates over to the only occupied table. "Go ahead and have a seat," the man said to Michael. "I'll be with you in just a moment."

Michael looked around. The tiny café left little room for privacy or options.

Michael whispered, "You want the counter or the table?"

"I guess the table."

They sat down at the table. Michael sat with his back to the pink-headed girl. He had glanced over at her as he sat down and raised an eyebrow at the sight behind him. Kate shook her head no.

"You alright?" he asked.

Kate whispered back, "I don't know." She motioned with her eyes to the couple behind him. Michael chuckled.

He whispered back, "We're from LA not the Midwest. They're nothing we aren't used to."

Kate kept to her quiet tone and answered, "I suppose you're right." It wasn't their appearance that held Kate's attention. It was that they didn't seem to be enjoying themselves.

The waiter came up and greeted Michael and Kate with a flashy smile. "Welcome. Can I get you a beverage?"

"How about two cervezas," Michael answered.

"No problem, sir," the boyish young man said with a charming dimpled smile. "Our nightly menu's on the chalkboard by the counter." The boy pointed to the blackboard that listed "Tonight's Menu" at the top.

"Our menu changes nightly," he continued, "depending on what my mom's got in her head to serve. We've got some great selections prepared tonight and in case you like what you have tonight, you can come back tomorrow and they'll be our lunch specials." The boy shined another one of his flashy boyish smiles. "Take some time and I'll get your beers and some chips and salsa. I'll be right back." As he walked away, he turned back and said, "Of course, we're small enough here that you can yell and I'll hear you just fine in the kitchen."

"Thank you," Kate said.

The boy immediately went behind the counter to a fridge and popped the tops on two bottled beers and brought them back to the table.

Michael grabbed his beer and took a swig. "That hits the spot. I could get used to this pace – low and slow." He looked over at the menu. "What do you feel like?"

"I don't know," Kate answered.

Written on the board were five selections; tamale pie, chicken enchiladas, chile colorado, shrimp tostadas and albondigas soup. The menu listed that all entrees were served with beans and rice, fresh tortillas and salad – all homemade.

As the couple looked over the menu, their waiter brought back the tortilla chips and salsa and asked, "You ready?"

Michael looked at Kate and Kate back at the board.

"No hurry," the waiter said. "I'll come back. Take your time."

He then went over and checked on the couple at the other table and the man at the table said something to the kid in a deep raspy voice. Kate wasn't able to hear it but she strained to listen anyway.

The waiter said, "No, no...you're family here in town. I understand. Don't worry about it. You can get it to me when you can. Mom won't mind."

The man said something else.

The boy then said, "She'll probably tell me that I should have told you not to worry about it at all. You know how she is."

The man mumbled something more and the waiter laughed. He looked over at the woman who said something quietly. "You got it," the boy said and then turned back to the kitchen.

"I think I'm going with the chile colorado. How 'bout you?" Michael asked.

Kate turned back toward the chalkboard. "I think I'll go with the enchiladas." She then turned back to the other couple. The woman had slammed something down on the table and the man said louder, "Not here. They're tourists."

Michael raised his eyebrows at the commotion while grabbing for another swig of beer.

The woman then said, "Why is this the only place we ever go?"

The man shushed her.

"Don't do that. I'm not one of the kids. You can't shush me."

"They can hear you," he said trying to keep things calm.

Michael and Kate didn't say a thing. They just listened.

"You think I care?" she said getting up. Her utensils fell on the floor in a clatter. "I can't do this anymore. We never get out of this pointless little town not even for dinner. I'm tired of it." Michael turned toward her as she grabbed her purse from the floor, turned and walked out.

"Tess," the man yelled, standing up. He didn't immediately go after her.

As the girl headed for the door, Kate looked right at her and for a split second the two women's eyes met. Kate could see she was very young. She could also see she had been crying as she dashed out.

As she did, the young waiter came back in. "Everything okay?"

The man stood there and apologized.

"Hey, no worries," the waiter said. "I know it hasn't been easy."

The man quickly walked toward the door and as he did, Kate looked right at him. His eyes met hers again and his hard exterior seemed to melt as a look of sadness covered his face.

"My god," Michael said to Kate. "What was that all about?"

The waiter heard Michael and looked over at Kate. He approached the table.

"I'm so sorry for that. I hope you're okay," he asked.

"We're fine," Kate said before Michael could answer. She then asked, "Is she okay?"

"Honestly, I don't know."

"You know them?" Michael asked.

"Oh yeah, they're local. It's a shame."

"I hope she'll be okay," Kate said.

"Me too," he said. "She just had a baby and I guess she's not dealing with it well for whatever reason. We'll have to see how it turns out...anyway what can I get you two?"

Postpartum. Kate understood its effects even though her own outcome wasn't as blessed.

"You okay?" Michael asked.

Kate shrugged her shoulders. *Am I?*

Michael reached across the table and grabbed her hand. His touch was reassuring.

"It's going to be okay, Kate," He said to her with a smile. She flashed him one of her appeasing smiles.

Kate wondered how two women with such different outcomes could share such similar feelings.

"Come on, Kate," Michael said, "don't do this. We're here to let go of it and that's only going to work if you let go of it. Even if only for the weekend."

Kate knew he was right. She grabbed her beer and forced herself to let it go.

The rest of the dinner went without incident. The addition of several more beers helped. Kate let her problems go and put some distance between the past and this getaway.

Michael and Kate stayed there talking and even laughed like what had been trouble for them in LA was long behind them. Truthfully, they both knew it was the effects of the beer but neither one of them cared. They talked while the kid cleaned up for the night.

CHAPTER 5

The next morning, Kate woke up first. She was surprised at how well she'd slept. Being the only guests, there was not much in the way of commotion. Both the silence of the valley and the comfort of the cottony bed allowed her to put much that circled in her head to rest.

She looked over at Michael still asleep, a pillow over his head in an attempt to block out the morning sun streaming in through the thin white curtains. His body facing her, his shirtless torso still got to her. She quietly slipped out of bed in panties and a t-shirt, walked across the room toward her suitcase, grabbed her bra and a change of clothes and headed for the bathroom.

Kate took her time getting ready. She did her hair and makeup and hummed the whole way through. The single frosted window streamed in a sunny glow to the bathroom. Brushing her teeth, she noticed the pale pink color of the paint. It reminded her of her mom's bathroom growing up. Times she'd watch her mom ready herself for the day. Her makeup, her perfume and jewelry all symbols of the womanhood that Kate someday hoped to be a part of. She'd dream of being a mom herself someday. The pale pink of the bathroom connected Kate to a happy memory.

The sound of the water running in the bathroom jolted Michael's attempt at furthering his sleep. He stretched out his hand to the cold side of the bed and realized Kate wasn't there. Rolling over, he reached for his watch on the nightstand. Squinting to make out the numbers, he couldn't believe his eyes. It was nearly twelve o'clock.

Michael sat up, looked around the room trying to avoid the shards of light from the large picturesque window.

He called for her, "Kate?"

There wasn't an answer. He realized he needed to get in the bathroom so he stood up and headed over in that direction. As he did, he came in contact with the large circular mirror above the dresser. Seeing himself in only his boxers, his age was immediately noticeable. The roundness of his belly and rolls over the top of his shorts seemed a disgrace to what he had once been. Any attempt to blame it on the lack of sleep he received was futile. Even well rested, he was sure he'd look older. He heard the water turn off in the bathroom and then heard the sound of Kate humming. He froze. Kate was humming?

With the pressure of his bladder encouraging him to knock on the door, he couldn't. He hadn't heard Kate hum in months. He didn't know what brought it about and didn't want it to stop. He took a step closer to the door and the old floor boards creaked under him. As they did, her humming stopped.

He knocked on the door, which Kate opened.

"Good morning," she said looking him over.

"Morning. How did you sleep?" he asked as he passed her on his way to the toilet.

"Quite good."

"Really?" he asked as he stood over the toilet.

"That bed was awesome. Plus, I think the heaviness of the food last night and quiet of the surroundings really helped."

"I couldn't get comfortable. Then that blasting sun came streaming in so early. Some black out shades would be nice."

"I don't know. I like the hominess of this place."

Michael looked over at Kate as he finished up. He couldn't tell if she was kidding. Seeing her face in the mirror as she applied makeup told him she was serious. He flushed the toilet and placed his hand on her to get her to move over slightly.

"Well, I'm glad you slept well. I need to take a shower. My neck is killing me."

He reached behind the pink shower curtain and turned the water on. Feeling the water, it was quickly tepid so he undressed and got in. Kate watched him from the mirror as he did.

The couple emerged from their room with their suitcases in hand. Seeing a grouping of family photos in the hall near the landing to the stairs, Kate stopped as her attention was drawn to two in particular. One appeared to be Lucy on her wedding day; the other featured Lucy with a young boy, most likely her son. He looked just like her. Kate was mesmerized by Lucy's noticeably genuine smile in each picture.

Another more recent photo depicted Lucy and Beck with their grown son on his wedding day. The three stood with the bride, each one smiling that same valid smile of happiness. Then Kate noticed the triangular-folded American flag in the glass case that hung next to a photo of the same young man in uniform.

"Come on Kate, I'm starving. We missed breakfast I'm sure. I hope we can get something for lunch."

Downstairs, they were greeted by a cheerful young woman. "Well hello, you two must have slept well," she said. She looked to be in her twenties with golden brown hair, a simple smile and uncomplicated complexion. The cheerfulness she exhibited was almost sickening to Kate.

Michael asked, "Sorry, what time is check out?"

The young woman answered with the hint of a southern accent, "There's no standard time here. You're fine."

Kate asked, "Where's Lucy?"

"Mom went into the city. She needed a couple of things so Dad took her into SLO, you know, San Luis Obispo."

Michael nodded as if he had known what SLO meant.

"So Lucy's your mother?" Kate asked.

"Oh, not really. She's my mother-in-law. I was married to her son, Ben."

Michael paid little attention. Kate, knowing full well the answer, asked, "Are you divorced?"

"Oh no, I'm a widow. Ben died a couple of years ago. He was a soldier. When he died, I came out here to live with them. I was raised by my Gramma and she died long before I met Ben. I was on my own before I met him. Lucy and Beck, they're my family now." There was silence between the two women for a moment.

The young woman continued, "Golly, where're my manners? I'm so sorry. I'm Danielle, but everyone, and I do mean everyone, calls me Danny." She reached out her hand to shake theirs.

Kate extended hers and responded, "I'm Kate, and this is my husband, Michael."

Michael said, "Glad to meet you." He turned to Kate and said, "I think I'll take the suitcases to the car. I'll be back."

"I'll bet you two are hungry," Danny said.

Kate answered, "Yes, but we don't want to be any trouble."

Michael went out the front door and looked around for Baby. This time, Baby ran happily up to him. Michael was relieved. Baby followed him to the car, his tail wagging.

Danny guided Kate into the living room, where a freshly set table awaited. "It's no trouble. Lucy expected you both to sleep in."

"Yeah, I don't know what got into us. We never sleep this late," Kate answered.

"It's the Harmony air. Seems city people always sleep in out here. I know I did when I first arrived and I'm not even from the city. There's a peacefulness to this place, don't you think?"

Kate nodded and asked, "Where are you from?"

"South Carolina. That's where I met Ben. He came into the restaurant I worked at while he was stationed there. He was so handsome. I couldn't take my eyes off him. And he was the same way with me. Practically ate there breakfast, lunch and dinner when he was off post."

Danny turned over the dust-free, upside down plates on the table and poured juice in glasses. Kate moved closer to the table as Danny continued, "And the food there was just awful so I know he wasn't coming in for that." Danny stopped what she was doing to think about him for a moment. "He always sat at my station and always left me a big tip. He was crazy like that. He finally got nerve enough to ask me out. I was dying for him to ask me. I said yes so fast he didn't know what hit him."

Danny went into the adjoining kitchen and promptly returned with a tray of muffins and placed them on the table. "Six months later we were married. Lucy and Beck flew out for the wedding."

Kate asked, "How long were you married?"

"Four years, nine months and six days. He was killed in a training accident. One of those freak things. Still he'll always be a hero to his mama, daddy and me."

Kate was surprised by her candor. Danny continued, "Hope you like banana nut muffins. Well, even if you don't, you'll love Lucy's. Everyone does. I can whip you up some eggs if you'd like."

"Oh no, the muffins and juice should be fine."

"How 'bout some coffee? I've already got it made," Danny said with a smile.

"That would be great."

Michael returned from outside to the set table and sat down. Danny returned from the kitchen. "Can I serve you both some coffee?"

Michael grabbed a cup off the table and lifted it to her. "That would be great." Looking over at Kate, he said, "It's gorgeous outside. The air crisp and cool. The sun hot. Picture perfect."

"Hate to say it. It's always like that here." After serving Michael his coffee, Danny turned back toward Kate. "Frankly, I was surprised Ben ever left." Danny shrugged her shoulders and continued, "Then again, he did grow up here. It seems like no matter where we grow up we always want to escape, doesn't it?"

Kate nodded in agreement.

"Anyway, since the moment I got here, I've loved it. I feel connected to Ben here. I'll probably never leave – no reason to." There was a momentary pause. "Anyway, I'll let you two enjoy your breakfast in quiet. I'll be in the kitchen if you need anything. I've already checked you out officially. If you'd like, pop your head in the kitchen and say good bye. I hope you two have just the most wonderful day."

Danny smiled and went on her way.

Kate sat there buttering the hearty muffin.

Michael asked, "You okay?"

Kate said, "Yeah, I feel a little foolish."

Michael, "Why's that?"

"Here I am, feeling sorry for myself and my loss. And here's this young girl as happy as a daisy after losing her husband. I just feel thoughtless is all." Michael touched Kate on the arm and then yawned.

"This coffee will do me some good. How about you?"

Kate answered, "I'm well. Actually, I feel surprisingly good today."

"Well, I'm glad."

The two finished the breakfast together. It had been years since they had actually sat down for breakfast together. The conversation was light and genuine.

As they got up to leave, Kate said, "I just want to stick my head in and say goodbye."

"Alright, I'll wait for you outside."

Kate walked to the doorway to the kitchen and leaned in. "Danny, we're going, I just wanted to thank you for everything."

Danny said, "You're welcome." She walked over to Kate and hugged her. It took Kate by surprise. Danny continued, "It was no trouble, really. That's what I'm here for. And if ever you come back this way, please stop in, okay?"

Kate said, "Oh, we will. We'll definitely be back."

CHAPTER 6

Driving away from the inn, there wasn't a cloud in the cornflower sky. The deep oaks were covered in alluring spring green leaves that flanked the drive overhead while tall wildflower grasses adorned the roadside. There had never been a more crystal clear day in their lives. With the car windows down, the splashes of cool air were invigorating. Kate bathed in the concert of warm waves of sun and cold breezes in a ceremony of impeccable temperature. She reached over and grabbed Michael's hand as he drove along the sun soaked winding road. Her hand surprised him. He was glad for her blissful affection but wondered if her mood would last when they returned to the realities of home.

Forging ahead, he asked, "Where do you want to go today? Farther north? Big Sur? Monterey?"

"Oh, I don't know. Anywhere, I guess." Her eyes skipped along the creek, trees and sunny foliage that held their path. The surroundings were reminiscent of the scenery from a luxury car commercial. As the curves straightened out, Kate spotted a lone sign in a thick pasture of high grasses on the right.

She called out, "Look, it's Raye's Realty!"

Michael laughed at its isolation. "Who'd see it way out here?"

As they approached, Kate stole a look at the lonely house Raye's sign promoted. The house with a broken appearance flashed Kate a memory from her past. That single flicker of happiness colorized the present condition of the house for Kate.

The house was a late 1800s design with a small front porch, just big enough for two. It had wood siding and a small stone fireplace that sat off the porch on the north side of the house. It was a forlorn one-story, painted white against the emerald landscape that surrounded it. Kate couldn't take her eyes off it. The remote memory of a house Kate knew as a child was shockingly pleasant. "I wanna stop and take a look," she said without thinking.

"Are you serious?" Michael asked. "It can't be safe. Look at it. It's probably haunted."

"It looks so much like Mom's house. The one she got when Gram died." As Kate talked about the house, visions of her childhood home reassured her. Scenes from a life in a simpler time when her mom was alive and she was as carefree as the summer days played in Kate's head; a swing, the dollhouse, eating cookies at the kitchen table, her mom's laugh, her own laugh. "It looks just like it, Michael. Please, I want to stop only for a minute."

Michael didn't argue. He pulled the car off the road into the long gravel drive that went down to the house. As they approached, the house's state of disrepair seemed even greater. There were shingles missing from the roof, chipping paint and broken windows – and that was just looking at the house from the front.

Michael pulled the car right up to the front steps where Kate noticed a hanging swing on the porch. One of its chains had come off so the left side of the swing dragged on the porch floor.

"Doesn't look like anyone has lived here in quite some time," Michael said. Kate undid her seat belt and opened her door.

"Come on, let's take a look," she said.

"You're getting out?"

"I just want to take a closer look." The resemblance to the house she had grown up in was eerie. There were details, like the swing, that weren't exactly similar, but there was sentiment to the house Kate couldn't ignore.

Kate stepped out and noticed yellow wildflowers pushing between the wooden porch and the gravel of the driveway.

"They're daisies. Mom always planted daisies." Kate marveled as she picked one. As she took a step up onto the porch, the floorboard on the first step cracked. Kate grabbed onto the handrail and twisted around, catching herself before she fell.

"Kate!" Michael called out from the car. He hurried out and went around to help her. Kate laughed, amused by her near fall.

"You alright?" Michael asked.

"Yes, just typically clumsy of me."

"Still, it isn't safe. This place could fall down on you."

"Michael, you're being ridiculous."

"No, I'm not. You never know with these old houses."

Kate ignored him. She skipped the first step, jumped to the second and then third. When she reached the top, she took precautions, as several of the porch floorboards were missing. She made her way up to the large front window. A dusty film coated the panes of glass, obscuring her view inside. She cupped her hands on the sides of her eyes and looked in.

"The fireplace is nice. The house we had didn't have a fireplace."

"Kate, let's go."

Still peering into the house, she answered, "Uh huh."

"Kate, we really should get going. You wanted to be closer to the ocean, didn't you? It's supposed to be one of the most beautiful drives heading north."

"I wonder what it would be like if we lived in this tiny little house – just you and me."

"What's got into you?"

"Just imagine for fun, instead of in LA; the peace and quiet, the sky, the breeze – the calm." She turned back around toward him. "Could you imagine?"

"It would be nice," he said, appeasing her. "But, back in reality, we have a pile of bills waiting for us at home."

"And that huge, empty house," Kate said, shaking her head. "How much is our house worth?"

Michael rolled his eyes. "I don't know. It was appraised at eight-forty, before we refinanced to use some of the equity for the business."

"You know, that place around the corner sold for nearly a million. How much do you think we could get for ours?"

"Our place isn't quite that big and houses aren't selling like that anymore."

"You think we could get maybe at least eight? Or even eight-twenty-five?"

Michael's puzzlement was turning into frustration. With all of Kate's ups and downs recently, it was impossible for him to know what she was really thinking. "I suppose. But you can't be serious. Just last night you hated all of this."

"I know I did, but today it feels different." She jumped down the porch steps with enthusiasm in her eyes. "Let's go look around back." She disappeared around the corner of the house before Michael could stop her.

Michael didn't know what to expect to find waiting around the corner. He hadn't seen her like this in forever. Her lows had outpaced any highs for so long that any eagerness from her was unexpected. He didn't know how to react. Bring her back to reality? Go along with her on this fantasy? It was impossible for him to diagnose. He had been wrong so many times before. Nothing he did helped or made her happy anymore.

In back of the house, torn and tattered screens blew in the breeze of a once screened-in porch. From inside the porch, there was a small door that led to what looked to be the kitchen. Kate tried to see beyond the porch into the kitchen. As she did, she heard the laughter of a little girl. Kate paused for a moment. She thought about how when she was a little girl, she'd sit there in the kitchen when her mom was getting dinner ready. It was just the two of them. They'd sing and laugh. Kate figured the sound was just a memory when she heard another giggle. This time, she paused to listen for it again.

"Is someone there?" she asked.

Kate waited for an answer. A breeze blew through the frayed screens and Kate remained silent. But only the sound of the wind in the nearby trees could be heard.

"Did you say something?" Michael said as he approached Kate near the back porch. Kate stood still listening again for the laughter.

Michael continued, "Would you look at this place? It looks like the last hide-out of a gang of bank robbers."

"Let's go into town and see if we can find Raye. I want to take a look inside." Kate smiled at him warmly. It wasn't her wiles at work, it was sincere.

"Are you okay? I mean, I'm not really sure what is going on with you. Don't get me wrong, I'm thrilled you're enjoying yourself so much. It's just…lately…this hasn't been you. What's going on?"

Kate approached him, "I don't know. Things just feel better today. Maybe it was something Danny said or the breakfast. Maybe even the weather. It put me in a different place. Then seeing this house, it reminds me of my mom's house, of happy times. I just want to see what it's like inside, that's all. We have time. We're heading nowhere in particular. We let the road take us and this is where it has led. I'm curious about the inside. Let me have this. Please?"

Michael couldn't deny her. Frankly, why would he want to? This was making her happy and that in itself was all he wanted. Yet, as much as he bought into the fantasy of Kate's newfound happiness, reality burrowed in and nagged him that this was dangerous. The further he let her play this out, the harder the fall would be. He had just bankrupted his business in their desire to have a baby and Kate's fall was so much worse because of it. Even with this reality harassing him, he gave in like he always did and agreed.

They stopped in at Gifts from the Sea hoping to find Raye there. Kate hopped out while Michael waited in the car. The bells on the door clattered and Ruth appeared from behind the green curtain of the backroom to greet her.

"Well, good morning, how are you?" Ruth asked with a smile.

Kate reciprocated the smile. "I'm fine. I was hoping to find Raye."

"She hasn't come by yet. But I'm sure you'll find her at her place. It's that first house you see coming into town."

"Great. Thanks." Kate flashed her smile at the kindly old woman and left.

The front yard of Raye's barn red house was littered with the tackiest of garden décor. Gnomes, flamingos, windmills and chimes, all formed a line on the picket fence out front. On the enlarged front door was a "Raye's Realty" sign mostly unseen behind a screen door.

Michael and Kate, together, walked up to the front door. Kate peered into the screen but the inside of the house was dark, making it hard to see in. Kate knocked and from the darkness emerged Raye, wearing a blazing golden caftan and matching scarf that held back her dyed inferno of red hair away from her face.

"You saw the house!" Raye said with a knowing smile.

Kate answered, "We were wondering if you could show us the inside."

Michael spoke up, "We're not really serious, just curious."

"Of course, hold on a minute." Raye turned back toward the darkness and picked up the receiver of a cordless phone. "Danny, I gotta run. I'm showing the house." Without a goodbye, she hung up the phone, grabbed her keys, and turned back to the front door to open the screen. "You wanna drive or walk?"

"Walk?" Michael questioned.

"Sure, it's just up the road."

"Can we drive?" Kate asked.

"Sure, but I don't have a car," Raye said.

"We can take ours," Kate volunteered.

As they walked to the car, Raye told Kate, "You're really going to love it."

"We're really just looking," Michael insisted.

"I understand. I do. But better to look than just drive by," Raye replied.

The three of them hopped into the car. Raye slid to the middle of the back seat and leaned up to get between the couple. "You'll find Harmony is a special place. We all know each other around here and look out for one another. You don't find that sense of community in LA, I'm sure."

Michael quickly reminded Raye, "As we've said we're not really in the market for a new house, especially not here in Mayberry." He was doing his best to not let things spiral any further.

Raye answered back, "Fair enough. But I gotta tell you, I knew you were the perfect couple for the house." She leaned over to Kate, "It really is perfect, you're going to love it here."

The wheels in Kate's head began to spin. *Why is this so out of the question? There's no denying we've been down the wrong path already.*

Raye sat back in her seat and checked her hair in Michael's rearview mirror. She peeled the auburn peaks back between her index and middle finger away from the silk scarf that corralled the flames from her sun-browned face. As she did, she casually asked, "So what do you two do for a living?"

Michael, seeing dollar signs in Raye's eyes, answered before Kate could, "I'm actually currently out of work."

Kate looked over at Michael. "That isn't necessarily true. You're working."

"As much as I can...I don't really have a steady job."

"Why would you say that?" Kate asked. Raye glanced back and forth between them both, amused.

"Because it's true. You know we have a mountain of bills at home."

Kate turned her attention back to Raye. "I'm a data manager and Michael's a graphic artist. He was the owner of his own design firm."

Raye said, "Say, that's not too bad."

Michael answered, "My business is in bankruptcy now."

"Regardless, you're both going to love it here," Raye said.

Michael rolled his eyes but didn't say anything. Caught between Raye's sales pitch and Kate's delicate state was no place he wanted to navigate. As he drove back to the house, he shook his head in disgust with himself. He hated how he continued to handle Kate.

Avoiding all the obvious repair issues outside, Raye opened the front door and said, "Welcome home!"

The interior of the house was alluring to Kate. The living room's only large bay window faced west. The ocean, while completely out of reach, was surprisingly visible between the pale green rolling hills in the distance. Between windswept trees, the diamonds of the Pacific danced on the sun's splendor. It was the room's crowning achievement. The practicality of the room was confining. Only a couple of pieces of furniture, not the sectional Kate and Michael currently had, would likely fit.

Raye stood center stage and pronounced, "The fireplace is original. And there's no getting over that view. Best view in Harmony. Nothing in town can touch it. The house sits higher up in the valley." Raye spun around and with a game show hostess gesture said, "Over here you have space for an intimate dining table." She crossed over from the center of the room and led the couple through a doorway. "Through here's the kitchen."

The kitchen was a long galley way. Narrow and lined with a small counter and sink on one side and unoccupied space for a refrigerator and electric stove on the other. At the end was just enough space for a small table for two. The kitchen had almost no cupboard space, but had a rustic farm style copper sink that faced a southern window that looked out toward a pasture.

Raye continued, "The kitchen may look like it has nearly no storage but with the sun porch and pantry out back it's actually more than adequate. With the right color of paint it could be a dream. You're going to love what full sun brings in here. It's beyond a cup of coffee in terms of energizing."

Michael took a look inside the ragged back porch. "There's a lot of work here. Plus, I don't see a dryer hook up?"

"No, just the hook up for the washer, but there's a clothesline out back. You could always get one of those top and bottom units. Or use the clothesline. You know, green is the new thing."

"So they say," he responded. He purposely checked his watch and walked back through to the living room, Raye not far behind him. Kate lingered in the kitchen. It wasn't exactly like the kitchen she envisioned. She visualized the small kitchen table her mom had with chrome edging and the pastel Formica top under the east facing window. She pictured the small girl sitting there making her mom laugh. At that table in her mom's place, the two of them sat the day her mom told her about the cancer. As Kate thought about that, she heard the giggle from the little girl again. This time it seemed close. Kate swiftly asked, "Is someone there?"

"Uh huh."

Kate froze.

"Kate, you coming?" Michael asked from the living room.

She couldn't answer right away.

"Kate?"

"I'll be right there." Kate looked around but didn't see anyone. She questioned it but the voice was so clear.

As Kate walked out of the room, her mom's voice played in her head. "Katie, don't worry about me. The doctor said there's a good chance I'll beat this. I don't want you to worry."

Kate turned back toward the space where she'd envisioned the table and remembered how hopeful her mother was then. How much her mom believed that it was going to all be fine. How happy she tried to look. Then Kate remembered that last day in the hospital and how frail her mom was. Her skin wrapped around her bones. Unrecognizable as a fifty-eight-year-old woman, her hope was long gone. Then, so was she.

"Katie," she'd say, "I swear I blinked and you were grown. How I long for those days when I'd hear you giggle in your little girl way and flash me that smile. All my worries would melt away in that instant and no matter what life was doing to me I could escape it in that moment with you."

Kate's heart warmed as she looked back into the empty kitchen. She took a deep breath to regain her composure before rejoining Michael and Raye.

The rest of the house was straightforward. To the left of the living room was a small hallway that led to two bedrooms. Wood paneling lined both the bedrooms which gave them a cold feel. Both rooms were too small for a California king-sized bed. Each room had a single north facing window but no closet. The closet space had been converted into the indoor bathroom that extended out toward the back of the house and butted up against the sun porch.

The claw-foot tub in the bathroom reminded the couple just how ancient the house really was. There was a pipe on the outside of the wall that snaked up from the tub to the rusty showerhead where a calcified last drop of water was forever frozen on the bottom rim of the head.

Wandering back into the living room, Raye told them, "Since the bathroom, like the sun porch, was an add-on, it's not fully insulated. And I need to tell you this addition is not up to code according to county records. So before the sale is final, you'll have to sign a disclosure stating that you knew the bathroom as well as that sun porch aren't up to code."

Kate asked, "Who owns the house?"

"He's a doctor on the east coast. His mother lived here in this house most of her life. He just wants to sell it for land value to pay off the estate taxes. He never even came out to see the house. Had a company come in and remove all the furnishings and clothes. I do need to mention before I forget that Gertie, his mother, died in the house."

Kate said, "She did?"

"It wasn't anything horrific, she died of natural causes. She was really old. She loved this place. Lived here nearly all her life. Even as a girl."

Kate asked, "Really?"

"Oh yeah, this house was built in the late eighteen-hundreds. It originally had an outhouse. The house was a caretaker's cottage. Gertie's father was the caretaker for a large dairy farm that included most of the properties in this area. Sometime in the forties, the farm was subdivided and the land sold off to other local farmers."

Michael commented, "You certainly know a lot about the history here."

"I have to, since I only sell the one or two properties a year." Raye smiled at Michael. She continued, "As for the history of Harmony, we're not really a town. We're just a small part of the county. Harmony itself got its name when a feud between dairy farmers ended in death. The remaining farmers called a truce and as a symbol of that truce they named the town Harmony."

Kate and Michael didn't say anything so Raye went on. "Just a little bit of town trivia I like to add in so you know you're getting your money's worth with me. Anyway, let me give you two a few minutes to talk about it. I'll wait for you outside."

"We don't need..." Michael began but Kate interrupted. "Thanks. That would be nice."

As soon as Raye was outside, Michael started in. "Excuse me, but what are we discussing here? I thought you were just curious. You know, get it out of your system and we head north."

Kate walked over to the picturesque window. "I don't know, Michael. Am I crazy? I feel like this old house is calling me. Just look at this view."

Michael joined her and they both stared out between the trees and grass at the shimmering horizon. "It is beautiful," he said, "but I don't understand. You know we can't get it."

"I know but...hear me out. What if we sold the house in LA and with that money bought this one? We could sell most of our stuff. Not much would fit in here anyway. What do you think it would cost to get this place in shape?"

"Easily a hundred grand and a ridiculous amount of work, back-breaking work, the type of work that neither of us has ever done before," he answered.

Kate's mind was racing. "A hundred grand, that's not bad. If we sell our house at its current market value that would probably be enough to buy this place and then some. Even with the refi we still have a good chunk of equity, we got that place for a steal, remember?"

"I do, but Kate we don't know a thing about this place."

"Raye said the owner is looking for a quick sale. Why not make an offer?"

Michael stared at Kate. "Honey, with all we've been through lately...this is crazy."

"Is it?" She looked at him wearing all her emotion on her face. "I know it is but something about it feels right to me."

"Honey, I love you, but I don't know about this. What about your job? I doubt very much there's going to be a need for a corporate data analyst here in town."

"Who cares? We'd pay cash for this place and then we'd have no house payment at all. How much money would we need then, monthly?"

"I don't know. What would we do for even the little money we'd need? What jobs are there?"

She looked at him hopeful. "I have no idea, but that's the fun part. Besides, we won't have to decide that for a while. We'll eat cheap, fix this place up, and then worry about getting jobs in town."

"Town? Kate, there are less than eighteen people who live here and less than a block of businesses, most of which are owner-operated. I doubt very much Gifts from the Sea has the need or means to pay someone even part-time to help out. If you sell one twelve dollar candle a day, I seriously doubt there is the need for bringing in additional help. My god, we could have blinked and missed this entire town!"

"I don't care. I don't." She crossed over in front of him toward the fireplace. She ran her hand along the painted wood of the mantel. "Michael, what do we have in LA? There's nothing there for us anymore. My mom is gone and we reached the end of the line for a baby. And your business is gone. I realize that. Can you? Getting away was a great idea. Not just for the weekend but forever."

Michael watched as Kate made her case. Her happiness was melting away and once again being replaced with brittleness. The light in her eyes only a flicker. It was only a matter of time before it would be snuffed out again. She hastily continued, "Michael, I can deal with the fact that we are never going to have kids. I know we've exhausted our options and truthfully, even if we had the money, which we don't, I don't think I could go another round of *in vitro*. I can't. It was just too hard, and having a baby shouldn't be that hard."

She rushed over to him, grabbed his hands and pleaded with him. "I want this. I do. I want to get out of LA. I don't want to work there anymore and hear all those women in the office talking about their kids and daycare. They have no idea what they have. And, I don't want the invitations to the kids' birthday parties anymore. I want peace, and this place offers peace. It has a peace I once felt, and, before you say it, I know I'm running away but so what. When I saw this house everything about it just felt right."

Michael couldn't see an easy way out. Having to face people he knew in advertising again wouldn't be easy. Making Kate happy wasn't easy either. Running was easy. "I don't know," he said. "I want you to be happy, but in this place?" He looked around and a list of repairs scrolled in his head. "I don't know. There's got to be an easier way."

"It's as if this has just all been meant to be. Us being here, me seeing this house, it feels right. It feels like home. Like Mom is here and I'm here and I'm happy. This makes me happy...and excited. I'm afraid if we go back to that oversized, empty house, we'll fall back into that life we were living. I'm afraid of the depression that lives there. And, I'm afraid that eventually it will pull us apart. I don't want that. I want us to work. You're all I have. I don't want to lose you, too."

She reached out and hugged him. He held onto her for a moment before breaking away. She gave him silence to think, knowing he needed time to get to where she already was. Too many words could push him back too far.

Finally, Michael admitted, "You know, the thought of going back to LA and looking for a job isn't exactly something I've been looking forward to. But are you sure you want this?"

She grabbed him around the neck. "I don't know what to be sure of. But this house is calling to me. There's too much here for me to ignore. This is what I want for us, a new beginning."

Michael thought some more before he said, "We'll have to ask them to accept a contingency that the sale is only viable if we sell our house in LA."

Kate grabbed him tighter. "Oh, I'm sure we'll have no trouble. Things seem to fall into place when it's the right thing to do."

"This is crazy!" he told her.

"I know. I know, but it's crazy exciting."

They both walked out to the porch. Raye was leaning against their car. She immediately started in, "Okay, so let's go back to my house and draw up the offer."

"Wait a minute," Michael said. "How do you know we want to make an offer?"

Raye said, "Honey, I had you in this house from the moment I saw you in Ruthie's shop. I knew it was for you."

Michael was curious. "How so?"

"Oh, stop fussin' over the details. If you want to know the truth, I'm psychic."

Kate wanting to believe asked, "Really?"

"No, not really, but I knew you were going to say that." Raye threw her head back and let out a giant laugh. "The truth is I saw you two hugging in the window. I've got most of it all written up already. Just waiting for you to say the word and fill in the details. I'm certain the seller will accept whatever I present to him. Just a couple of things I want to cover with you. The house has its own well for water. Only one telephone line. We don't offer any sort of DSL or IPS Internet, whatever you call it, this far out of town. And, cable TV isn't available out here either. But..." Raye said with excitement, "there's satellite being offered. Except I'm not sure you can get a signal from the house, so we should probably add a disclosure for that as well now that I think of it. Anyway, it's the perfect house for you. You're going to love living here. You really have no idea."

CHAPTER 7

Going from a 3500 square foot home to one with not even a thousand square feet was a huge adjustment. Kate and Michael sold what they could during back-to-back weekend yard sales and donated the rest of what they wouldn't need to a local charity that Michael had done some pro bono work for.

They traded in both their cars and bought a used Ford pickup instead. No longer would there be time-killing commutes to and from work. They even downsized their wardrobe. No more power suits, ties and office attire. They kept only jeans, t-shirts and casual clothing for working around the new house. With the funds they cleared from the equity and minimizing their lifestyle, they had enough money to make the needed improvements to their new home and just enough to live on for about six months.

With truck and rented trailer loaded, they headed out. Traffic on the 134 was heavy as usual. It was midweek and Kate watched out her side window as commuters inched past them. Kate wondered about each person they passed; none looked happy. Many tried to accomplish what they could during their long, stale commutes. Some shaved, read the paper, ate a McMuffin, while others applied makeup, studied reports and talked on their cell phones. All of them with the same look on their face. The look Kate had seen in her own rearview mirror for longer than she wanted to remember. It was no way to live.

Whether it was the stirring anticipation of a new beginning or just a typical California coastal day, the scenery on the way up was better than Kate had remembered as their journey hugged the pallid sand beaches of Ventura. With traffic now behind them, nothing appeared to be holding them back.

When they hit northern Santa Barbara County, they ran into seasonal wildfires along Highway 101. Traffic crawled to a stop, with fires overlooking a ridge above the highway on the right. The couple watched as helicopters with large buckets dipped down into the Pacific on the left and poured a flood of water on the flames, again and again, to aid the firefighters on the ground digging a fire line. With the dark smoke and rising flames to the right, it appeared as if they were passing through hell.

"Is this safe?" Kate asked as she thought about their trailer full of all that remained from their lives in LA.

"The highway wouldn't be open if it wasn't," Michael answered as he watched the action above them.

Kate wondered if sacrificing everything to make this move was the right choice. She didn't dare say anything to Michael about her doubts because she knew she was responsible for it. She didn't want him to hate her for any of this. Hadn't she done enough to make them miserable already? Now they had given up anything that remained, and for what? Her breathing quickened as her fears got the best of her.

"You alright?" he asked.

She took a slow, calming deep breath, trying to be inconspicuous about it. "I'm fine. I just want us to get through this unscathed."

"It'll be fine. Believe me, if it wasn't safe they'd have this road closed. We're going to be fine," he assured her.

Just beyond San Luis Obispo, a sense of tranquility washed over Kate, putting her fears of the moment to rest. They didn't pull off Highway 1 into Harmony until nearly seven o'clock that evening. It was the height of summer, and Daylight Saving Time would give them another hour before sunset.

The town looked smaller than they remembered. As they pulled up to Raye's house to get the keys, she greeted the couple from her doorway with a huge wave, as if greeting long missed relatives. Coming down to the road, Raye hadn't changed – she wore a tribal print robe, a wrap in her hair and a coiled snake bracelet wrapped around her forearm. A couple of other women filed out of the house behind her.

Kate got out of the truck first.

"Welcome to Harmony!" Raye shouted. "This is the Harmony welcoming committee." Michael joined Kate on the sidewalk as Raye introduced the three women with her to their new neighbors.

"This here is Holla. She and her husband, Sunny, run the pottery shack." Holla was a tiny girl barely in her twenties. With a tie-dyed Harmony shirt, peasant skirt and hemp fishbone headband, she looked every bit the hippie that modern times had long forgotten.

Raye continued, "They're both talented people. Sunny's dad ran the pottery shack for a great number of years before he passed on. You'll have to stop by their shop as soon as you can. It's absolutely fabulous!"

Holla greeted Kate with a wrapped gift. Her smile was shy and so was she. In a tiny voice, she said, "This here's a vase to contain all of the earth's natural beauty you can collect, for inside your new home."

Lucy, standing behind her, interjected, "She means flowers, if you don't speak Holla."

Holla added, "It's a gift from a new friend."

Raye was quick to add, "You know, they say friendships are like fingerprints. No two touch you the same. You'll come to find that's true even when there are only eighteen of us."

Lucy pushed her way in front of Raye and Holla to greet Kate and Michael. "So good to see you two again but by God, you both look god-awful tired. That drive from LA is a real pisser. No worries – Harmony will have you rested up in no time. You need anything – anything at all – you give Beck and me a holler."

The third woman stood quietly behind the others, nearly hidden by Lucy's large frame. The couple recognized her from the gift shop. Raye said, "And of course, you two know Ruth from Gifts from the Sea."

Ruth approached the couple with a wide smile, her walk more of a shuffle. Michael watched the other women monitor Ruth's every move. They appeared ready to catch her should she need their balancing arm. Ruth came to Kate and touched her hand, gaining her balance in the process.

"Good to see you again, my dear." Ruth's hands were cool and papery. "You two enjoying that candle?"

At first, Michael and Kate were confused, and then it dawned on Kate that she was talking about the candle Kate had purchased on their last trip. "Why, of course. It's somewhere among all our stuff here in the trailer."

Ruth said, "Good. I'm glad you two have enjoyed it." She squeezed Kate's hand one more time before letting go. Without another word, she turned, putting a hand on Raye and then on Lucy's shoulder before walking back down to her shop.

Raye dug into the pockets of her robe, the pockets so deep she had to bend down to reach what she was looking for.

"Here it is...the key to your home!" She pulled it out and there on a ring was a single key with a strand of beads attached to a white feather. "Holla here made the key ring for you as a gift."

"It's really nothing," Holla said. "Just something I do to pass the time."

Lucy said, "Well, don't let us hens keep the two of you from your home. You have plenty to do, I'm sure. Oh, and don't you worry about dinners. The three of us, along with Juanita and the rest of the ladies in town, have you covered for the week."

Kate said, "Oh, you don't have to go to any trouble."

"It's no trouble. It's what we do in Harmony," Raye chimed in.

Before Kate could say another word, Michael spoke up. "Thank you ladies, thanks to all of you for such a warm welcome."

As they drove up Harmony Valley Road, the house seemed to glow in the shadow of the blazing ginger sun, as it came into view. Michael backed the truck and trailer up to the front porch. Kate could hardly wait. She scurried out, leaped up to the top of the porch and quickly turned the key in the door as Michael followed.

"We're home," she said as she opened the creaky door. Inside it was cold, damp and earthy. With the glowing sun streaming in through the open front door, it was as if life was returning to the house.

That first night proved to be a trying one. Michael laid the mattress down on a bed sheet that Kate used to cover the cold living room floor. The two lay there side by side looking up at the water damaged ceiling. There in the stillness of the house was a crackling sound like that of the silent interlude between songs on an old record album. They listened as the old house settled in around the two of them.

CHAPTER 8

The next morning, the windows were delivered that Michael had ordered a few days prior. It was easily one of the first things that needed to be done. A house with broken windows lacked any security.

As Michael carefully balanced one of the windows on the outside of the house, Kate was positioned inside the window opening to help get it in place. Heavier than he had anticipated, Michael steadied it as best he could.

"Hey let me give you a hand with that!" a shout came from behind. A startled Michael jumped and lost his hold on the window. Beck reached around and grabbed it just in time.

"Beck, my gosh!" Lucy shouted just as loudly. "That was loud enough to wake the dead."

"Nah," Beck said, waving her off. Spying a how-to book sitting on the ground, Beck asked, "You ever done this before?"

Michael replied, "No, but the man at Home Depot told me it was no trouble. Made it seem fairly easy."

"Probably never installed a window himself in his life. You can't trust those superstore clerks nowadays. Next time you go into SLO, I'll go with ya. I'll show you where there's a real hardware store."

The two men set the window down on the ground leaning it against the house.

Lucy called in to Kate. "Well, since you have my husband here, I'm taking you to town."

Kate looked down at herself. She had on her grubby sweats and her hair was pulled back in a careless ponytail. It hadn't even been washed. "I'm really not prepared to go anywhere today," she replied.

"Well, I'll wait. Get yourself ready. I'm sure you could use a pair of hands somewhere in that house. I'll just nose around a bit inside and see what I can do."

"Oh no, I wouldn't expect you to do anything," Kate answered, almost embarrassed.

"I know you don't expect it. But it wouldn't be neighborly of me to sit and wait for you without doing a thing in the meantime. I don't work that way. I gotta keep myself busy." Lucy didn't wait for Kate's permission. Waving off Kate in the window, Lucy headed for the porch. "It's settled then. Go get dressed. I'll keep myself busy inside."

Lucy, with her heavy gait, made the entire porch shake as she ascended each stair step.

"Careful with the steps," Kate called out. "They need to be replaced. It's probably best if you just wait outside. The house is a mess anyway."

Beck laughed. "Don't you worry. We knew the condition the house was in when you bought it.

And besides, without Danny's help, Lucy wouldn't be able to stay on top of our place. Trust me."

Kate reluctantly nodded as the front door flew open. She quickly ran to the bathroom and closed the door behind her.

Beck chuckled and said to Michael, "Well, they'll be out of our hair soon enough. I'm confident that between the two of us, we'll have your windows done in no time. Let me grab my tool box. I'll be right back." Beck patted Michael on the back and then turned toward to the road to get his tools from his truck, which was parked up the gravel drive.

Several minutes later, Kate was ready. Lucy continued to busy herself sweeping up the place. The house was wall to wall hardwood floors. "Sometimes I think wood floors are tougher to clean than carpets. The dust shows so much more. Give me the days of shag carpet. My gosh, you never saw dust, dirt or near anything else in that long nap."

"Thanks for your help," Kate answered, grabbing for her purse.

Lucy didn't seem to hear her. "The thing was with that shag carpet, I can remember Ben's Legos getting hidden in the waves of the long strands. Oh, how it would wreak havoc on my Hoover. Those darn little pieces of plastic. I bet we lost a Lego fortune in that shag. And those things aren't cheap!"

Lucy turned her attention to Kate and gave her an up and down glance which made Kate a little self-conscious. "Well, you ready?" Lucy asked.

Kate hoped she was. "Yeah, where are we headed?"

"I thought we'd walk downtown. You need to meet your neighbors. They've all been asking about you and Michael."

Kate said, "We're planning on going into town once we get things, you know, settled. It's just there is so much to do."

"Oh, no one cares. We're a small community here. Everyone knows everyone. And you've been the talk of town since your last trip. Raye and I were gabbing about it yesterday, so I told her I'd swing by and get you and bring you to town."

Kate thought about the anonymity of LA. Sure, you'd wave to your neighbors in and out of your driveway but that was the extent of it. And most people in LA liked it that way, including Kate.

Lucy continued talking, but Kate wasn't paying attention. It didn't seem to bother Lucy. She just kept right on talking. Kate picked up what she was saying mid-sentence. "…gone before any of us knew it. She'll be missed. Nonetheless, with you and Michael here there are nearly eighteen of us again. No need to change the sign. That's the good thing about Raye, she keeps us busy. Someone moves out or dies and someone else moves in. 'Cept we don't want too many here. You know, some time ago, they wanted to turn this town into a Hyatt. You know, being so close to the coast. Golf course and everything. Well, we wanted nothing to do with that. We all, and when I say all I mean all eighteen of us marched into SLO and told the county we wanted nothing to do with a Hyatt. We liked our town the way it was. Of course, we're not really a town. We don't have no government here so to speak. We kind of make our rules up between the eighteen of us. Whoo! I've been talking non-stop again, haven't I? Beck tells me all the time that I need to slow down. I think I'm just excited to take you to town. Someone new! How exciting that is. It was ages ago I came here and was someone new. Can't hardly remember a time when I wasn't here in Harmony. Anyway, you got what you need?"

Kate slung her purse over her shoulder. "Ready when you are."

"Well, good, it's a great day. Of course, you'll find all days here are..." and without even looking at Kate, Lucy continued to talk as she walked right out the front door and down the steps. Kate followed her somewhat reluctantly. From inside Kate could hear Lucy go on, "Yoo-hoo! Boys, we're on our way to town." Beck hollered something back to her and she replied, "Oh don't mind him, Kate." Descending the porch steps, Kate looked over at Michael. He looked at her and smiled back at her. He wanted to laugh. Kate shook her head at him. Turning back, she saw Lucy was now fifteen feet in front of her, heading up the gravel drive, arms flailing in the air as she continued to talk. Kate jogged to catch up. Michael watched the two women walk down the road.

"Sure is a pretty thing," Beck said.

"Kate?"

"No, silly, Lucinda. Don't know what I'd do without that woman," Beck said as he eyed her walking down the road, hands in motion, talking away. Michael watched Beck looking at his wife. He could see the love in his eyes for the woman he had been married to for what Michael assumed was decades.

Kate and Lucy turned down Old Creamery Road toward town. As they approached, Kate took her time studying the place. The big black and white "Welcome to Harmony" sign on the left was the hopeful speed bump to those on Highway 1 jetting by.

On the right side of the street was the barn red house where Raye lived. Kate could see Raye standing out by her front picket fence talking with some tourists in their car. Lucy waved to her from a good distance. "Yoo-hoo! I've got Kate. We're coming."

Raye wrapped up the business she had with the tourists, and they were off. With Lucy walking down the center of the road, and Kate behind her, the car was forced to go around them. Kate wondered what the tourists thought of the sleepy little town. The fact that they sped back onto the highway was a good indication that they found nothing special about Harmony.

"Well, hello you two," Raye said. "I was wondering when you might make it to town today."

Lucy answered, "Had to wait until she got ready. They were putting in new windows. Beck's there now. He'll have it taken care of."

Raye looked at Kate, "New windows? What a great way to add resale value to the house!"

Kate nodded politely, not quite sure what to say. Raye came through her garden gate and met them on the sidewalk. She and Lucy walked ahead as Kate followed behind. The two women chatted nonstop back and forth as they walked.

In between Raye's house and the old creamery was a tree-shaded courtyard. The courtyard was rich with colorful flower blooms of yellow, orange and purple tucked along tiny paths adorned with benches. Pushed back into the courtyard was the Pottery Shack. The shop was in a good-sized brick building adorned with a tarnished corrugated tin roof. It looked like it had been a milking barn in the dairy era. Just outside the shop were assorted pots, vases, urns – all one-of-a-kinds in rich tapestry colors.

The women turned into the courtyard toward the shop. Raye turned back to Kate. "We'll stop by and say hello to Sunny and Holla. They're second generation here in Harmony." Kate only nodded, unsure of what to expect from her new neighbors.

As they approached the doorway, Lucy spoke first. "Hello! Anyone home?"

Holla was inside arranging pottery in a central display. Holla said in her hollow voice, "Hi there, ladies. Out for a walk I see."

Lucy said, "Nope, we're here on official business. You know, showing our new neighbor around. Well, Holla don't be shy. Here she is."

As Holla approached the women, Raye and Lucy parted, and Holla came between them. Kate reached out her hand to shake Holla's, but Holla came in for a hug. Kate was taken aback by it. "Hand shaking is for strangers. Hugs are for neighbors," she said. The girl's body felt like that of a bird.

Holla wore a peasant skirt with a simple t-shirt with the "Pottery Shack" logo on it that she tied up at the bottom. She smelled faintly of body odor and lavender. "I want you to meet Sunny, my life partner, and our son, Mason. Let me go get them." Holla walked over to another room which was open to the shop.

Lucy filled Kate in. "Sunny and Holla are second generation hippies too. They never married but say they are committed to each other by nature. Which I think means sex."

"Lucy!" Raye shouted.

"What else could they mean? Nature as in carnal nature. Their son an obvious product of that carnal involvement."

Raye interrupted Lucy. "Sunny is our honorary mayor. His father was also a potter and was one of the founders of the artist colony that revived Harmony back in the sixties."

"Well, it's strange to me, and I lived in the sixties. Never had no use for that hippie-dippie if you know what I mean," Lucy said as she raised her forefinger and thumb together to her mouth.

Holla returned, followed by Sunny with Mason in his arms. Sunny wore cut-off jean shorts, tire-treaded sandals and a blue-green tie-dyed shirt with a long beard as an accent around his neck. He was likely only in his late twenties, but the length of his beard and the slightly balding head made him look much older.

Mason was a beautiful towheaded cherub. He looked to be slightly under a year. He wore a shirt similar to his father's and a cloth diaper with colorful coverlet.

As Sunny approached, he handed Mason off to Holla. "Welcome, my sister, to our humble commune." He gave Kate an uncomfortable hug. He too reeked of body odor. "It's my awesome pleasure to welcome you to our interwoven family. I, uh, like to think of all of us as nature's family. And it's great to get another young couple in town."

Raye and Lucy looked at each other somewhat offended. Holla picked up on it. "But all are welcome and play an important part in our community, right Sunny?"

"Oh yeah, absolutely. By all means, we all serve a purpose here. Like gravity we are all drawn to this place for a reason. It's aligned in the stars and the moon holds us in balance. It's totally universal."

Just then a large, loud woman with dyed black hair, a long witch's nose and rows of wrinkles burst into the shop. "Sunny, I've got a bone to pick with you!"

Holla sighed. "What now, Della?"

Della focused on Sunny. "That dog of yours crapped on my lawn again. Now I'll have to insist you keep that mutt on a leash in your own yard."

Holla answered, "He can't help it." Turning her attention to Kate, she continued, "It's just her lawn is so lush and green. It's his perfect place to potty."

Della interrupted her. "It's not going to stay lush and green with crap and piss stains on it. It's already looking spotty."

Raye, embarrassed, tried to calm things down. "Della, now, now."

"Now, now, nothing! I've tried. Lord knows I've tried to make the peace. And Lord knows his father and mother were dear friends to Dobb and me. But for heaven's sake, that dog uses my lawn as his toilet. My lawn! He comes all the way across the highway and Lord knows how he hasn't gotten hit yet. I had hoped it would have come soon enough."

Holla said, "Della, that's not nice. You be nice."

"What? Be nice? I've tried nice with you people. I have. But you haven't done a darn thing about your dog."

Sunny finally spoke up, "Holla, we may not have a choice. We may just need to keep Buddha tied up."

Holla wasn't having this. "Oh, no. We're not tying up one of nature's animals. This isn't a zoo and just because she keeps animals fenced in doesn't mean we have to."

Della looked at Lucy, throwing her hands up. "There you have it. This is why I have to get the sheriff involved."

Sunny said, "No way, Della. I promise you I'll, uh, keep Buddha away from your lawn. There's no need to bring the law into Harmony."

Della shook her head. "You've said that before, and I still have crap on my lawn. I nearly stepped in it myself this morning. Besides what're you feeding that mutt? I thought someone had died the smell was so wretched."

Raye stepped in this time. "Della, we've all got to get along here. Let's give Sunny and Holla another chance." Raye motioned her head toward

Kate who was standing behind the other women to avoid getting involved.

Della hadn't even noticed her. Now that Raye had made her more aware, Della, with her round stomach and high waist band, sashayed over to Kate. "My dear, are you a tourist?" she politely asked with a grin.

Raye answered for Kate. "No, this is Kate. She and her husband bought Gertie's place."

"That place? You bought that place? Probably paid too much for it, too." Della shook her head back and forth. "Tsk-tsk."

Raye jumped in. "Pay her no mind, Kate."

"I'd tell you to run," Della offered. "Run away from this place. There's nothing here worth living for, you'll only be disappointed. Of course, life is nothing but disappointment."

Della turned her attention back to Sunny. "As for your dog. You keep him off my lawn or I'll get the sheriff involved. Oh, how I wish we could settle things like we did back in the day. Back in the day, I'd just take my pistol out and shoot the darn thing – dead on the spot."

Holla was upset. "Oh, Della! How could you even think such a thing?"

"Think it! Honey, I've lived it. I've lived on a dairy farm my whole life. One time, I saw Papa take his pistol to a lame calf. I saw Mama shoot a rat the size of a dog. You do what you got to do to live your life."

It had been a while since Della had gone off the deep end like this.

Sunny tried to placate her. "Miss Della, you have my word. You won't see Buddha on your lawn again."

She shook her head and answered sternly, "I'd better not." She turned her attention back to Kate. Grinning at her, she calmly said, "Pleasure meeting you. If you have the need for any dairy products, our dairy farm is just across the highway. I also own the wine shop in town as well as most of the buildings here. Thought you should know that. If you need anything, give me a call. I'll be as neighborly as possible."

Kate answered her, "Thank you, and it was, um, nice to meet you, too."

Della went on, "This town meant a lot to my husband, Dobb. His family lived here for years. It's too bad I was never able to give him a child. Now, there's no one after me to carry on his family tradition." She looked upward and sweetly said, "Oh Dobb. How I wish I could have given you a son." She then got angry again, and went on, "A son who could work that darn farm and tell the Mexicans what to do. I hate dealing with farm hands. Disgusting people. You don't get the kind of help like you used to." She stopped talking for a minute and everyone was silent. They all hoped she'd leave. She continued, "Well, no need to stand around with you people not saying a thing. I better get back to the shop. You never know when someone might pull off the highway and want a bottle of wine and some cheese to take out on the lovely bluffs. Yuck. I hate those kinds of people. Sappy! But you gotta pay the bills." And with that, Della, with her hands on her high hips, swaggered out of the pottery shop and back down to her own. Everyone could hear her continue to talk to herself. From the sidewalk. "Why Dobb, why?" she repeated. "Why'd you let this town be infested with these types of people?"

Lucy apologized to Kate. "You'll have to forgive her. Della can be rather abrasive. She's had a tough life. Her husband died some six years ago, and she was never the same."

Holla said to Lucy, "A tough life is no reason to be so nasty. It's not good to the harmony of this town, all that bad mojo."

Raye said, "Now, let's not dive into the Della debate again."

"All right," Lucy replied. "I won't say another word about her."

Raye said, "Thank you." Raye then turned to Kate to tell her, "Her husband Dobb's family was one of the last of the dairy farmers from the old co-op that was here. The family owns the old creamery and most of the land around it. Dobb was a good man. He allowed artists like Sunny's father to set up shop here and make a living. He didn't want to see his town die like the creamery had."

Holla added indignantly, "That doesn't give her or anyone else the right to be so nasty. Truly, truly nasty. Probably why she never had children. Karma can be like that."

Holla's words stung Kate but she stayed quiet. She too had often thought that maybe it was something she did in her past that caused her infertility or maybe God knew that she wouldn't be a good mother.

Lucy said, "Well, we'd best be moving along. I know that when Beck and Michael are finished, ol' Beck will be expecting something to eat. I'm sure he'll be sore, I can count on that. Probably want me to get him a bath ready. And I do love bathing a man."

Holla was embarrassed. "Lucy!" she squealed.

"What? I'm a married woman, and I admit I enjoy the sight of my man in his altogether."

Sunny laughed. Now everyone was embarrassed. Raye looked at Kate in awkwardness. She then said, "Well, Holla, Sunny, we'll be on our way."

Kate approached them with her hand out, "It was certainly nice meeting you," she said.

There was no stopping the hug. Sunny and Holla with Mason in her arms approached her. Holla said, "Family hug." And the three of them wrapped their arms around Kate, Holla adding, "Surrounded by a family's love is the heart's security."

Sunny added, "This is awesome. I love family hugs." He tightened his reach in an inappropriate way toward Kate.

Holla proclaimed, "May the warmth of our family's hug fill you with warm thoughts for yours."

It was all overwhelming, both the hug and the smell.

Lucy, Raye and Kate made their way across the courtyard under the shade of a huge flowering tree. Kate studied the buildings closely. All were a mismatched vision of old wood, brick, mortar and stone. The town looked like a patchwork quilt with varied textures and colors. Like the locals themselves, some were young and free-formed. Others were older pillars of the community.

Growing vines of morning glories stretched over some of the older buildings like nature's coat of paint, covering up the rundown parts of town. The courtyard itself was filled with golden California poppies and various other free growing native plants.

Behind the front of the Creamery building, Kate remembered, was Juanita's café.

Raye said, "Let's stop in and say hello to Juanita."

Lucy asked, "Did you and Michael like the food here?"

"Oh yes, Michael loved it. More than he ever liked mine," Kate joked.

The two other women politely laughed. Lucy said, "Wait 'til he gets as old as Beck. Beck can't eat Mexican food for the life of him."

Raye said, "Really, I had no idea."

"Oh, you'd have an idea if you had ever come within twenty feet of our bedroom on a night when he ate Mexican."

Lucy and Raye howled with laughter.

Kate added, "Oh you don't have to be that old. Trust me, Michael does damage himself."

Lucy started laughing so hard she couldn't catch her breath but tried to get out, "Well...it doesn't do our guests...it doesn't do our guests any favors when they stay over. I mean light a candle already." With that, Lucy bent over grabbing her sides with both arms as she let out a huge guffaw. Laughing uncontrollably and bending over to catch her breath led Lucy to pass some gas of her own. "Well excuse me. I guess I can't even get *close* to Mexican food without it affecting me."

All three women screamed with laughter. Kate couldn't remember when she had laughed so hard. Raye was struggling, herself, to stay upright.

Raye said, "Oh Lucy, you crack me up. Where do you come up with what you say sometimes?"

Wiping tears from her eyes, Lucy said, "Well, I don't know. I just say what comes into my head, that's for sure."

Still laughing, the women opened the door to the café and stepped in.

They were greeted by the same young man that waited on Kate and Michael during their first visit.

"Good morning, Miss Raye and Miss Lucy," the young man said.

Raye answered him, "Good morning, Hijo. How are we today?"

"Oh, we're fine. Care for a table?"

Raye responded, "Oh no. We just stopped by to say hello and introduce you to our new neighbor here."

Hijo looked over at Kate and smiled, his dimples in full effect. "Hello," he said.

Raye continued, "This is Kate. She and her husband are the ones who bought Gertie's place.

"Welcome to town," Hijo answered as he flashed his dimpled smile at her again.

Lucy said, "Oh you and those cheeks. Don't fall for it Kate. Hijo here is a terrible flirt."

"Oh, I don't know about that," he said still smiling.

Raye said, "That's how he gets his biggest tips. He learned quickly."

Hijo added, "I think I remember you and your husband being here before."

"You remember us?" Kate asked.

"Sure. It's a small town. Plus that was the night Stan and Tess were in here." He looked over at Raye and Lucy. They both nodded like they knew what he was talking about. He continued, "I'll be sure and remember your name. We're like that around here."

"I've noticed. It's nothing like LA," Kate answered.

"Oh no! It's nothing like LA. The people there are cold. Don't even treat people like they treat their own dogs. People there treat service people like dogs and dogs like family. Here in Harmony, it's all family."

"He has that right!" Raye answered. "Now, if we could just find Hijo a woman to settle down with. I bet I could come up with something in the way of a house."

Lucy argued, "My goodness, Raye. The boy is not even, I'd say, eighteen."

"I'm nineteen, in fact," Hijo corrected her.

"You see, Lucy. Nineteen. Didn't you and Beck get married when you were nineteen?"

"Oh yes, but I was a fool."

"A fool in love," Raye added.

"Oh yes. A fool in love," Lucy said. "Besides, I got Hijo here picked out for Danny."

"Danny?" Raye asked.

"Sure. When Hijo gets a little older I think he'll be perfect for Danny."

Hijo blushed.

Raye said, "Either way, a house will be needed."

"You see, Kate," Lucy said, "she's always got an angle, this one. You gotta watch her."

Raye, looking back at the open kitchen, asked, "Your mom around?"

"She's in the back. I'll go get her," Hijo said. He grabbed a tub of dirty dishes from the counter and walked back through a door to the side. Out of sight, he spoke in Spanish.

A small head peeked out from the corner. She was short with flecks of gray in her dark hair, her smile big and caring. When she saw who it was, she shuffled over to the counter.

"Hola, Miss Raye and Miss Lucinda," she said with the flair of a beautiful accent.

"Good morning, Juanita," both women said. Juanita came closer to them and reached out both her hands to the two women. Her hands were aged but strong looking from years of hard work.

She said to Raye, "Your hands are warm. Always warm, just like your heart." She turned around and called out to Hijo. "Get them some tortillas to take home." She turned back around and said to the women, "I've made too many. Way too many like I was cooking for an army." She then looked over at Kate and smiled. "Hello."

Kate said, "Hello."

Raye told Juanita, "This is Kate. She and her husband bought Gert's old place."

"Oh?" Juanita said with a raised eyebrow.

Raye continued, "Yes, they are settling in nicely."

"Just the two of you?" Juanita asked.

"Yes," Kate answered.

Juanita came closer to her and put her hand on top of Kate's arm. "No children?" she asked.

"No ma'am," Kate politely answered to the question she knew she would hear for all her life.

"You should have children. This is a nice town. We need children," Juanita said. "It keeps us young," she continued, looking at both Raye and Lucy.

Lucy spoke, "That it does."

"This town is getting too old. We need young couples to have more children," Juanita insisted.

Raye asked, "What about Hijo?"

"Ay dios mio! If we wait for Hijo to have children, we will be a ciudad muerta – a ghost town."

The women laughed.

"I'm not kidding. That boy won't leave me a minute. I doubt he'd find a woman while tied around my apron." She looked over at Kate. "He's my only son, so I babied him too much. Oh, his father, madre Maria que me ayude, he would turn over in his grave if he were to see Hijo. He'd say, 'you made my boy into a mujer – a woman.'"

"Oh, Juanita, he's a good son," Raye said.

Shrugging her shoulders, she replied, "I guess."

Hijo came out from the back with foil-wrapped tortillas and handed them to Juanita. "Ay dios mio. You are too stingy. Go back and give more."

Hijo immediately turned around and went in back to wrap more tortillas.

Juanita said to Kate, "My son says I would give the world away and I say, yes, I would if I owned it." She laughed. "My son needs to go to Mass more. I tell Ruth to work on him," she said with a wink.

Hijo quickly came back out with larger wrapped rounds of tortillas. Juanita looked at them. "There. That's better." She grabbed Hijo's cheeks with one hand and squeezed them. "Oh, this one, he'll learn."

Hijo smiled. A little embarrassed, he went in the back to work. Juanita handed the ladies the foil-wrapped tortillas. They were still warm. Kate thanked her and Juanita smiled back. Patting her on the arm, she added, "You bring your husband back here to eat, and I'll make sure you have children in no time. I know this spell my aunt told me. It is guaranteed to bring you children pronto."

"We'll definitely be back," Kate answered.

"You don't believe, do you? It's the truth," Juanita reaffirmed.

Kate felt like now was as good a time as any to tell them. "Michael and I found out we can't have children. We conceived last year through *in vitro*, but we lost the baby. So try as you will Juanita, I doubt very much you'll see any success. I'd hate to disappoint you."

"Nah, you won't disappoint me. I'll say a rosary for you. Who knows?"

Kate quickly said, "Don't worry. We're okay with it now. It has been a tough year, but we're doing fine. Please don't feel sorry for us."

Lucy hastily said, "Well, you're certainly brave. I admire your spirit. After all, life is about living with what you are dealt. When Ben died and I lost my only son I thought my world would end. But it didn't. I ended up with a wonderful daughter in Danny. I tell myself every day how grateful I am to have her here with us. It's like Ben sent her to us because he knew Beck and I would have a hard time going on. Life seems to bring you what you need in order to get through those tough times. And who knows, you and Michael may come out of this with someone like Danny. Someone who can fill your heart back up after it's been emptied by the pain."

Lucy smiled at Kate with a shiny tear in the corner of her eye. Kate grabbed her hand tightly. "I hope so. I hope we will be as lucky and happy as you and Beck are."

"Happy?" Lucy said. "Who said we were happy?" And she let out another of her now famous laughs.

"Oh Lucy, you're terrible," Raye said, shaking her head.

The ladies left the café, warm tortillas in hand, and moved down the sidewalk. As the three women continued on their way toward the end of the road, a menacing head-shaved man with multiple piercings and tattoos emerged from the shop across from them. Kate recognized him from that night in the restaurant. He approached with a baby in his arms and a Mohawk-wearing toddler in tow.

"Raye am I glad to see you," the man said in a smoky voice as he approached the women.

"Okay, here it comes," Lucy said under her breath.

"Quiet. He'll hear you," Raye answered. "What is it, Stan?" she asked.

"Here's the thing," he said. "I gotta run down to get some materials. Can you watch Rocket and Harmie? I swear I'll be back in an hour."

"Stan, you know I'd love to, but I'm busy this morning." Raye motioned to Kate as she said it.

"Uh sorry, who are you?" he asked.

Lucy said, "No need to be rude, Stan. This is our new neighbor, Kate. She and her husband Michael bought Gertie's old place."

"No frigging way. That dump?" he said.

Raye said, "Yes, we're all aware it's a fixer upper."

"And haunted," he added. His toddler son stood close behind him with his face buried in a portable game console. Kate noticed not just the Mohawk but that the boy had his ear pierced. The word *haunted* caught the boy's attention.

"Stan, the house is not haunted. How many times must we go through this?" Raye asked.

"Say what you will but old Gert died there. And just by looking at the place you can tell it's haunted."

"Kate, pay him no mind," Raye said.

Lucy added, "Mostly because he has no mind."

"Now, Lucy," Stan said. "Let's not go there today. I need some help. Look at me. Look at these kids. I'm doing the best I can."

"Stan, give her to me," Lucy replied, taking the baby from him.

"Take her. She's been a handful lately. She's so spoiled that I can't put her down a minute without her crying."

Kate leaned in for a look at the baby's small face. She had pale pink skin like a doll. "She's beautiful," Kate told the father.

"Don't think she don't know it," he replied. Now with his hands free, he reached out to shake Kate's hand. "By the way, I'm Stan the stain-glass man." He pointed across the street to his shop. Then he pointed to the baby in Lucy's arms. "That there is Harmony, but we just call her Harmie." And pulling at the boy behind him, he added, "This here is Rocket. Say hello to Kate."

The boy shyly looked up from his game and said hello.

Stan said, "Sorry if I seemed a little rude there a minute ago. Thought at first you were one of those yuppie-type tourists who blow into town with their frigging sixty-thousand dollar car and ask for a discount on everything."

Raye said, "Stan, that's no way to talk about our town's customers." To Kate she explained, "Stan's a talented artist. He does pretty cool stained glass art, and he blows. Glass that is. We're just working on his people skills."

Lucy added, "Yeah, he's got some lovely stuff in the gallery over at the Creamery."

"We all do," Raye said. "But Stan's stuff really stands out."

"Yeah but we pay most of it to Della on the rent she charges us," Stan grumbled. "Not like she pays anything on it herself. She owns it free and clear and yet she charges us frigging rent on it. Wait 'til you meet Della."

"Oh, she's already met Della," Lucy said.

"Oh yeah?"

Raye answered, "She came by when we were at Sunny's, complaining about Buddha again."

"Right on!" Stan yelled out with a fist in the air. "You get 'em Buddha. You crap on the establishment!"

Raye said, "Now, be nice."

Stan said, "And she's nice? My god, I haven't met a woman before who needed so badly to get laid."

Raye said, "Stan, what are we going to do with you?"

"Well, hopefully watch the kids while I run to get some supplies."

Raye said, "Give me some time here with Kate, and I'll come by and watch the kids at your place. Take the kids back over there, and I'll be over as soon as I can."

"Thanks, Raye. You're a life saver," he answered.

Lucy handed the baby off to Stan.

"Come on, Rocket. Let's get home." Stan with Harmie in hand and Rocket in shadow marched right back over to his house behind the glass shop as the three women watched.

Kate asked, "What happened to his wife?"

Lucy explained in a hushed tone, "She left him. Just up and ran off. Of course, Tess was like that – flighty. I mean who runs out on a six-month old?"

Raye added, "She was confused. It had to be postpartum."

Lucy answered, "It doesn't really matter. She's been gone now for over a month. You'd think her mothering instinct would have kicked in by now."

"She may have been too young," Raye said.

"That's poppycock. It don't matter how young you are. It matters how much you care and, frankly, she didn't care. I could never imagine walking out on my kid. And look at that poor boy. With a haircut and name like that. It doesn't fit him. He's such a sweet boy."

"Lucy, Stan's just as sweet. Don't judge the book by the cover. He's got a lot to handle."

Kate looked down at her watch, and Raye noticed it.

"It's getting to be lunch time isn't it?" Raye said.

"Yeah, I'd like to get back and make sure I put lunch together for Beck and Michael."

Lucy said, "Getting hungry myself."

Kate added, "I would like to stop in and say hello to Ruth since we're here."

Raye said, "That's a good idea. I should check on her."

The women walked the last remaining steps of the sidewalk to the last shop on the street. Raye went in first and the bells rang. The smell of Ruth's shop was more pleasant than Kate had remembered. The mixture of the candles, incense and other fragrant gifts Ruth sold was becoming a cheerful sensation.

Ruth appeared from behind the forest green curtain. Instantly she smiled and said, "Well, what do I owe this honor that all three of you would come at once?"

Raye and Ruth met each other halfway down the middle of the crowded aisle and shared a hug. Raye pulled back and said, "We're showing Kate around town. You know, introducing her to the neighbors."

Ruth looked over at Kate. "Sounds like fun."

Lucy said, "Yeah but we ran into Della."

Ruth said, "Oh...how was she this morning?"

Raye said, "Ruth, you know how she is. She was in rare form this morning."

Ruth said to Kate, "Honey, she means no harm."

"No, she means it. She's mean," Lucy interrupted.

"Oh Lucy," Ruth explained. "She's just a lonely woman trying to make her way in a world she thinks no longer needs her. She's had a difficult time of it. Dobb did everything for her. It's been a tough adjustment."

"Adjustment? Dobb has been dead over six years now. How long of an adjustment does she need?" Lucy wasn't affording Della any leniency.

Ruth reasoned to Lucy, "Some people don't adapt as well as others. We all deal with our losses differently. It's harsh to judge someone else for their reaction to their individual grief."

Lucy replied, "We've all had to deal with some major loss in our lives. I just don't see why someone needs to be nasty about it."

Raye said, "Enough about that," and then turned back to Ruth, "We only wanted to stop in to say hello."

Kate said, "It's good seeing you again."

Ruth smiled and patted Kate's hand with her own. Kate noticed how light and feathery it felt up on hers. Ruth said to Kate, "Stop by anytime. More often is better than not."

Raye wanted Kate to know a little more about Ruth. "Kate, did you know Ruth here also runs the Harmony Chapel behind the Creamery? She performs weddings here all the time."

"Well, I don't know about all the time," Lucy chimed in. "Whenever Raye sets something up. Raye is good at finding the perfect weddings for Harmony."

Raye said, "Well, I can't just sell houses in this market. I'd never afford my rent. So I help plan weddings on the side. Keeps our town abuzz. Weddings bring in wedding guests, and guests come and spend money."

"Even need a place to stay like our inn," Lucy agreed.

"It's good business for all of us," Raye added.

"Well Kate, I think you met just about everyone. You glad you moved here yet?" Lucy asked.

Kate didn't hesitate this time. "It's a different pace than living in LA but I feel like I can actually catch my breath and breathe. When you're so used to going, going, going, you assume that's how the whole world lives. Come to a place like this and you realize that not everyone runs the rat race."

Ruth said, "Some of us even take a turtle's pace."

"Exactly," Kate answered. "I think it's just what Michael and I need."

Ruth concluded, "Well, we're all glad you are here. Raye did a fine job finding you for our town."

"I should say so," Lucy added. "We thought we'd never find anyone for Gertie's place."

Raye said, "And now when people read our population sign on the highway, we don't have to count the cats and dog."

Everyone laughed. But amidst the warmth and kindness she'd felt today among her new neighbors, Kate still felt that somehow she didn't quite fit in.

CHAPTER 9

Everything from the kitchen but the microwave was still in boxes. Cooking never really thrilled Kate but with Michael working so hard on the house, she felt an obligation to put something together.

She opened up the foil-wrapped tortillas from Juanita's which weren't the uniform rounds Kate was accustomed to. None were exactly the perfect circle. Some were oblong like eggs and others had the slightest imperfections. Kate tore a strip off one and put it in her mouth. There was a natural buttery flavor to it like no other tortilla she had tasted before.

With the tortillas, Kate added some cheddar and pepper jack cheese along with some tomatoes she sliced to near transparency. She heated them in the microwave before adding fresh sliced avocado to both their plates. Lunch was as good as it was going to get with the limited utensils currently available.

Kate pulled two folding beach chairs up to a table height of boxes that she had covered with a bed sheet.

"I was able to find the plates, but not any forks or spoons," Kate said as she placed the food on the makeshift table. "So we'll have to eat with our hands."

"Whew," Michael said wiping the sweat from his head as he sat down. "No problem. I'm starving. I don't know how Beck does it. It was all I could do to keep up with him. How old do you think he is?" He looked down at his plate. "Hey, this looks good."

"I don't know…maybe sixty. Really?" Kate answered.

"Yeah. You made this?"

"I did. Juanita gave us some tortillas when we stopped by."

"You went by Juanita's?"

"There wasn't much we didn't hit in town."

Michael grabbed one of the quesadillas and smeared it with some of the avocado. With a mouthful, he announced, "This is awesome."

"Really?" she asked.

"Oh, yeah," he said stuffing another round of tortilla, cheese and tomato in his mouth.

"Here, let me grab you a beer from the cooler." Kate maneuvered her way through the maze of boxes in the house until she reached a small dorm-sized cooler they were using as a refrigerator in the kitchen. "I've got to get this kitchen taken care of. I didn't expect to lose half the day today, you know what I mean?"

Michael shouted back at Kate, "Yeah, as it turned out, though, Beck was a huge help."

Kate returned and sat back down. She handed Michael the beer. "I still haven't found the bottle opener."

"No problem," he said as he reached over for a screwdriver from the floor. With it he popped the cap off and took a giant swig. "Anyway, I couldn't have gotten it done without him. I really couldn't. Beck's a good guy." Michael kept the bottle of beer in one hand and grabbed for a slice of the quesadilla in his other. He ripped into it and with his mouth full said, "So you think he's sixty, huh?"

"I guess. I figure he's around my mom's age. Lucy was a riot."

Still with food in his mouth, he asked, "How'd that go?" Strings of golden cheese hung at the corner of his mouth as he inhaled another bite.

"I felt like a precious lap dog with Lucy and Raye showing me off around town. I met just about everyone."

"Oh yeah?"

"There are some real characters here in town. This place used to be some sort of a hippie commune or something."

"What makes you say that?"

"There was this young hippie couple in their twenties."

"In their twenties?"

"Michael, I'm not kidding. I guess the guy's dad helped found a colony here in the sixties and his kid, Sunny, and his wife, girlfriend, life partner, I don't know what, look like they're keeping the hope alive. It was a real trip."

Michael asked, "So were they tripping?"

"I don't think so. But I wouldn't be surprised. The guy reminds me of your cousin, Todd."

"Oh, a pothead?"

"Lucy somewhat indicated it. She gave me all the inside dirt on everyone we came in contact with. Remember that couple in Juanita's on our last visit? The ones who had that fight?" Kate asked, handing a beer for herself to Michael to open.

"Oh yeah, punk rock chick," Michael answered. He popped the top and handed it back to her.

"Well, I guess they live or lived in town. The girl walked out on the guy and their two kids. She had just had a baby around the time we saw them. Lucy said it was postpartum but who knows. I can't imagine walking out on a baby," Kate said as she put the bottle of beer up to her lips.

Michael watched Kate with the bottle.

"Anyway, I guess she's been gone and the poor guy's struggling." Kate put her bottle down and noticed Michael's plate was almost empty.

"Would you like me to make some more?" Kate asked.

"There's more? Sure."

Kate made her way back to the kitchen. Michael watched the curve of her body as she went through the doorway. "There's something sexy about you cooking."

"Really?" she asked with her back to him at the microwave.

"Yeah, I'm not sure what it is but it works for you."

Kate didn't say any more. She was a little afraid that Michael was hoping something would happen between them tonight. She knew she owed it to him but the thought still terrified her. She couldn't get past it.

Michael said, "I don't know, maybe all this physical labor's got my testosterone pumping."

Kate knew it was the effects of the beer as well.

He continued, "Whew, I'm way too tired to do anything about it whatever it is. After this, I just want to take a shower and take it easy. Beck's coming over again tomorrow."

Kate returned with more quesadillas. "I ran out of avocado. We'll have to make a run to the market when we get a chance."

"Thanks. I've gotta run into SLO tomorrow morning before Beck gets here. I could pick up some things on the way back. Just make me out a list."

"That would be great," Kate told him. She touched his arm. She always found his forearms sexy. His arms were built and had just enough dark hair on them to make the statement that he was a man without being too hairy. Kate smiled at Michael. He leaned across the improvised table to kiss her. This time she didn't turn away. She allowed his chapped lips to touch hers. She could taste the beer on his mouth, and it was intoxicating. She continued to kiss him and Michael pulled her closer. The kiss was passionate, but he pulled back and kissed her quickly one last time before sitting back in his chair. The kiss had left Kate wanting more. But she would have hated for it to continue any further for fear she would have to be the one to stop the action once again.

The two sat in silence for another minute before Michael asked Kate about who else she had met. They sat, ate and laughed there in the crowded living room with boxes of their work-in-progress home before Michael went to clean up. Kate began to clear the table. As she reached over for Michael's plate, she felt something caress the skin on her arm. The feeling made the invisible hairs on her arm stand up. Startled, Kate turned around expecting to see Michael, but he wasn't there. She heard the old pipes turn on in the tub and water begin to run. She stood there silently and waited several seconds but nothing happened so she went about the business of cleaning up the dinner mess.

The entire time she couldn't help but feel like she was being watched.

CHAPTER 10

The drive between Harmony and SLO was nearly an hour but Michael didn't mind the commute or the solitude. The distance between hadn't become routine enough yet to grow tired of it. Plus, the combination of coastal blue hues and hearty cool air were a shower of calm in a life still struggling to find its buoyancy.

As Michael came around the hill leaving Cayucos, the line between windswept pallid sands and grassy hills ruled the final landscape toward Harmony. As he flew past the tranquility toward home, he spotted a man standing atop one of the small seaside hills up ahead on his left. Except for the exaggerated movements, the man seemed to blend into the natural surroundings. His clothes were ragged and soiled. His hair and beard were long and flowing in the breeze, wrapping around his face as the man danced with what looked like a discarded pizza box in one hand. The man held the flat box out away from him balancing it in his palm with his thumb. As Michael approached, he noticed in the other hand the man held a long, slender paint brush and there next to him was a makeshift easel and a half-painted rectangular piece of plywood.

As Michael sped by, the man noticed Michael and waved at him. Michael automatically waved back only to realize he had never seen the man before. Feeling foolish for waving, Michael wondered if the man was someone Kate met in town but forgot to mention.

As he approached the drive to the house, Michael spotted Beck's truck out front. He then spotted Beck standing on the roof of the house; hammer in hand, holding nails in his mouth, and in search of something. Michael pulled around the drive behind Beck's truck. Noticing, Beck waved at him.

"You're up early this morning," Michael said as he got out.

Beck shouted down from the steep slope of the roof, "Just thought I'd get a jump on the roof for ya. It ain't going to fix itself and I smell rain."

Michael looked around. The sky in the valley was solely blue with not a cloud in view.

"You can't tell by looking at the sky," Beck responded to Michael's upward glances. "The skies here are liars. They'll turn on you faster than a rat trap turns on its prize. You'll come to find that out the longer you live here. You get to a point where you smell the rain coming in the onshore breeze. Something the gulls alert you to. You'll see them flying inland and know they're one step ahead of nature."

As Beck finished, a single seagull flew overhead, squawking down on the men.

"What'd I tell ya? Hear him? Rain…rain…rain, he cries." Beck couldn't contain himself and started to laugh at what he was certain he sounded like.

"Plus I know you don't even have a roof ladder yet," Beck continued, "and I know you have plenty to do yourself here. I figured you wouldn't mind me climbing up here and banging around a bit."

Michael smiled, "No, not at all. Let me get up there and give you a hand."

"Nah, you go about what you planned on getting done. I'm almost finished here anyway. Then I'll be down to help you with whatever you got going on."

"You know," Michael said, unloading the truck, "I don't want to put you out. I'm sure you've got plenty to do over at your place."

"Truth is there ain't much I can do there anymore. And if I hang around the house too long, Lucy's going to find things for me to do. Things she and Danny could easily take care of themselves. Lucy don't like to see me with nothing keeping me busy. I'm sure you know how that is."

Michael smirked. Truth was Kate wasn't really the type to nag. In fact, this past year, she barely asked him to do a thing. Mostly he had to do what she wouldn't or couldn't do. Things like laundry and dinners and ironing his shirts.

One time, he'd been running late for an important meeting at the bank regarding his business loan, and he couldn't find a single dress shirt to wear. Kate went on and on about it, saying, "I'm sorry. It just slipped my mind to take the clothes to the cleaners. I'm such a terrible wife."

Beck began to shimmy down the ladder. "Well, at least it's cool today. Hate working when it's hot. Not that it ever gets real hot around here. Not like your LA. Hotter than Hades, that place can get." Beck paused a minute. "Only place I've been that's worse is South Carolina. The humidity there is hell. Makes you want to die." Coming over to Michael's truck, Beck noticed lumber. "What's your plan with all these planks?"

"They're for the porch. I want to get the steps shored up. That wood is rotting away all over. It's not safe."

Without thinking, Beck started in, "Well, you should have gotten that treated wood. It'll last longer for outdoors."

Michael didn't say anything. He hadn't thought about that.

"No matter, I've got some sealant over at my place. We'll use what you got and then seal it up. It'll be fine, son."

There was a moment of silence between the men as that last sentence hung in the air between them.

Beck moved on. "Let me help you unload this truck and see what else we might need from over at my place before I run over there. Wouldn't make much sense to be running back and forth all day. How much help would I be then?"

Beck grabbed some pails of paint from the back of the truck and carried them to the porch. Michael grabbed a couple of bags from the back and asked, "Are there a lot of painters around here?"

"You don't need any professional painter, trust me. You and I can take care of this house without the high cost and delays from any professional painters."

"No, not house painters. I meant artists. On my way back, I saw this guy up on one of the hills painting."

Beck answered, "Oh, you saw some guy painting up on a hill, you say."

"Yeah, he was up on one of the small crests of pasture on the west side of the road. He waved at me as I went by like he knew me."

"He did, huh?"

"Yeah, I waved back at him. I just figured it was someone in town Kate met."

"I doubt Kate met him in town. Doubt Della would let Pete anywhere near town."

"Why? What's his story? Is he from around here?"

"You could say so, I guess. He wanders up and down the coast between here and Monterey for the most part. They sell his paintings down in the gallery in town. Once he earns a bit of money, Sunny runs the money out to him along with some food from Juanita's, and he's on his way." Beck paused for a moment. "So I guess he's back then. If that's who you saw."

Michael asked, "Is there a problem?"

"No, not at all. I hadn't seen him in a while. You know I shouldn't be surprised. It had been a while since anyone had seen him around here. I'd heard he's gone as far north as Frisco Bay. I don't want you and Kate to worry. He's harmless as much as I can tell. His timing is always peculiar, though."

"How so?"

"Oh, I don't know. Not worth getting into I suppose. Some will make more out of it than they should, that's for sure. Pete's nothing more than a drifter. Don't let anyone convince you of anything more than that. Just a wayward artist trying to make a buck here in town and then he'll be on his way. Never stays long enough to get into any real trouble. He'll get what he's come for and be on his way."

"So there's a gallery in town?"

"Yeah, the hippies convinced Dobb some time ago to turn the old creamery into an art gallery. Pete's got some stuff in there. None of it's anything I'd like. If you're into art, you should check it out."

"Well, the truth is I used to paint back in college. Always thought I'd be a painter but art doesn't really pay the mortgage, you know."

"Especially a mortgage in LA."

"Very true," Michael answered.

"But weren't you an artist of some sort back in LA? Lucy mentioned something like that."

"A graphic artist, all computer stuff, not traditional brush and palette."

"What's a graphic artist do?"

"Mostly advertising work. I'd put ads together, logos, campaigns, all commercial stuff."

"Hmm. I had no idea there was a call for something like that."

Michael laughed. "Well, in my case, I don't think there was much of a call for it. I went out of business."

"Did ya?"

"Yeah, no big deal. It was a few months ago, although now it seems like a lifetime ago. It was something. I was really on a roll there for a while. Won a couple of awards, got jobs with the big guys, and even hired a staff."

"What changed?"

"I thought the rush would last forever. I planned poorly and got caught with my pants down when the economy turned. I priced myself out of the market. I guess I thought I was worth it. Maybe I was for a time. Then the work stopped flowing. I took good clients for granted, and they went elsewhere. As they left, one by one, I'd convince myself I didn't need them. Then when I couldn't afford to pay vendors, I realized I did need them but by then it was far too late. Too many of my clients were happy elsewhere. I was left in a hole that I had no way to dig my way out of. Money I should have saved or invested had long been spent. And more money than should have been spent went toward us trying to get pregnant. What a waste that turned out to be."

"I doubt very much that you trying to have a baby was a waste."

"Well, we have nothing to show for all the money we put into it. We knew it was a gamble but didn't think the odds were so stacked against us. I should have been shrewder than I was. I should have been more level-headed when she wasn't able to be."

"I think you're much too hard on yourself."

"Nonetheless, we threw away a lot of money on our dreams."

"Well, you two look happy to me."

Michael chuckled. "I'm sure we do."

"No, I mean it. It may take you two some time, but you'll find it. Why, look at me and Lucy. We've never wanted to be anywhere else. We've traveled here and there but we always find we're happy just being here. I know I probably sound simple to someone like you but I guess I enjoy simple. The modern world makes things so complicated with their eighty-hour work week, two hour commutes and constant updates to the latest thingamajig. Instead of looking down at the screen in your hand, look up and out at the world around you. Do that and I guarantee you'll get there."

"I hope you're right. Kate really wanted to come here and start over. I was willing to do just about anything to get her back. That's the least I can do, considering."

"Considering what?" Beck asked.

"Considering all that went wrong for us."

"You know, you aren't the only one in this life that's failed at something. You gotta look a little bit farther than the tip of your own nose sometimes to see you aren't the only one in the boat you're rowing. Everyone has dreams that went unfulfilled." Beck carried an armful of lumber to the front of the porch and dropped it with a clatter.

Michael had forgotten all about Beck's son, Ben.

"You're right. Seems like I get so entrapped in my own problems I forget the rest of the world has its share as well."

"Well, what did I expect? You LA types are so wrapped up in yourselves. I think they call you the me generation, don't they?"

Michael laughed. "True enough. I should have thought more about it before I said all I did."

"It's quite all right."

"How is it you were ever able to get over your loss?" Michael asked.

"It wasn't easy. Lucy cried for days. People round here were mighty helpful. It was a few years ago. Gert, the woman who lived here in your house, was a big help to Lucy. She'd lost a daughter some time back. Told Lucy to hang on to the good she remembered. It was part of why she never left Harmony, she said. She wanted to stay here where she could be closest to where she would remember her daughter most. Playing around this house, laughing, living. It's important to a parent to hang on to that."

"What happened to her daughter?" Michael asked as the two men leaned against the side of the truck.

"You know, I'm not too sure. I can't say there's anyone around here who would have known what happened to her daughter, that was a long time ago. It's not really something you ask. If a person's moved on beyond their loss, there's no sense in dragging them back through it. Gert's son never stuck around long enough to care. He took off and never looked back. Never even came back to clear out the house after his mom died."

Beck watched the traffic whizzing by on Highway 1 down in the valley. "The truth is loss often has a bright side. Danny's been a blessing. We get to see every day what our son saw in that girl. She's been the greatest gift our son ever gave us." Beck rubbed at the corner of his eye. "Aw, look at me. Let's just get your truck unloaded so we can get that porch put together."

CHAPTER 11

There was no question in Kate's mind that a farmhouse kitchen is yellow. So whoever painted the kitchen its current peachy flesh color had no idea that this kitchen should be yellow. "Sunlight Yellow" was in fact the color her kitchen was meant to be. The color was cheery but with a slightly pale tone. It was exactly like Kate had always wanted the sun to be in the morning – bright but calm. On her commute to work, back in LA, she drove east and that early morning sun was brutal. She wasn't a morning person, but there was no way around the fact that this kitchen was to be yellow.

With Michael and Beck back in SLO, it was the perfect time to paint the kitchen in the peaceful quiet of her developing home. She put on a pot of coffee and cranked up the volume on the stereo. That was something nice about this house. She could listen to music at the volume she enjoyed without having to worry about any neighbors. The one problem was getting something decent to tune into on the radio. She tuned the stereo to the only station she could get. It was a local station out of Morro Bay. They played a combination of the real oldies like big band and standards; Frank Sinatra, Benny Goodman, Rosemary Clooney, along with hits up through the seventies. It was nothing like what Kate would have ever thought she'd listen to but the silence in the house was deafening. Besides, at the top and bottom of each hour, the station would report on the local news and weather conditions. The newscasters, like the music, seemed to speak to an era long gone.

"Twenty-two after the top of the hour, you're listening to KMOR. They're calling for rain but the weather outside says nothing but sun. Surf's mild with the winds coming up on us out of the southwest. From where I sit, I see no sign of a cloud in the sky. Those predictions of rain from the big boys don't look to be true. Leave it to your local station, KMOR, where you're sure to get more local coverage, more local weather and more of the music you just can't find on the superstations. I'll be back with your world news after these important messages. Don't change that dial. Always come back for KMOR."

Kate opened the front door, latched the screen door shut and went about her work in the kitchen. With the sun streaming in, it was clear "Sunlight Yellow" was the perfect match. With her back to the window and the sun, Kate saw her own shadow on the wall in front of her. She still carried an extra twenty pounds on her figure. Not baby weight – depression weight. Exercise like painting would likely do her some good.

She painted the door and window trim first, humming along as she evened out the streaks the brush left over the well-coated wood window sill. As she painted, she watched the shape of her figure as she moved back and forth, up and down. No matter how she moved, she was disgusted by what she saw. *How'd I ever get like this?* Kate picked up her pace, hoping to increase her heart rate. She watched her shadow as if looking for the weight to melt away. As she turned back to dip her brush, out of the corner of her eye she saw a small shadow pass by her. She turned around but didn't see anything. *A hot flash?*

The heat of the sun was magnified by the kitchen's window. Kate quickly shoved the window open to cool herself down. With a breeze coming through, she looked out to the field grasses next to the house and for a moment found the expanse suffocating. Too used to the close proximity of the houses in Southern California she guessed.

Fleetwood Mac's "Over My Head" came on and she began to sing. It was a song she knew well. She belted it out while continuing to paint and let the music carry her away. As she sang out during the first chorus, she heard something. She stopped singing and painting to listen. Not hearing anything more, she figured it must have been the wind. She returned to work and picked up at the second chorus until the song was done.

In the silence between songs, she heard something else. In mid stroke, she froze and turned her head toward the living room, certain someone was there. As the next song came on, she lost track of the sound in the house. The music seemed too loud. She was afraid to move so she called out to see if someone was out there. "Hello?"

She paused, straining to hear an answer over the music. With no reply, she worried her solitude was getting the best of her. She couldn't think of a single time in her life when she had this much space to herself. This much time to just do anything non-work related. In their house back in LA, she didn't paint a single room herself. They always paid some painters to come in and do the job. In fact, they paid everyone to come and do the things around the house; the painting, the gardening, the cleaning, even the shopping. Their careers had them too busy to do much of anything other than work.

Living in a town with only eighteen people, it would be hard for any service person like that to make any money. She laughed at how much they would be left to do for themselves here. She resumed her painting. Getting the painting done was easy. She was certain Michael would be proud. With the trim done, she poured some "Sunlight Yellow" into the roller pan. She wanted to get the flat surfaces done before Michael returned.

As the next song ended, there in the moment of silence came laughter through the breezes of the open window. Kate didn't think anything of it until the next song came on and the volume dropped. Kate hadn't heard the door open but called out anyway, "That was fast. Did you get everything you needed?"

There wasn't a response. "Michael?" Still nothing. She stopped painting and walked over to the doorway to the living room. The volume of the stereo was clearly much lower. She wiped her hands on a rag and called out again, "Michael?"

No one answered. She looked over at the screen door as it bounced in the breeze. She knew she had latched it. She walked over to the hall to see if Michael was in the bedroom or bathroom – still no one. Her heart racing, she walked back to the front door and looked out. His truck was still gone. She could feel her heart pounding in her throat. She shut the door and locked it. She then went over and turned the volume back up on the stereo. *Could it have turned itself down?*

She went back to the kitchen and as she continued painting, she no longer sang. Instead she listened. She was listening to see if she could hear anyone. She then remembered the laughing she had heard and realized she wasn't in the city any more so she questioned it. Back in LA, it would be perfectly normal to hear the laughter of a neighbor in their backyard with the window open. But here there were no neighbors around.

She was certain it was a child's laugh. *Maybe some kid was playing around and came in and turned the music down and left.* It made sense to her. *Except what kid?*

The kids she had met were young and lived in town. *I must be tired…or hungry. Now I'm seeing and hearing things. Maybe I'm crazy. Wouldn't surprise me a bit. Wouldn't surprise Michael either. He already thinks I'm crazy. If not crazy, clinically depressed. I gotta get out of here. Just get out of the house for a while. Go see someone in town. Who? Ruth – go see Ruth.*

She started down for Gifts from the Sea and pushed the door to the shop open. The clanging of bells summoned Ruth out of the backroom.

"Well, hello. How's the house coming along? You two getting settled in?" Ruth's calm voice reassured Kate's silence.

"We are. It's a lot of work, though."

"The work is good for you, I know. Work like that, with your hands, is always gratifying. Not at all like paperwork that binds the mind. No, the act of physical labor is freeing."

Kate wandered from table to table in the store. She realized there was nothing there she hadn't seen before. Feeling Ruth's eyes on her, Kate looked up and smiled at her. "You've got some real interesting things here."

"Oh thank you. You've been here a couple of times before, so I'm sure you've noticed not much has changed. Was there something you were looking for today in particular? I'm never really sure what people expect to find in a lonely old spiritual store like this."

"A spiritual shop?" Kate questioned as she looked around the shop.

"Why yes, you couldn't tell?"

"Not at first, but now that you mention it, it does make more sense. I'm curious, what made you want to open a shop like this in Harmony?"

"Well, believe it or not, I used to be a nun."

"A nun?"

"Oh yes, Christ's bride, but that was ages ago. I came through Harmony some time ago and fell in love with it and never left. Anyway, I had to make a living. Vows of poverty don't afford the glorious vista views here on the central coast. So I opened up this shop and took over the chapel here in town."

"So you left the church?"

"Yes, some time ago for other reasons. But I am still an ordained minister, the only one in town, in fact. You should go out back and see the chapel. It is a really nice one. There is a lot of promise here in Harmony. Although I am sure you are finding that out on your own."

"Of course," Kate answered continuing to walk around.

Ruth continued, "It's that hope of a new place that is what I felt when I first passed through here. Those majestic bluffs and the waves and the green pastures. No more perfect a place here on earth, I am certain. Once I stumbled upon it, there was no denying that I couldn't leave it. I had to stay."

Ruth's head began to bob a little from her advanced years. Her eyes begin to well up. She continued, "So much in my life I gave up. I gave up my vows to my Lord and made new ones." She wiped a tear from her eye. "Oh would you listen to me go on...you didn't come in here for that."

"Oh, it's all right. As it is, I just needed to get out of the house today. The isolation was getting to me. Thought I'd come down to town and window shop a little."

"Perfect day for it with the sun and all. Besides, we don't get much foot traffic here during the week. You're likely to be my only shopper today. No worries or expectations though. Feel free to look around or just talk."

Kate knew she meant it. She stayed and chatted a little more with Ruth before grabbing some scented candles, and made her way home. As she approached the house, Michael's truck was there. She picked up her leisurely pace. He was unloading the truck at the foot of the porch.

"Hiya," he said cheerfully.

"Hiya."

"You go into town?" he asked.

"Yeah, needed to get out a bit. The quiet of the house was more than I could take today."

"Oh yeah, having second thoughts?"

Kate replied, "Not at all. Just needed to get out."

"The kitchen's looking good. I like the color."

"Thanks."

"You think you'll have it done today?" Michael asked.

"Now that you're here I'm sure I will. I would love for us to get the kitchen unpacked and settled. Although I'm not sure how great I'll be in the kitchen."

"Oh, I'm sure we can get Juanita to teach you a thing or two," Michael said with a smile.

"Oh really? Well thank goodness for Beck and his teaching you a thing or two."

"What?" he said laughing.

"Yeah, we'd have no windows and holes in the roof if not for Beck."

"Is that how it is?"

"Yeah that's how it is."

Michael stopped what he was doing and crept closer to Kate. "No Michael, there's work to be done." He didn't care. He grabbed her from around the waist and lifted her up.

Kate said, "You're all sweaty."

This was his invitation to wipe his wet brow against her neck.

"Michael stop, yuck, there isn't enough hot water for us both to take a shower. By the way, when are you going to replace the water heater?"

"As soon as you cook me a four-course dinner."

"So never?"

"Oh yeah?" Michael spun her around in a dizzying motion and lost his balance. Michael fell to his knees, but managed to hold Kate up so she wouldn't hurt herself. He lowered Kate to the ground and the two lay down on the dirt and gravel driveway. There was a moment of silence and then they both began to laugh again.

CHAPTER 12

Progress on the house wasn't coming as quickly as Kate and Michael would have liked. Michael never professed to be the handiest of handymen. He reminded Kate as often as he could when they were preparing for the move that he was comfortable with the aesthetic changes in the house, but those that required plumbing and electrical expertise would be far from his domain. Nonetheless, Kate reassured him that she was confident that they would be able to figure it out. What they didn't know could be learned from the library of how-to books they purchased at the local home improvement supercenter.

When time came to replace the outdated toilet, the step-by-step installation instructions that came with the new toilet looked simple enough. With every book that Michael consulted, it seemed easy enough for him to take it on himself. He wouldn't need to rely on Beck for everything.

The project started off well enough. He wasn't even concerned when the old toilet cracked as he removed it. The problem he ran into was that the sewage line in the house was run sometime in the nineteen-thirties and connecting the new toilet to the ancient sewer line required a custom coupling. As Michael waited on the coupling, the couple was without a working toilet.

Luckily, Beck had a plumber friend in Paso Robles who could make the custom piece but even the two days he needed to get to it seemed extreme. Beck told Michael, "You're a braver man than I living with a woman who hasn't a toilet to do her business on."

Michael consoled Kate by saying it would only be a couple days before the guy could get the connector made and reminded her they still had use of the bathroom sink. He also created a makeshift bucket commode with disposable bags that they would use in the meantime. It wasn't ideal but it would get the job done until the new toilet could be installed. Michael couldn't have foreseen the problem with the sewer line. It wasn't his fault and he was making the best of the situation.

While they waited on the part, the two made use of the time by finishing up the patching and painting in their bedroom. They had removed the previous wood paneling and in its absence were countless cracks and nail holes in the plaster. With music blaring, Kate sanded the layers of paint off the trim and woodwork while Michael worked on filling in the cracks and holes in the plaster. With weeks of remodeling already behind them, they jadedly worked without conversing to the point where Kate couldn't keep silent any longer.

"Any word on the part for the toilet?"

Michael kept working. "No, I'm sure he'll call when it's ready."

Kate sanded the wood door frame with a more vigorous pace. "Perhaps you should call and check in. Let him know the urgency."

"I'm pretty sure he's aware. He said he'll call us as soon as it's done."

Kate stopped sanding. "You know, it wouldn't hurt to call him. I mean, it's been four days already. It was only supposed to be two. It's kind of getting old using your bucket."

A little exasperated, Michael answered, "Kate, I just talked to the guy yesterday. He knows we're waiting on him. He's got a big job he's trying to get done, remember? You just need to be patient. It's not going to be forever."

"That's easy for you to say – you're a guy. You go out back and piss openly out in the weeds behind the house. It's not so easy for women. You have no idea." She threw down her sander, ripped off her disposable gloves and continued. "You couldn't. It's just like before." She stopped herself from saying anything more and grabbed her bottle of water.

"Like what?" he asked.

"Oh never mind. It's not important anymore. It's over." She lifted her water bottle to her mouth so she couldn't say anymore.

Michael stopped what he was doing. "You know, this isn't even my fault. We needed a new toilet because the old one didn't flush the way you thought it should. I wanted to wait on the bathroom but no you wanted it and I tried to give it to you. I'm sorry it didn't work out this time or anytime. I'm doing the best I can."

"Oh give me a break! Every time something doesn't go your way or work out you say 'I'm doing the best I can' as if I'm asking for the impossible."

Michael laughed. "Sometimes you are."

"A working toilet is asking the impossible?" she said with voice raised.

"In this case, yes."

"Geez, I didn't know a working toilet was the impossible – my mistake."

"You know, some things that seem easy don't always turn out that way. You, of all people, should know that."

"Screw you!" she told him throwing her bottle down. She walked out and down the hall to the bathroom. He watched her go. He knew her well enough to know she wasn't finished. Sure enough, she turned back to him. "You know what? You don't get it. You're a smart man, Michael, and you think you know everything there is to know about women and sex and the biology of it all, but you don't. Sometimes life is graphic in a way that you could never understand. You think a period is just that – a tiny dot or interruption. Well, it's not always like that. And it doesn't take a miscarriage to make matters messy. Am I really so bad for wanting a flushing toilet?"

Michael didn't say anything.

"I'm not. When you told me it would be two days I believed you. I'm sure you hadn't thought about what time of the month this was for me but I had. I believed that when you said it would be two days that it would be just that. Here it is four days and I'm now in the midst of a heavy period and it isn't pretty. And yes without the use of water to dilute the situation it brings back memories of losing the baby. It isn't easy for me. Maybe it is for you because you're a guy and you stood there and held my hand through it and you don't feel it."

"Don't give me that. You have no idea what I feel," he was quick to answer.

"You're right. You're absolutely right. I have no idea because you don't tell me," she yelled at him.

"Don't tell you? Don't tell you?" He yelled right back. "I couldn't tell you. I can't tell you. Your grief consumed the both of us. There was only enough room for your grief in our marriage so that mine didn't even count."

"Don't put it back on me. You watched me break down in total rawness and didn't give anything back. All I got back was this façade of a man, who like his father, didn't give anything back."

Michael's anger boiled over. His face turned ruby red. Kate saw it. He moved one step forward toward the hallway to the living room.

"Go ahead, Michael. Walk out. That's what you want to do," she egged him on.

"You want me to run?"

"No. I want you here. I want to know you're committed to being here."

"My god, Kate, I moved all the way out here didn't I? How much more do you want from me?"

Kate approached him ignoring the bodily feelings she had for the bathroom that first started the argument. "I want more than the façade you give me. I want you to talk to me."

"That's just it, Kate. All that's been allowed was for you and your loss. I lost a lot more than you did."

"How so?" she asked without thinking about it.

"Really? Well, I lost a baby but I also lost my business and my wife."

Kate approached Michael. "No you haven't. I'm right here. Let me in."

"I wish I could but you're always so over a cliff all the time that someone has to hold you together. There isn't room for me to be anything but the guy holding you together."

"I'm not sure I know what you mean."

"Are you serious? Sure when we first came here, you were so excited and I thought that maybe this crazy idea of us moving was what we needed. Now, you seem like you're slipping away again."

Kate didn't know what to think about that. She thought she was doing much better. With a sullen look on her face she asked, "I am?"

"Yes, you are."

Kate thought about it. Then she thought about the voice she heard when they first came here. She hadn't heard it in a while. She hadn't felt anything in the house. Maybe it was all in her mind.

"I don't understand," she said. "I thought I was doing so much better. Maybe it's just my..."

"Hormones?"

"Yeah. My period's really heavy this month. Maybe it's just that."

"It can't always just be about that and if it is you should see someone. This isn't normal for you. I'm not sure what to make of it anymore."

"Just work on getting us the toilet working again would you?" She turned around and marched down toward the bathroom. Shutting the door behind her, she worried that she was losing her grip on reality. She dropped her pants and positioned herself on the crude toilet and let the tears flow out of her like they had so many times before.

The rest of that night it was like the two of them were back in their house in LA. They didn't talk. The scars of past fights were still very evident. The demons of their past once again reared their ugly heads. It was their first fight in Harmony. Kate was sure it would not be their last.

CHAPTER 13

The space between a conflicted couple only intensifies in a smaller house. There aren't as many places to hide. The next day, the custom coupling arrived and Michael and Beck were able to get the toilet working again. To avoid letting Beck see how bad things were between her and Michael, Kate decided to go and see Ruth. Ruth was easier to talk to – didn't ask a lot of questions like Raye or Lucy did. There was a peacefulness to Ruth that Kate sought.

The store was vacant as usual. Immediately recognizing Kate, Ruth greeted her. "Hello, my dear, so good to see you again."

Ruth's cheerfulness warmed Kate. It reminded her of her own mother.

"Thought I'd stop in and see how you're doing. You need anything? Between Michael and myself we always seem to be going down to San Luis Obispo for something."

"No dear. I have everything I need right here. But thanks for asking. Would you like some tea? I just brewed some Earl Grey. Care for a cup?"

"I'd love some," Kate replied as she approached the counter.

"Have a seat," Ruth said. She motioned for Kate to sit down at the stool at the end of the counter.

"How are things coming with the house?" Ruth asked as she poured the tea.

"Slow, actually. Michael and Beck are finally getting the toilet back up and running."

"You were without a toilet?" Ruth asked from the backroom.

"Yes. It hasn't been pleasant."

"I should say not."

Kate didn't get any more into it. She sat there in silence. She looked at the sameness of the shop and then out the window to see if there were any cars around. Nothing as usual. "I can't seem to get used to the quiet around here."

"I imagine it does take some time to adjust, especially with being from down south and a more vigorous pace."

"That's for sure. Even in the silence of LA you heard something; sprinklers or car alarms or dogs barking. Here there doesn't seem to be much of that. Sometimes it gets so quiet I swear I hear things."

"Oh?"

"You know, voices, laughing, I guess just about anything I can imagine in the silence."

"Oh I see," Ruth responded as she brought the tea service over to the counter.

"Thank you," Kate said. As she stirred cream and sugar into her cup, Kate couldn't help but ask, "Does the quiet around here ever get to you?"

"Oh no, can't say that it does. To me everything here seems perfect. I am certain of that."

"I don't mean to be rude but does anyone ever come into your shop?" Kate said.

"Why, of course. You're here now and Raye is sure to be by sometime later. Danny and Lucy stop by every now and then."

"No, I mean customers. I'm sorry if that seems rude. I'm just curious. I never see anyone around town."

Ruth laughed. "Well, we definitely don't see the traffic of say a shopping mall but I get enough people in here to make it work. I make it work because it is where I want to be."

Kate asked, "How is it that you are so certain?"

"Are you having second thoughts about the move here?"

There was a pause as Kate took a sip of her tea. The flavor was subtle. She wasn't a tea drinker to say the least. But there was an almost familiar quality to it. "I guess I am. When I saw the house it reminded me of my mom. She had a house she got from Gram that was just like the one here in Harmony. When I saw it I felt immediately connected to her again. I miss my mom."

"Your mom is…"

Kate interrupted Ruth so she didn't have to hear it. "Ovarian cancer."

"Oh, I am so sorry," Ruth sympathized for Kate. She reached out and placed her hand on top of Kate's, rubbing it slightly. This was becoming a habit with Ruth, reaching out to touch Kate. Kate didn't mind it. Ruth's touch was soft like her mom's always was. A tear formed in Kate's eye that she immediately wiped away.

"Oh here they go. Me and tears seem to go hand-in-hand lately. It's probably just the hormones. I keep saying that and haven't even taken them in months now."

"Hormones?" Ruth questioned.

"Michael and I were trying to get pregnant and the doctor had me taking all sorts of hormones. They aren't quite out of my system yet. Or so I tell myself. It can sometimes take up to a year to get back on track and feeling yourself again."

Ruth, not wanting to be too intrusive, asked, "I take it you decided not to have children then?"

Kate took a deep breath. "That's a tough one." As another tear formed, she continued, "Oh Michael wouldn't want to see me like this. It's been such a long time since I've felt like this. I don't know where it's coming from." Kate quickly composed herself. Ruth reached for a tissue box under the counter and handed it to Kate. "Thank you," Kate replied.

"I certainly didn't mean to upset you."

"You haven't. You've been nothing but sweet to me. It's tough for me to even think about, let alone talk about."

"Well, no worries. You don't have to say anything more."

Kate thought about it and said, "No. I want to talk about it. I need to talk about it. Certainly talking about it with you seems my best option. Michael doesn't want to talk about it anymore. The whole thing is a growing wedge between us that neither of us wants to talk about. It hurts too much and neither one of us wants to hurt the other one anymore."

Ruth pulled up the other stool next to Kate to give her full attention. Kate continued, "Except it's something I need to talk about. I think holding it inside is what is making it all so difficult. I know for men it is easier to just hold on to it. But I think women need to get it out. Don't you agree?"

"I think it is a matter of both men and women needing to get it out. I don't think it does anyone any good to hold on to something that is hurting them. Hold on to the love. That is what we should all hold on to."

"You're right. It does no one any good to hold on to what hurts us. You see, Michael and I wanted so badly to have a baby. My career wasn't exactly what I had hoped for. While a career can be fulfilling and even be an accomplishment, it's not what ultimately defines you in your life especially when you're not exactly thrilled with how your career turned out. I was sure being a mommy was something to be treasured. Like every little girl, I wanted to be someone's mommy."

Kate grabbed for a tissue and wiped the corners of her eyes before it was too late.

She continued, "When we couldn't seem to make a baby ourselves, the situation became stressful. I wasn't getting any younger. Or so others reminded me."

"Oh that is just awful. Sometimes people say the most stupid things," Ruth interjected.

Kate continued, "Years went by and we tried everything in the book and still nothing. When mom got sick, I wanted so badly to get pregnant. I had hopes that if she had something to live for, like a grandbaby, she'd make it. So we pushed on and were referred to a fertility specialist who ultimately told us that I was not ovulating. That while I had my periods, there did not seem to be a detectable time of ovulation. My periods have always been extremely irregular." Kate paused. "I'm sorry. Is that too personal? That's not something you share, is it?"

"Honey, it's only personal if you make it personal and we're far beyond that," Ruth assured her.

"Good. Well, as it turned out, our only choice was to try *in vitro* fertilization."

"Oh, I see," Ruth said stirring her own tea but never taking a drink.

"So we poured a bunch of money into it. The first embryos didn't take and I lost the babies. There were five of them. I wasn't handling it all very well so Michael decided we should borrow money against my 401k to pay for another round. He even took a loan out on his business so we could try again. We decided together we would give it only one more go. This time I carried one embryo eight weeks. Everything seemed like it was going well." Kate paused a moment. Ruth, seeing her distress, held her hand. "I lost the baby. That was just over a month before we came here that weekend. I was so depressed. I felt like such a failure. I failed Michael and myself and I left us broke. I knew when I lost that baby it was the end of the road. We couldn't afford another round. At the same time, Michael's business was suffering and soon he had to close up shop altogether. I felt like it was my entire fault."

"My dear, it was no one's fault. It just was. You said yourself you both decided to do this together. Certainly Michael doesn't blame you."

"He doesn't. I just feel guilty about it all."

Ruth spoke up. "Oh, guilt is from the devil. We owe it to Christ to let go of that feeling. We are all sanctified by the blood of Christ for whatever we do in this life. Ask and you shall receive his grace."

Kate stared ahead in silence. Then Ruth added, "I'm sorry. I know religion makes some people uneasy. It is all I know. It is how I relate. I wanted you to understand that the guilt you feel is self-induced. It is something you can rid yourself of. It does not have to be who you are. No one blames you. Certainly not Michael or God."

"I know you're right. But it's so hard to let go. To let go of everything I dreamed life would be. Nothing mattered more to me than being a mom. And when that was taken from me, I didn't know what I was supposed to do with my life. Even now, I'm not sure if this is where I am really supposed to be."

Kate blew her nose before saying, "How do you know what you are doing here is right for you?"

Ruth said, "Because it feels right. This is exactly where the Lord wants me. If you ask me people don't appreciate where they are enough. It really is best to enjoy where you are, knowing full well it is where you are meant to be. Think about it. When you came here to Harmony what compelled you to want to stay?"

"Well, there was this peace about the place. The house reminded me of Mom and home."

Ruth asked, "And does it still?"

"It does. I'm just confused I guess."

Patting Kate on the arm, Ruth said, "That is because you are still young."

"Young? I'm thirty-six," Kate said.

"Youth is relative. When you are as old as I am, you'll see that. Too often with young people, the clouds get in the way of the sun." Ruth got up and walked over to a painting of Christ she had on the wall near the counter. "Those who focus on the sun only see its glory. Those who are lost among the clouds will remain there for eternity should they not keep their eye on the sun's glory."

Kate didn't say anything.

Ruth asked, "Does talking about religion bother you?"

"No, not necessarily, you know, just growing up with my mom, we weren't religious. Mom used to tell me that Gram was always on her about religion and I think it turned my mom off. Mom never talked about it...not ever."

"Did you know your grandmother well?"

"Oh no, she died when I was a little girl and Mom went out to her funeral alone. 'A funeral is no place for a kid,' she said. I remember her saying that so clearly. Then when she died a year ago, I wondered what she would want. Did she want me there? I couldn't be sure. I went of course. But it wasn't what I expected it to be. It was cold. I felt detached from her and everything. After all, Mom wasn't really there. Her body was there but she wasn't. I couldn't feel her. She was already gone."

There was a long pause between the two. Kate got up from her stool and walked over to the front window and stared out to the highway. Ruth felt it was best to give her the solitude she needed. Too often, Ruth had seen weary travelers come through Harmony and rush through the shop so they could get on to their next destination. It wasn't often she saw people stop and dwell in their solitude. Ruth went about cleaning up the counter of the tea service.

After a couple of minutes, Kate turned back to Ruth and asked, "Why would a God make it so I couldn't have children? What's the point in that?"

"Well, the Lord sometimes works in mysterious ways. What we may not understand now we generally find out later. I know, because you're still so close to that pronouncement it's hard for you to understand, but what you have been through has reason in it. You may not know it now but someday you will."

"I guess," Kate said. "I just don't understand how I could miss something I never really had."

Ruth approached Kate at the window. "I can't be certain but maybe somewhere out there you have it – maybe not in this earthly vessel but on some other level. So your heart aches for what it knows is out there already. Maybe that's some silly old lady logic. I don't know but that's what came to me in the moment you asked it."

"Are you saying that maybe somewhere in heaven there's a baby waiting for me, you know, for when I get there?"

"Perhaps. The thing is, on earth, we're always changing, chasing a dream, sometimes there is success and sometimes there is failure. In heaven, there is no failure. There is no fear. No dream. Heaven is the dream."

"How can you be sure?" Kate asked.

"I feel it. It's the same certainty I have in being here. It's all I need."

Kate thought about it for a moment. "Thank you for listening and for the tea. I appreciate it."

"It's no problem. I've enjoyed it."

"I should get back to the house. There's more there for me to do."

"It was my pleasure, dear. Stop by again soon. I love the company."

CHAPTER 14

Back at the house, Michael was out front putting the finishing touches on painting the porch. With the wind zipping through the eucalyptus trees, he whipped the brush along the white wood railing of the landing. The work he was doing was a great distraction from the problems he had with Kate. The simplicity of the work was satisfying for him.

Michael began to hum to himself without even realizing it. As he thought about the song he was humming, he didn't even recognize it. He stopped for a minute to try and place the song. As he did, he heard the humming continue. Someone else was humming.

"What song is that?"

The humming stopped. There was no answer.

"Kate?" Again no answer. Feeling like maybe the heat was getting to him, he decided to take a break and get a drink. He stood up and walked down the steps of the porch to where he had placed his bottle of water. He took a swig and looked out over the grassy valley in front of the house. In the distance, the trees continued to sway in motion of the coastal winds. He started to hum again but this time caught himself and stopped. Again, the humming continued uninterrupted. It wasn't even Kate. He heard it. The humming was behind him. He turned but no one was there. He walked around the corner of the porch to see if anyone was on the side of the house. As he came back around to the corner of the porch, he saw the porch swing move as if someone had just gotten up. Michael shook his head in disbelief.

"Is someone there?" he asked.

Getting no response, he turned completely around in every direction. The lush landscape revealed no one. As he turned back to the porch, he heard the faintest laugh so he turned around again but nothing.

"Alright! Who's out there?" he demanded. "I heard you. I heard you laugh. I heard you hum. Now come on. Show yourself. This isn't funny."

He scanned the landscape again hoping to see something, anything. But there was nothing there.

"Michael, who are you talking to?" He turned back around and there was Kate in the distance walking up the drive to the house.

"Was that you?" he asked.

"Me? What?" she wanted to know.

"Are you playing some sort of joke on me? Was that you laughing?"

Kate laughed and said, "You hearing things?"

Michael didn't know what to say. He knew he heard both the laugh and the humming. He even saw the swing move but he didn't know what to say to Kate.

"I guess I was just talking to myself."

Kate laughed again. "I guess all this solitude is getting to you, too."

"Yeah, and maybe the heat."

"You'd better come in. It's getting pretty warm out here."

Michael followed Kate up the steps. As he ascended the steps of the porch, he turned around one more time just to make sure no one else was out there.

"The toilet is all done," he made sure to tell her.

"Thank you." She walked down the hall to see for herself. "It looks good," she called out from the bathroom. She flushed the toilet to see it work.

Coming back to the living room she said, "That's a sound I never thought I'd treasure this much."

"Yeah, I know what you mean."

"When did Beck go?" she asked.

"Shortly after we were done. He was taking Lucy in to see the dentist."

"Is she alright?"

"It didn't seem like she wasn't. He didn't really say anything about it. I assumed it was something routine."

Kate thought about it. "Well, once we get the kitchen together we should have them over for dinner."

"As long as it's nothing big, it should be alright," Michael replied. "You know I'm not crazy about entertaining."

"All too well," Kate answered.

Michael turned to walk back out to the porch.

"Michael," Kate called.

"Yeah."

"Before you go out, I want to say I'm sorry about yesterday. I overreacted. There's no excuse."

He smiled and said, "I understand." She came over to him and gave him a hug.

He told her, "Thanks for apologizing. It means a lot."

She looked up at him and kissed him and asked, "You want my help outside?"

"Sure."

As they worked on painting the porch, Michael asked, "Have you noticed anything strange going on around the house?"

Kate asked, "Like what?"

"Like, I don't know. Have you heard things?"

Kate again, "Like what?"

"I'm not sure. When I was outside here earlier I thought I heard humming. Like a girl humming."

"A girl?"

"I know it sounds strange but it's playing over and over in my head. It sounded like a little girl to me. Are there any kids around here that you have seen in town?"

"There are just the two babies and Stan's kid, Rocket. But he wouldn't come out here all this way on his own."

"That's what I thought."

"You know, when I was painting the kitchen, I thought I heard someone laughing. I actually thought it was you playing a joke on me but then I remembered you had gone to town. It sounded like a little girl to me too. Michael, you don't suppose that maybe this house is haunted?"

"Haunted, oh no."

"Why not? Maybe the house is haunted. Raye could have unloaded this house on us."

"Kate, you can't honestly tell me you believe that."

"I don't know. Maybe I do...that's all I am saying."

Michael laughed. Kate wasn't amused. "Is it really that hard for you to believe?"

He answered, "I don't think it's logical is all."

"Then what is it? What else could it be?"

Michael thought more about it. "I don't know, but not a ghost."

"Well, I saw a shadow cross behind me when I was painting. I looked around and no one was there."

Michael laughed. Kate still wasn't amused. He said, "Come on. It could have been an illusion."

"Well, I got so freaked out I went into town. I didn't want to be alone."

"I'm sorry. I didn't realize."

"Why are you sorry?"

"Because I shouldn't have left you alone."

Kate got up and walked over to the door.

"Kate, stop it. Don't get mad at me."

"Why, Michael? Why not! I'm not this fragile thing that you have to guard. I'm not. Besides it's not just me. You heard something too. It's not just fragile little Kate. It's you as well."

Michael said, "I just think there has to be a rational reason for all of it. That's all."

"And the whispers and laughing and unlatched screen door? Sure, what is that, then? Why can't it logically be a ghost?"

"Because there is no such thing, Kate."

"Says you! But what do you know. What do you know about anything, Michael? You know, Michael, that day I went into town to meet everybody, someone mentioned that the house was haunted. You don't know everything, you know."

"That's the problem with you, Kate. As soon as I or anyone else says something to you that you don't agree with, you make it personal. Can't you ever argue your point on a level playing field? That's the difference between men and woman. Women can't argue on the same level so they make it personal."

Michael got up and walked off down the drive. It was silent. There was no humming or laughing or singing or talking. No one was there. No one but him and he was alone. He was sure of it. He wondered if they'd ever find their way back to the way it was before.

CHAPTER 15

There were a couple of days of silence between the couple as they continued working separately on projects around the house. On the anniversary of her mom's death, Kate wasn't about to give Michael the satisfaction of bringing it up. However, she needed to talk to someone about it and her now routine visits with Ruth were the cherished part of her day.

Kate sat herself on the stool at the end of Ruth's counter as Ruth appeared from the backroom carrying a huge stack of boxes.

"Can I give you a hand?" Kate asked.

"Oh no honey, I've got it. I feel terrific. The sun is shining, the ocean breeze cheery and all is good in the world."

Kate looked down. Ruth offered, "How about a cup of tea?"

Kate replied, "Sure." It wasn't a convincing response. Not saying anything more, Ruth walked over to her electric teapot and poured two cups.

"Ruth, can I ask you something?"

"Of course," Ruth answered.

"What's heaven like? I mean, I know there's peace there and it's this golden place with streets of gold. All that stuff the movies show us. But beyond the physical elements what is it like to be there?"

Ruth turned around slowly. "Honey, do you think I've been there?" Ruth smiled as she amused herself.

"Oh no, of course not! I'm asking because of, you know, your past and because you're so into religion."

"I know, dear. I am just having fun with you. The truth is I don't think heaven is a physical place at all. Heaven's not up in the sky like so many think. It's a place of mind. It knows no boundary. I believe a soul is at peace once it arrives in heaven. It does not wander or wonder. It knows. And when we die, our soul goes to that place of peace. The soul is in harmony with the spiritual realm and all its elements. Void of time, pain and distance. It's unlike anything we could imagine."

Ruth brought over the cups of tea on saucers for the two of them. "That's probably more than you asked, I know. But heaven is hard for anyone to define. It is beyond our comprehension. Even the greatest minds of this earth have tried to comprehend the alternate universe that heaven is. Describing it as an alternate universe isn't even correct. Heaven is beyond us, yet it is still a part of us."

Kate said, "I never really thought of it that way. What part of it is with us?"

"The part we hold in our hearts. The hope and happiness for a brighter future." Ruth sat down next to Kate. "I'm curious as to why you would ask such a heavy question today. Is it your baby you're wondering about?"

"No, it's not that. Today's the anniversary of my mom's passing. I woke up knowing it. It was the first thing I thought about. I just want to know she's okay."

"Honey, she's in heaven. She is more than okay. She is perfect."

"I hope so. I miss her. She was all the family I had. Being an only child is lonely enough and once your parents are gone, it's even lonelier."

"I can only imagine. But you still have Michael," Ruth said.

"I do. That's the trouble with me, Ruth. I worry way too much and think of what was."

Ruth interjected, "And what can't be changed."

"I can't help it. It's who I am. My mom was a worrier too."

"But you can, Kate. You just need to choose not to worry."

"How so?"

"I mean you don't have to worry so much. It may be how you are made, but we have choices. We can make changes in ourselves if we choose to do so. Now, I'm not saying it is easy. Changing is never easy. Especially if we are fighting those things so imbedded in us that we think they make up who we are. It is like fighting the very nature of our being but the reward can be oh so glorious if we can just reach beyond that which we think we cannot do.

"I read a passage once about songbirds. No matter what happens the songbird sings. Though it may rain or winds howl or its enemy steal its eggs, the songbird rises with the sun on each new day and sings. Happy only for a new day and its new beginning."

"Of course, it's far easier for something as simple as a bird."

"Why?" Ruth asked. "Why do you think it is easy?"

"I don't know. I suppose because life is so much simpler for the bird."

"Life is only as complicated as we make it. Make it complicated and it is complicated. Make it simple and it is simple. It really is as easy as that."

"You're so confident. How can you be so sure we can be who we want to be?"

"I am confident because I have seen the signs that what I believe is true."

Kate sighed, "I guess I just don't get it."

"Take Harmony here; I believe Harmony is a spiritual place. I like to think of it like a little piece of heaven on earth. You can't look at the majestic surroundings and not be moved. There's a legend about the Piedras Blancas Lighthouse up the road. The legend says the light's beacon calls souls here for the beauty we all cherish. It calls us out further west to what lies beyond the shore. Above the waves and clouds lies a life beyond this one."

Kate said, "That legend about souls...is it talking about souls as in ghosts?"

"In a way, I think it does."

"So are you saying Harmony is haunted?"

"Oh no, not haunted. That is such an overused term."

"Do you believe in ghosts?"

Ruth said, "I don't believe in ghosts the way you think of them. There's the Holy Ghost. And there are angels and demons alike. Those are real and can certainly give the illusion of being ghostly. I don't want to get too far ahead of you, Kate. Spirituality is a precious gift. It is not something I can answer for you. I have been on my journey a lot longer than you have. If there is anything to be learned it is patience. Patience, patience, patience. Anne Morrow Lindbergh wrote that."

"I was never good at patience. Michael can attest to that."

"I think patience is something that is learned with age. Soon enough, time will move faster than you want it to. And your impatience will disappear. Then you'll be longing for things to slow down."

"Right now, I can't wait until the house is in order."

"I don't doubt that."

Kate said, "The pace here in Harmony is much slower, but I'm learning to enjoy it. It's hard when things at home are going so slowly."

"Renovations can be difficult but in time things will get done and you'll be able to look back on the journey and be all the more proud at what you accomplished. You need to treasure times like this in the midst of the journey."

"That's easier said than done," Kate said. "As much as I enjoy the pace of Harmony, it's the pace of getting things in order here that I'm having trouble with."

"That is because you compartmentalize these two areas of your life separately when they should be joined together. If you think of it all being connected, then those things that bring you peace should balance out those things where peace seems impossible."

"I'm not sure I understand."

Ruth, without much thought, answered, "It isn't easily explained. It is something you have to experience for yourself. There's a harmony between things in life even between the physical and spiritual. Take the beach. When I first set my eyes on the coastline here I thought I had died and gone to heaven. I stood there with my naked feet in the warm and soft sand and curled my toes in it, connecting with it. Then the onshore breeze hit my face and I closed my eyes. The breath I took in was like a baptism. That powerful, cleansing wind, I had not felt anything else like it. I knew then and there I was finally home. Everything just made sense in that moment."

Kate watched as Ruth closed her eyes as she told the story. Ruth licked her lips and tried to taste the salty air of the beach. "That day on the beach, I had my gift and I knew this was where my Lord wanted me to be."

Kate replied, "Wow. I wish that I could know my every move is a right one."

"Honey, my every move has not always been correct. I've made my mistakes – plenty of them in fact. But the past is past. Life should be about taking from our mistakes what we can and using them to move us on. Take beach glass for instance. Certainly, the thought of someone throwing litter in the sea is a mistake, but the ocean takes it and tosses it around until it becomes something of beauty. Something someone walking along the beach will stop and pick up and carry away with them."

Kate said, "But there are some mistakes I doubt you can really walk away from."

"You're wrong. I've made my share of mistakes that I thought weren't forgivable. For instance, walking away from the church. I made a commitment to God in marriage to my Lord and yet I walked away. I was chastised for it and felt a level of guilt for it no one should. Now, I look back at that and over the course of my life it wasn't even the biggest mistake I made."

Ruth turned toward the window and watched as the traffic sped by on the highway. "The truth is I think it takes time for things to come into perspective. Time slows you down so you can think about things. I can't tell you all the hours I have sat and thought things over at the beach just taking in the inspiring landscape. The beach is a gift from God. A gift to be taken in over long periods of time. Time alone. Time to think. Time to appreciate."

"I've always just thought of it as a nice place to hang out, work on a tan, you know, soak up the sun."

Ruth continued, "When I see the beauty in a landscape or in the face of a child or in two people sharing a moment together I think it is awe inspiring."

"I wish I felt the way you do," Kate said.

"Well, don't say that. Go down to the beach. Go and experience it for yourself. Go and feel the clarity. Connect with that spirit inside yourself that is yearning to come out. There is power and peace in moving beyond our own reality to a power greater than ourselves. Go now! Don't sit here sipping tea with this old woman. Go on. The beach is calling."

Ruth shuffled over to Kate and with all her might attempted to move the girl to the door. Kate didn't resist. She was eager to experience something.

Kate took her time in walking down to the beach. As she reached the coastline, she noticed she had the windswept shore to herself. She sat there looking out at the sparkle and the endless expanse. For what seemed like endless minutes nothing seemed to happen. Before she knew it her mind began to wander as the rhythm of the waves mesmerized her. In a natural state of meditation, she cleared her mind and forced herself to feel the serenity of the moment. Her mind cleared of thoughts of her mom and concerns of Michael. Before long, the sun began to drop in front of her. Its endless copper circle pulled at her from inside.

It's calling me. What does it say?

Kate surrendered to its trance. Her eyes fixed on its glow. She couldn't move. She didn't think. It had erased her thoughts. Nothing came to mind and she slipped willingly into its preeminence. She had moved to a place she had never been before. It was as if her mind was no longer present and euphoria washed over her.

"Kate."

The hairs on the back of her neck came alive. *I am here.*

"You alright?" the voice called out.

I am.

She felt the comfort of a hand on her shoulder. The hand shook her. "Kate." She turned and there was Michael.

"Michael?"

"There you are. I was worried about you."

Kate smiled at him. She stood and hugged him around the neck. "How did you know where to find me?"

"I stopped by Ruth's and she mentioned she sent you down here. You okay?"

"I am." A breeze washed over the two of them. Kate closed her eyes and soaked it in. She opened her eyes to see Michael looking at her.

"I saw you here and worried that you were crying."

"No. Nothing like that," she said.

He smiled. "I'm glad you're okay."

"I am."

CHAPTER 16

Over the next week, Michael and Kate worked on getting the bathroom in place. They removed the old claw foot tub and exchanged it for a tub and shower enclosure with tiles they laid themselves. Michael and Beck put the tub in place and had all the plumbing together in a single day. Kate was impressed at how handy Michael was becoming. Each morning, Kate made a big pot of coffee and off they were, tiling away. Both of them working together, laughing and enjoying each other's company again as if nothing had happened.

Michael didn't know what to make of the sudden transformation so he remained slightly guarded. As the week went on, more and more of the fragile Kate vanished. She never even mentioned her mom and all signs of depression were gone. Not wanting to stir up the past, Michael ignored every opportunity to talk about it and ruin where they were heading. He chose to accept how well things were going.

Their time together had helped release some of the guilt and hopelessness Kate still carried with her. Plus, watching Michael work was actually sexy to Kate. She hadn't said anything to him but her feelings for him physically were gratifying. The fact was clear that Kate wanted her husband in the physical sense for the first time in a long time. The feelings were freeing and impulsive.

At the end of the week, when all the tile was laid, Kate polished up some of the grout work while Michael mopped up the floor.

"Finally, we have a new shower without that old rusty pipe!" Michael declared.

"And it looks great," Kate said. "You do great work."

"Thanks."

"I have an idea," Kate said. "Why don't we break it in?"

Kate didn't wait for his answer. She approached and kissed him. Michael willingly returned the kiss, pulling her close. As the kiss continued, his hands wandered. Kate immediately ended the kiss and stood back from him.

For a second, Michael was confused. Without warning, Kate pulled her top over her head and headed toward the shower, her body glistening with the sweat of her hard work. She then unclipped her bra and let it fall to the ground. Michael without hesitation reached out to grab her. He held her and kissed her passionately. Michael's hands all over her, Kate pulled at the bottom of Michael's shirt and raised it over his head. Michael continued to kiss Kate all over.

Instead of taking a shower, Michael carried Kate to the bedroom.

On the bed, Michael slipped Kate's pants off. He then slid off his own and climbed on top of her.

"I love you," he said.

"I love you!" she said back. They kissed as he positioned himself and as he did, Kate sighed. As they moved together, suddenly there was a giggle. Michael immediately stopped moving.

"Did you hear something?" he whispered.

"I think I did," she replied. They lay as one for a few seconds not making a sound, but they didn't hear anything. Michael started up again and they were back into their rhythm. They continued to move as one when they heard it again. Without finishing, Michael stopped, rolled off Kate and looked behind him. Embarrassed, Kate pulled the blanket over her naked body. Michael was on the opposite side of the bed from where his shorts were.

He stood up. Covering himself, he walked toward his shorts. Again there was a girl's giggle. The giggle came from right in the room. He rushed to grab his shorts and pulled them up.

"Damn it!" he said. "Who's here?" He went to the bedroom doorway and looked down the hall. Seeing nothing, he went in the living room. No one was there and the front door was still closed and locked. From the hall, he heard creaks on the wood floors.

"Kate?"

"Yeah Mike." He heard her reply still inside the bedroom. He went into the kitchen. The back door was also locked. He raced back and checked the bathroom. Still no one. Returning to the bedroom, he found Kate with a t-shirt and a pair of shorts on.

"What was it?" she asked.

"I'm not sure but you heard it too?"

"Oh yeah. That was freaky."

"What did it sound like to you?"

"Like a kid or something. Laughing," she replied.

"Like it was coming from inside the ..."

"...room," she finished.

"Right. Did it sound like someone was at the window watching?"

"Could have been. Did you look outside the window?" Kate asked.

"No, it sounded like it was inside. I'm sure of it. But no one's here and both doors are locked."

Kate answered, "This is so weird."

The two of them looked at each other, drawing the same conclusion without saying a word. Everything they had heard or seen before was questionable. But there was no denying it this time. This was real.

"Michael, I'm scared."

Kate walked toward him and put her arms around him. She held him tightly around the waist, resting her head on his bare chest. Michael's silence offered her no comfort. She knew it meant he was scared too.

The two of them sat on the bed, watching, waiting for something to happen. Nothing did.

As night fell, they decided to sleep in shifts and hope that whatever, whoever it was, would return. Kate took the first shift. Kate decided keeping busy would be best so she lined the new kitchen cabinet drawers and shelves. Instead of putting the stereo on in the living room, she plugged in a smaller radio in the kitchen, keeping it low. She tuned it to KMOR and a song came on that Kate liked. She started to hum then stopped herself, remembering the humming had elicited the sounds before. She kept quiet. Then a crackling album version of "Moonlight Serenade" came on the radio and it gave the house a creepy feeling. Kate became uneasy. She stopped lining the top shelf of the overhead cabinets and got down from the step ladder to turn the station. As she tuned the radio, behind the static, she heard crying. Startled, Kate continued to turn the radio knob in an attempt to make the crying stop. She tuned in an easy listening station way down on the dial that was playing current pop music.

Kate turned back toward the step ladder and the radio began to tune itself back up the dial. Kate froze. She listened to the static between stations as the dial finally settled back on "Moonlight Serenade."

Kate was panic-stricken. Without thought, she went over and pulled the plug on the radio. In mid-song, the music stopped. There was silence. Kate didn't move for what seemed like minutes and listened until finally she sighed in relief.

Just as she turned back to her work, there it was again, the crying. With no radio, there was little to be confused about.

Kate listened to the crying. It was a young girl. Kate's heart pounded hard against her chest. The crying was clear. It was close. It wasn't in the kitchen but it was close. Inside the house for certain. Kate remained still but wasn't completely afraid.

Without thought, she muttered, "Why are you crying?"

The crying continued. Kate asked a little more loudly, "Hello?"

The crying stopped. Kate held her breath and there in the silence she heard "hello" in a hauntingly breathless voice.

Kate shook her head back and forth in denial and asked again, "Why were you crying?"

Kate held her breath some more not wanting to confuse any sounds, not even her own breathing, with what she might hear.

Still nothing so she asked, "Are you there?"

"I'm here," the voice said.

Kate was taken with goose bumps.

"Where are you?" Kate asked as she moved toward the voice. She was certain it was coming from the screened porch.

"I'm here with you."

Kate approached the screened porch. The door between the kitchen and porch was open. It always was when she was up. The night air coming in from the screened porch felt good. The porch screen door was latched and locked. She made certain before Michael went to bed.

"Who are you?" Kate asked as she approached the porch.

"I'm me, silly." It was a girl.

Kate tiptoed closer to the doorway between the two rooms. "And why were you crying?"

"Because you turned off the music."

"Oh," Kate answered, her heart now in her throat. "I'm sorry but you scared me. I didn't know you were here."

"Where else would I be? I've been here the whole time."

Kate was now just outside the doorway. The light was off in the porch. Frozen with fear for what she would see, she was afraid to move forward, but not enough afraid to do nothing. Kate mustered up the courage to step into the doorway. As she did she asked, "Who are you?"

She saw nothing in the porch but heard the voice as clear as if it was standing only a few feet in front of her. "It's me, silly -- Ruby."

Kate looked back and forth in the screened in area. She looked toward the pantry – nothing. She looked at the washer – nothing. She looked at the small table by the door – still nothing.

"Well, I'm Kate. It's nice to meet you."

"I know you're Kate. Michael calls you Kate all the time."

Kate turned her head every which way possible to see through the light coming in from the kitchen doorway. She hoped to see something without moving. As she strained to see something, there behind the table was a figure.

It was silhouetted.

It scared Kate.

"My God!" she called out and put her hand over her mouth. She didn't move and the silhouetted figure moved from behind the table. "Why are you afraid?" the girl asked.

"I...I...don't know," Kate answered. Kate's entire body began to shake uncontrollably. The figure was now in plain sight. From the light streaming in from the kitchen behind her, Kate could make out the figure of a very young girl around four years old. The vision was so clear that Kate could see her blonde hair and rose-patterned dress.

Kate screamed out, "MICHAEL!"

As she did, she switched on the porch light from the switch by the doorway. As the light came on, the vision of the girl was gone. Kate cried out again, "Michael. Come quick!"

She heard him running across the old creaky floorboards of the house. He reached the kitchen, squinting his eyes from the intense lights. "Kate, what is it?"

Kate screamed at her husband in fear. She came toward him and grabbed on to his arms. She was shaking. "Michael, there was a girl. Right here...in front of me." Kate turned back to the screened porch and pointed. "She was in there....right behind that table."

"What?" Michael asked.

"A girl. It was a girl. I saw her. She was in the screened porch by that table. She started to walk toward me. I talked to her and she answered back. Then I just freaked out."

"Who? What? I don't understand."

"I don't either," Kate said. She grabbed onto Michael tighter. "Michael, I saw it. I am telling you. You have to believe me. She even knew our names like she had been watching us the entire time we've been here."

Michael, unsure whether he was actually awake or still sleeping rubbed both eyes with one hand.

Taking Michael by the hand, Kate went over to the doorway. "Michael, come see. She was right here. I saw her with my own eyes."

Michael came over for a look and saw nothing. He was unsure what to think. Certainly they had heard other things. But he didn't know what to believe. Without thinking he said, "Kate, there is nothing here."

"I know, Michael, there is nothing here now. But she was right here. She was talking to me. She said her name was Ruby." Kate pointed back to the radio in the kitchen. "She even turned the station back on the radio to the one I was listening to. She was listening to it and when I turned it off she was crying. Michael, I think she lives here. She even knew my name and yours."

"What?"

"She did. She said she heard you call me Kate. She even called you by your name. I think she was watching us earlier in the bedroom. She's just a little girl. It made her laugh."

Without much thought, Michael went to the locked porch door and flipped on the outside light. He grabbed the flashlight he had stashed next to the door. He unlatched the door and stepped outside. He shined the light back and forth across the yard into the endless darkness. The coastal fog had rolled in and was lying thick over the green grasses giving the landscape an eerie feel.

Kate followed behind him, staying inside. Michael saw nothing. He scratched his head and turned off the flashlight. He turned back to the house and said, "Kate, there is nothing out there."

"Michael, she wasn't outside. She was in the house. Right here in the screened porch. She was blonde and wore a sundress with roses on it. It was a simple dress. Homemade, I think."

Seeing her husband's unbelief, she continued, "Michael, it was clear as that. She was here in this house."

Kate then turned back toward the kitchen and called out for her, "Ruby? Ruby? Where are you?

Michael is here. Don't be afraid. We're here with you." There was no response.

Kate was growing upset. "I'm not crazy. I know you think I am but I'm not." She insisted, "Michael, you know you heard her laugh earlier and the humming on the front porch. There is a girl here with us. She is here in the house. I am not crazy."

He thought more about it. He wasn't sure what was going on. He feared Kate was possibly seeing what she wanted to see. But then again, maybe Kate was right. The two pulled chairs out at their small kitchen table and waited it out. Kate even put on the radio again in hopes of luring the girl back out of hiding. Michael put on a pot of coffee and the two stayed up all night. But nothing happened. There was no crying or laughing or visions the rest of the night. As the sun came up, the two, unsure of what had happened, agreed to finally go to bed. It had been a long dark night.

Michael fell asleep quickly while Kate stayed awake in the morning light. She couldn't get the exchange out of her mind. With the sun up, the house felt its cheery self again. The kitchen with its sunny yellow was aglow in the pure light of day. Gone were the shadows of the darkness and the mysteries of the night. But even with the light of day, Kate was unsettled. She walked around the house looking and listening.

Kate had to get out of the house. She kissed her sleeping husband goodbye, leaving him a note on the night stand. She was hopeful Ruth could help shine some light on the matter.

CHAPTER 17

Ruth's shop was in chaos when Kate arrived. Nearly everything had been moved to one side of the shop. The door to the shop was wide open and plumes of dust spiraled out. Through the empty window, Kate could see Raye and Lucy dusting everything in the place.

"You know, Lucy," Raye said, "I told Holla about those snoring mouth guard thingies you say Beck uses."

"Oh yeah?" Lucy answered. "What'd she say?"

"She said that Sunny doesn't put anything artificial in his mouth."

"I wonder if they make one out of hemp."

Raye laughed.

"I'm serious," Lucy went on, wiping down the now empty front window box. "You'd think with all the smoking that boy does he'd be so relaxed that he wouldn't even snore."

Raye answered, "Now, you're only speculating. We don't know the personal practices of our town's honorary mayor."

"Yeah, right, speculating."

From behind the counter, amongst the clutter of countless knickknacks, Ruth noticed Kate entering. "Ladies, we have company," she said.

Lucy and Raye glanced up from their work to see who it was.

Raye was first to say, "You're out early this morning."

"I know," Kate replied. "Thought I'd get a jump on the day. I wanted to talk to Ruth about something but I see you're busy so I'll come back."

Lucy chimed in, "So busy we could use the help. Grab a duster and get to work."

"One thing about being so close to the highway is that the soot is a constant reminder that the road is there," Raye added.

"Go on," Lucy insisted, "there's a duster, use it and gab away. Besides, we need something or someone new to talk about."

Raye added, "The problem with a small town is new topics are hard to come by."

Kate didn't really know where to begin. Before she could think, Lucy threw the duster at her. "Here ya go."

Kate caught it and put it to work.

Lucy scooted out from between a table and the window. "Now that Kate's here, think I'll go check on Danny. She's over watching Stan's brats. I don't like her to be over there too long alone. I'll be back."

Raye said, "Stop worrying about Danny. She's fine."

"It's not Danny I'm worried about. It's that Stan. I don't want him to get too comfortable with

Danny that he finds her a permanent replacement for Tess."

"Why not?" Raye asked. "He's a good father and he'd be a great husband."

Lucy looked over at Raye. "For someone else maybe, but not my Danny. Anyway, Kate's here. She can help fill in for me for a while. I'll be back later to catch up on the gossip. Take notes."

Lucy quickly grabbed her purse over at the counter. "See ya Ruthie. I'll be back." Kate watched through the window as Lucy walked across the vacant street to a door at the back of Stan's glass shop.

Raye said, "That's just like Lucy to find someone else to do her share of the work. I swear Ruth that woman hasn't worked a day since Danny got here. Between that girl and Beck, Lucy manages to avoid every lick of the work."

Ruth noticed the seriousness on Kate's face as Raye spoke. "What is it you wanted to talk about, honey?"

"Oh, it can wait," Kate said as she made her way around the front of the empty shop.

"Either you start talking," Raye said, "or we are obligated to start asking you questions. It's either what you came in to talk about or we pry something else out of you."

"It's about the house," Kate said. "And the previous owner."

"Who, Gertie?" Raye answered. "What do you want to know about her?"

"Did you all know her well?" Kate asked.

"Honey, there is only eighteen of us here," Raye said. "We know everyone pretty well."

Kate smiled then said, "Did she ever mention hearing things in the house?"

"No, she lived alone," Raye said looking over at Ruth as she dusted the tiniest of knickknacks.

"Did she ever mention any ghosts?"

"Ghosts? You think Gertie's haunting you?" Raye asked.

"Well, not exactly. I was wondering if she ever said anything to you about seeing or even hearing things in the house. Things that weren't really there."

Everyone was silent for a minute. So Ruth asked, "Are you seeing things in the house?"

"I'm not sure. That's why I'm asking."

"You think you're seeing things then?" Raye said.

Kate answered, "I know I'm seeing things. And not just seeing them but hearing and talking with them."

Raye's painted on eyebrows raised nearly to her hair line. As soon as they went up, they came back down with a questioning frown. "What is it you are seeing?"

Kate thought about it before answering.

"I think there is a child living in our house."

"A child?" Raye said first.

Ruth added, "Glory be."

Kate continued, "I saw her last night. She was a vision of some sort. She said her name was Ruby and she knew my name and Michael's. Am I crazy?"

Raye quickly insisted, "No, you're not crazy."

"Honey, could it be you're grieving for the baby you and Michael lost?" Ruth asked. "Or maybe you were dreaming."

"I didn't think about the baby," Kate said. She thought about it for a moment. Then she said, "I know I wasn't dreaming. And this isn't a baby. It's a girl. A little girl."

"Amazing grace," Ruth said in astonishment.

Raye and Ruth came closer to Kate as she continued talking. "I saw her as plain as day last night. I don't know, maybe she's a little girl who died."

Raye answered, "I don't know of any little girls that died around here."

Kate asked, "Maybe Gertie's daughter?"

"That was ages ago," Raye answered. "Besides Gert's daughter was an infant when she died."

Kate then asked, "Well, has anyone else around here seen anything peculiar like this before? Is this place haunted?"

The two tenured residents of Harmony didn't say a word.

Then Ruth explained, "As far as ghosts are concerned, in the way you mean, people don't come back. Once you leave your life here on earth and go to the heavenly realm, there is no necessity to come back. Once you're there, you'll never want to leave. So ghosts in the way you are thinking about them don't really exist."

"But what about this girl? If she's not a ghost what can she be?" Kate asked.

"Well, maybe she's a sort of holy ghost?" Ruth asked. "God does send his messengers to earth with special purposes. Are not all ministering spirits sent to serve for the sake of salvation?"

"I don't know," Kate said. "I, actually, hadn't...this is a little girl not something spiritual."

Ruth continued, "Kate, you're misguided if you think children aren't spiritual. They're actually more open to it than adults. Adulthood hasn't robbed them of the pure innocence of believing."

Kate wasn't following Ruth's logic.

Seeing her aggravation, Raye told her, "Kate, I told you Harmony is a special place. Why I'm never surprised to hear about supernatural things like what you have seen. So if you say you saw a girl and you truly believe it then I believe you."

"So do I," Ruth said.

Their confidence in her was a comfort. "You really think a messenger could take on the form of a little girl?"

Ruth answered, "They can take on almost any form. That of a person, an animal, even a child. There is nothing outside the realm of what God is capable of doing. He sends us his holy spirit in various forms to guide us, lead us and advise us."

Raye explained, "We're more likely to be comforted by people or things we feel most relaxed with."

Kate thought about what they were telling her.

Raye added, "Nothing surprises me about what is possible. Not even this. This isn't the first time something like this has happened in this town. Those of us here are drawn here by its lure of contentment and peace. Then there's that legend of the lighthouse. Who's to say that isn't true?"

"Are there others who have seen similar things?" Kate still wanted to know.

"We've all seen things," Raye answered. "The thing is some of us accept it. Others suppress it. Either they don't understand it, are afraid of it or they do know what it is so they fight it."

"So it's not just me then?" Kate asked.

"I bet it has been like this for centuries," Raye said.

Ruth added, "Who knows, maybe that old lighthouse out there *is* a beacon."

Kate wondered what Michael would think. She sat there in a daze.

"You alright?" Raye asked her.

"Yeah I'm just wondering what Michael is going to think of all this. He's very skeptical of things like this."

Raye replied, "He does seem that type. But I wouldn't put too much worry into what he thinks."

"Has he always been so reluctant," Ruth asked, "about things like this?"

"Not always. In fact, when I met and married him it was his optimism that made me love him even more. He was so positive and confident."

"What changed?" Raye asked.

"I guess me. I became obsessed with having a baby and he obsessed with giving me one. The more I sunk into my dark places, the more he pushed himself to get me what would make me happy."

"It's so like a man to have to fix things," Raye said.

"It's in their make-up," Ruth said. "A man is wired to lead, protect and assure his family that he has everything under control. That the wife and family can count on him. It's a survival thing much like every other species of animals."

"Well, when he couldn't fix me and things started spinning out of control for us, his optimism faded."

Raye asked, "What do you think it was that set him over the edge?"

"I shouldn't say this," Kate said looking at Ruth, "you being an ex-nun and all, but Michael blamed God for the lot of our problems. He believed that God should have come through for us with the baby and his business. And when things got worse, in Michael's words, we were on our own. He'd say things like 'There's nothing out there supporting our lives. When we die we die and more people are born and more people die. There is nothing greater out there.'"

Ruth asked, "And what do you think?"

"That's a tough one. Ruth, you're a nice lady and all, but my mom raised me, I guess, to be as skeptical as Michael is."

"That's interesting. You obviously have had an effect on what he believes, or doesn't believe."

"I never thought about it that way," Kate said. "It's funny how it all turned out. My mom fought so hard against religion her whole life. You see Gram was very religious and Mom didn't see the point in any of it. So she raised me without any religion at all. I mean, there were rules to be followed, but we never talked about or set foot in a church. I think that maybe when Gram died my mom blamed God as well. I'm not really sure. We never really talked about that."

"I know your grandmother died when you were young. Did you know your grandfather?" Ruth asked.

"No, my grandfather died before I was even born. I think that was the reason my grandma was so religious. She turned to religion as her solace."

Raye asked, "Why?"

"My mom told me that after he died, Gram dedicated her life to her church. My mom wanted nothing to do with that. That's why she ran off with my dad for a while. They never married. By the time I was born, my dad was long gone. I know Gram came for a visit at some point. I believe there's a picture of me and her from when I was a baby. I wish I could find those pictures. I still can't find everything from the move. In fact," Kate said looking at her watch, "I should really be getting back. I'm sure Michael's awake now. He'll be worrying about me."

"Oh, don't let us keep you," Raye said returning to the dusting. "We shouldn't have kept you here this long if you have work to do."

Kate smiled. "It's okay. I knew if I came down here Ruth could help me get back on track. It's funny. You remind me so much of my mom. I could talk to her for hours on end and every time I did I felt so much better because of it. Anyway, thank you, you both gave me a lot to think about."

"What did I have to do with any of it?" Raye asked.

Kate laughed. "I'm not exactly sure but you're just easy to talk to. You seem to get me. You know, I regret all that I had taken for granted before coming here."

"It doesn't have to always be like that," Raye said.

Ruth chimed in, "Don't let regrets from the past hold you up from events of tomorrow."

Raye to Ruth, "Anne Morrow Lindbergh?"

"Oh gosh no," Ruth said. "I just made it up I think."

The women laughed.

"You're right. No more regrets," Kate said. "I'm just going to march home and tell Michael what you told me about the girl and see what he says. I'll convince him it's nothing to worry about. It's a good thing, right?"

"It is," Raye said.

Ruth added, "It is a blessing, my dear. You will see."

"And so will he," Kate said turning toward the door. "Thanks again, ladies. Have a great day."

CHAPTER 18

Michael woke up alone. Afraid something had happened to Kate, he got up quickly. He threw himself back on the bed as soon as he read Kate's note. He laid there thinking about what had happened the night before. He couldn't wrap his mind around any of it. As close as he and Kate had gotten, he worried that deep down she was slipping further away.

After a while, he headed into the kitchen, poured himself some coffee and seeing the radio decided to turn it on. He stood there a moment waiting for anything out of the ordinary. Nothing.

Michael decided to install the new dishwasher in hopes it could distract Kate from last night. He ripped open the box and dug in for the instructions. Unfolding the booklet of step-by-step directions, he realized the project was actually tougher than he would have liked. With his recent advances in working around the house, he was confident, nonetheless, in his abilities and wanted to take it on himself.

Michael went to work. He cleared out the cleaning products already stashed below the sink and turned off the water from underneath. Lying on his back, he slid in under the sink. Grabbing his newly purchased plumber's wrench, he began to loosen the ancient pipe fittings. Obvious to Michael was that this was the first time in decades anyone had tried to loosen the pipe fittings. The plumbing was old and calcified from years of a slow leak that had sealed itself up. Years of droplets of water running down the outside of the pipes made it difficult to grapple with his wrench.

With the shiny wrench clamped over the rough and grainy fitting and with all his strength, the wrench torqued around the pipe. Michael grasped the wrench tightly but the shiny teeth of the jaws slipped from the aged fitting. He made a tighter attempt and as he applied pressure, the wrench slipped again. Only this time, when the wrench slipped so did his hand against the rusty hot water valve. His knuckles cracked with the strike and the rawness of the valve tore the skin off the top of his knuckles.

"Damn it," he said in anger as he grabbed his hurt hand with the other. Michael sat up quickly from under the sink and in doing so hit his head against the top of the inner cabinet. The pain was quick and sharp to the top of his head. Again, loudly, "Damn it!" Moving his good hand from the throbbing one, he placed it on top of his head. He winced from the steady throbbing pain.

Michael scooted out from under the sink and sat up on the kitchen floor. That was when he heard, "You know you shouldn't say that."

Michael, without thinking, said, "What?"

"That word. You shouldn't say that word. It's a bad word."

Michael realized someone was there. The voice was clearly a child's. He looked around and saw no one. His heart raced. Michael sat up taller. He looked around the sunny kitchen and didn't see anyone.

"Who's there?" he asked.

"It's just me, Ruby."

Michael didn't move. He waited another minute unsure of what to say at first. "Ruby?"

"Yeah silly."

The voice sounded like it was right next to him.

"Where are you?" he asked.

"I'm right here behind you."

Quickly, Michael turned around one way and then the other. Still seeing no one, he finally turned all the way around facing the sink and window above it. With the blinding sunlight shining white in from the window, it was hard for him to see anything there. He stood to face the window.

"Where?" he asked again squinting into the light.

"Right here!" And just as soon as he heard her, he could see darkness pass in front of his face. "I'm waving my hand right in front of you. Can't you see it?" The darkness continued to move back and forth in front of eyes. Michael leaned back adjusting his eyes to the bright light and blurry vision before him. He finally made out a tiny silhouetted figure sitting on the counter next to the sink just above where he had been. The glowing sunlight around the figure made the details ominous.

Looking right at it, he heard, "Can you see me, Michael?"

Now he could make out the figure waving at him again. The sight shocked him. "My god, who are you?"

"I just told you. I'm Ruby."

Michael approached the figure and as he did she became less clear. He reached out his hands trying to touch the image that seemed close enough to reach. He felt nothing.

He stepped even closer -- his heart continuing to race.

"Are you okay?" she asked.

"I don't know. Am I?"

"I don't know but I bet that hurt. You know, you shouldn't say that word. It's a bad word."

Michael waved his hands in front of himself. The figure was gone. There was nothing there on the counter anymore.

"Are you still here?" he asked.

"No. I'm over here next to the table now."

Michael turned around and there standing next to the kitchen table was a young girl. He could see her clearly now; her golden hair, her smile, her dress. She looked no older than five years. She smiled at him. She looked real. Michael rubbed his eyes. He shook his head sure that he had hit it too hard. Sure that this was all just his imagination.

He said, "I don't understand. Where did you come from?"

"I didn't come from anywhere. I live here."

Michael didn't approach her. He stood perfectly still afraid if he moved she would disappear. "You live here?"

"Yeah, I live here with you and Kate. I'm glad you're here."

"You're glad I'm here? Do you know me?"

"Of course I do. I told you I live here. Before I was all alone, now I'm here with you and Kate. I'm not alone anymore."

Michael thought for a minute. He couldn't believe any of this was happening. And, what was it that was happening? "How long have you been here?"

"Oh, ever since I was born." The girl began to walk around the kitchen in front of Michael and depending on the sunlight she would come in and out of view for him. He kept his eyes on her unsure of what he was seeing.

"Have you always lived here alone?"

"Oh no," she laughed. "I live here with you and Kate. I'm not alone."

"Was that you there on the porch that day when I was painting?"

Ruby laughed, "Yeah, I love that swing."

Michael remembered, "I heard you laugh."

"Yeah, I thought it was funny. You chasing after me."

"Is that what I was doing?"

"Yeah, it was a lot of fun," she said.

"I can't believe it. I can see you, sort of," Michael said straining to see her. "And Kate, she saw you last night."

"Yeah, but that was scary. Kate was yelling. I don't like yelling."

Michael said, "I think she was scared because you surprised her."

"Yeah, well maybe. I just don't like yelling," Ruby said. Ruby then noticed Michael's hand was bleeding. "Oh no, you got a boo-boo."

Michael looked down at his hand. With the shock, he had forgotten all about it. "Uh...yeah...a band-aid. I wonder if we have band-aids?"

"You have band-aids don't you?"

"I'm not really sure. I think Kate has some....but where?"

"You sure you're alright?"

"I think so," Michael said, a little unsure himself. He grabbed for a paper towel on the counter to stop the bleeding.

"That's not a band-aid!"

"I know...I'm not sure we have one. I don't really know where to look."

Ruby just shook her head at him. "Where's Kate? I'm sure she'd know."

Kate would know. That was true. Kate would know what to do in a situation like this. Michael didn't know what to do. Either Kate was sane or both of them had gone crazy. *Could it be the paint fumes?* He laughed at that. He knew Kate would laugh about it as well.

"What's so funny?' Ruby asked.

"Oh nothing. I'm sorry. I shouldn't have laughed. It might not even be funny at all."

CHAPTER 19

Kate returned home energized by her conversation with the ladies. As she approached the house, she could see Michael. He was back to painting the porch when she walked up.

"Hiya," Kate said as she approached him.

Michael looked up at her. "You back?"

"Yeah," Kate answered. Michael seemed perturbed. "Something wrong?" she asked.

"You know there's a ton of work here to do. And it would get done a lot faster if you stayed here more than four hours during the day and worked on your projects."

Kate asked, "Where's this coming from?"

Michael stopped painting. "Where is this coming from? It's coming from the fact that I don't know what I'm doing here. I don't know how to fix a house or install a dishwasher. God knows what we are doing here. I'm tired and frustrated and just want all this work to be behind us."

"Well, so do I," Kate said.

"Then help me."

"Help you?"

"Yeah, help me. I don't know what the hell I'm doing. I mean heck. I don't know what the heck I'm doing. I tried to install the dishwasher and couldn't figure that out so I came out here and decided to paint. At least that's something I can do – paint."

Kate didn't know what to say.

So Michael continued, "I never even changed the oil in my car before this. Installing a dishwasher…I'm not made for this."

"Okay, what do you want me to do about it?"

"I want you…no…I expect you to be here and help me. I need your help and I'm always working around here alone. I need your support here. Like I did, oh never mind, it isn't worth it."

"Like you did what? Oh never mind. Rolling her eyes and frustrated, "And I was having such a great day too. I didn't need this today. Did you even realize that it's been weeks since I thought about the miscarriage? Weeks! I was actually feeling better."

"I could see that," he said.

"Then why are you taking your frustration out on me? I'm sorry you're frustrated with the house. I am. I just wanted to ask Ruth about last night."

Michael didn't say anything. He dipped his paint brush and went back to his work. He looked down at the shadows each of them was casting on the gravel driveway. Two shadows reaching out beyond them as one. He looked up at her. "I'm frustrated. I didn't get much sleep and I know, neither did you, but it's been a rough morning. I cut my hand."

Kate asked, "How did you cut your hand?" She came toward him to look at the hand he had wrapped in paper towel and duct tape.

"It's no big deal. I was trying to tie in the dishwasher to the pipes under the kitchen sink and the wrench slipped. I cut it on the water valve."

"It looks pretty bad. Did you put anything on it so it wouldn't get infected?"

"No...I didn't know where stuff like that would be."

"Did you look in the medicine cabinet in the bathroom?"

"No, I wrapped it up and came out here. Don't worry about it. How are you handling what happened last night?"

Kate responded, "I'm fine. I told Ruth and Raye about what happened. Neither of them was surprised by any of it."

"I had a feeling Raye wasn't telling us something about this house. She knew, and I'm sure everyone knew, that the house was haunted."

"It may not be haunted."

"May not be haunted? You're kidding right? Raye knew. Now we're stuck with this house. We should get a lawyer and get out of it. Raye had an obligation to disclose something like that I'm sure."

Kate laughed. "A lawyer? Michael, what lawyer do you know? And even if you were to call someone what would you say? My realtor didn't tell me that the house I bought has a little girl in it?"

Kate in a deep man voice, "A real little girl?"

Kate now doing an imitation of Michael's voice, "Uh...not exactly. It's not what you think. It looks like a girl and sounds like a girl."

Back in the deep voice again, "Then it's a girl!"

In her own voice, "Who's going to believe you?"

Michael laughed about it. "I guess you're right. But I know I've heard about legal disclosures about haunted houses somewhere."

"Michael, the house isn't haunted."

Pointing at the house behind him, "You mean to tell me that you don't think we...you saw anything in there?"

"No, I know I saw her."

"HER! See you admit the house is haunted," he said pointing at her. "I rest my case."

Kate said, "The house isn't necessarily haunted. At least not in the way Ruth explained it. Oh you're making me forget what I wanted to tell you. I had it all planned out on the walk up here. Now I don't remember exactly how she explained it."

As Kate thought about what Ruth had said, she realized what he had admitted. "Wait a minute. You said we saw her. You saw her?"

Michael didn't say anything at first. Kate approached him. "You saw her? You saw her!"

Michael frustrated again, yelled, "I don't know what I saw but whatever she is was here this morning."

Kate took the paint brush from his hand and threw it in the paint can. "Oh Michael, you really saw her."

Calming down, he said, "What did I see? What did we see?"

"Ruth said something about maybe it's a spirit or a messenger. Oh I don't remember. But it's nothing to worry about. Nearly everyone in town sees them."

Michael rolled his eyes. "Oh, nothing to worry about because everyone in crazy town sees them. Look at these people Kate – not one of them is normal. We're just as crazy as they are now."

"You know what Michael, if seeing her and feeling her is lunacy, then I am okay with it."

"How can you say that?" he asked her.

"Well, because Ruth says it's a blessing."

"Oh, a blessing. What do we really know about Ruth? Isn't she an ex-nun? Who gets kicked out of being a nun? She's probably crazy too."

Kate responded, "She's not crazy, Michael. Ugh! I'm sorry I made you so skeptical about things. That's all my fault. But at least I'm trying to make a difference. I'm getting better. I know you see that. I know you see me. And I'm asking you to believe me when I tell you I believe Ruth. I'm not going to worry about it. I'm going to accept Ruby and try to figure out what she needs from us. I want to try and help her, Michael."

"You're not her mother, Kate."

"I know I'm not her mother. I wasn't saying that I was. I'm just saying that I'm not afraid of her. Maybe she needs something and if we help her maybe she'll go away. So for now, we, and that includes you, just have to accept that she is here living with us."

"Oh great! And what about sex, Kate? You know how long it's been since we had sex?"

"Of course I do."

Michael was getting angry again. "Just last night, for the first time in a long time we were close. My god, you were ready and lord knows I've been ready. I was almost there. Almost. And then this kid shows up and laughs. I don't know maybe it's a guy thing but I can't have sex when I know someone is laughing."

"Well, I don't know what to tell you. I don't have all the answers. We'll have to figure something out."

"I've been doing that for close to a year now," Michael snapped. He picked up the paint brush again.

"Wait a minute," she said grabbing his arm. "What is that supposed to mean?" She thought about it. "No, never mind. I know what you mean. I'm sorry. I'm sorry, Michael, for everything this last year has been for you. But it hasn't been you going through it alone. I've had to go through it too. I love you and I know I have been hard to live with but so have you. You know what I loved about you when I met you? Your optimism and that belief you had that everything would work out. And now, you're nothing like that. You're losing yourself and I take responsibility for it. I know I made your life hard. I know my losses overshadowed your losses. But please understand that we got to this place in our lives together. To this place and this house, these are the answers to us getting back what we lost together. I know you find it hard to believe so let me be the one who believes enough for both of us. Let me be the one who is optimistic. Let me be the one who believes that in the end it will all work out."

He didn't know what to say. There was so much in what she said about his own self-pity that he never realized she noticed. He took her hand in his. "I know I've spent so much time blaming you but you're right. I have just as much to share in what we have become. I'm really glad to hear you talk this way. I love you. I'm just not sure where we go from here. Plus, to tell you the truth, I'm tired."

"Well we, especially you, have been working so hard since we got here. We haven't had a break in a long time."

"You're right," he said, "working this hard and putting everything into this house and now it seems like it may have all been a waste. How can we live with this thing, this girl, in our house?"

"I'm not sure but I am willing to see," she told him.

Michael wasn't sure of how he felt. But he liked how much Kate was vested in it and their relationship again. He agreed to let her be the one to believe in the good for the both of them.

CHAPTER 20

Later that day, Kate helped Michael install the dishwasher. It was a challenging task but together it seemed less complicated. As they worked, both waited for Ruby to make another appearance but she never did. When they were done, they went into town together for dinner at Juanita's. The two of them together hadn't come into town since they first arrived.

As they turned toward the courtyard heading to Juanita's, they ran into Sunny cutting through it on his way to relieve Buddha somewhere else. "Hiya Kate," Sunny said.

Kate said, "Hi Sunny. This is my husband, Michael."

Michael stretched out his hand and without warning, Sunny came in for a hug. "My brother, it is good to finally meet you." Kate stood back behind Sunny and watched as Michael kept his eyes on Kate the entire time.

Finally able to break free, Michael said, "Well, it's good to meet you too. Heard a lot about you and your wife."

"Oh Holla? She's not my wife, man. That's man's law, not nature's law. We try as best we can to shelter ourselves from as many of man's laws as possible."

"We're all aware of your avoidance of laws," the three of them heard coming from behind them in a big voice. It was Della. She was walking at a brisk pace wagging her finger. "But be sure you clean up after that mutt. People don't want to step in crap when they visit Harmony. I hope that's a law you can live up to."

Buddha barked continuously and pulled on his burdensome leash at Della. She returned an acid stare toward the dog.

"No worries, Miss Della, got a dime bag here somewhere," Sunny replied. With Buddha going at her nonstop, Sunny turned back to Michael and Kate and said, "Well, nice to see you. I better get going. I assured Holla I would keep the peace and that isn't easy when Buddha's as fired up as he is."

Kate and Michael said their goodbyes and watched as Sunny walked the dog over to the grass on the other side of the road.

Della frowned at Sunny as he passed her. She turned and watched his every move. As she watched after him, she backed herself up next to Kate and Michael. "That beast and his dog! Both mangy beyond humanity," Della said keeping her eye on them. Della, Kate and Michael watched as Buddha found a spot and squatted. Sunny waved happily at them, bag in hand for picking up the waste.

"Disgusting. His father was barely any better. There's a reason those types hide out here in

Harmony," Della said. "Dobbs was wrong to let them stay. All that crap art and the tourists. Oh the tourists. This place was so much better with nothing but cows."

Realizing the stranger in her presence, Della abruptly asked, "Who are you?" of Michael.

Kate spoke up, "Della this is my husband, Michael."

"Oh," Della said. "What do you do for a living Michael?"

Michael retracting his automatic outstretched hand said, "Well, I used to be a graphic artist."

"Oh god, not another artist," Della said rolling her eyes.

Michael answered, "Not really that kind of artist. I'm more of a corporate one."

"Well, that's an oxymoron if I ever heard one – a corporate artist?"

"He works for businesses, Della. You know logos and advertising," Kate said.

"Oh, you mean junk mail. Great. That's even worse."

Before Michael or Kate said another thing, Della noticed a homeless man with a canvas painting under his arm walking down the road into town just beyond where Sunny was. Marching toward the man, she yelled, "Oh no, you don't! You get out of here! We don't want your type here in town. Go on and get before I call the sheriff."

The man, fearing for his life with the big burly woman coming at him, turned and ran away holding his painting with one hand and his pants up with the other. A partially exposed buttock as her view, Della turned back toward Michael and

Kate. "Would you look at that? No underbritches. How uncivilized is that?'

Sunny walking back across the street, tugged his jeans up and said, "You know, you don't really need to wear underwear, Miss Della. It's actually quite freeing."

Della looked back to Kate. "What'd I tell ya? Totally uncivilized."

Unrelenting, Della followed the man all the way down up to the main highway. She wasn't going to take any chances and have him sneak back in when she wasn't looking.

Buddha barked at Della.

Sunny crossed the road near the couple. "Would you look at her? And she says we're whack. She's crazier than all of us. Well, now that Buddha's cleared out his tank, I better go check on Mason. I'm sure he's ready to clear out his. See ya!"

"See ya, Sunny," Kate said.

Michael watched Della run the man out of town. "I've seen that man before."

"You have?" Kate asked.

"Yeah, he was out painting on a bluff one morning when I was coming back from SLO and he waved at me. It was strange since I'd never seen him before. I mentioned it to Beck and he told me not to worry about it. He said not to worry about him – Pete's harmless."

"Harmless?"

"In fact, Beck said I shouldn't believe what some of the others would say about him. As if some people thought he was more than just a man."

"What do you mean?"

"I'm not sure. It just got me thinking about Ruby and your impression from Ruth that she was harmless and not something to worry about."

"Yeah, both Raye and Ruth said other people have had similar interactions. You think this Pete guy is something like Ruby?"

"I'm not sure but it makes me think there is more going on here than anyone is really saying."

The couple walked up to Juanita's and noticed both tables were actually occupied at the time.

"Looks sort of busy," Michael said.

"Hey, let's go pass some time in the Creamery," Kate replied. "They have an art gallery in there. Let's go check it out."

They walked around to the front of the Creamery building that anchored the town in Harmony. On one end was the Harmony post office and the other was Gifts from the Sea. Juanita's was anchored behind it. With a gallery at its center, the art of Harmony was really at the heart of the town.

The inside of the Creamery was enormous. It was an open beam warehouse all washed in white like it had been painted with milk.

"Hey stranger," Holla said recognizing Kate.

Kate returned the hello. "Holla, this is Michael, my husband."

"Nice to meet you," she said but didn't approach him. Looking back at Kate, she said, "Haven't seen you for a while. Everything okay?"

"Oh sure, busy with the house," Kate replied.

"You looking for anything in particular or just out browsing?"

"Sort of out browsing. Waiting on a table over at Juanita's."

Holla asked, "Is this your first time in here?"

"Yeah, we've been meaning to stop in," Kate answered first.

"Lots to do over at the house," Michael added.

"Well, take a look around, we have some great stuff in here."

The couple proceeded to stroll through the open gallery. In the back corner, there was a small display of equipment left over from the old dairy days. Kate and Michael looked at the plaques and pictures next to the discarded equipment. Kate noticed one of Della and her husband, Dobb.

"There's Della and that must be her husband Dobb," she said. "He looked like a strong man. Nice looking for his day. And look, Della's smiling. Happier times, I guess."

"And thinner," Michael added.

"Michael!"

"Well, I suppose she does enjoy her dairy cream and whipped cream...and heavy cream ...and ice cream," Michael went on in amusement.

Kate laughed. Her laugh got the attention of Holla from behind the counter. She looked over at Kate who covered her laugh with her hand. Kate felt obliged to apologize.

Holla in a quiet tone said, "It's alright." She then went back to writing something.

The gallery had a lot of paintings to be seen along with some great blown glass pieces.

"These must be Stan's," Kate told Michael.

"They're quite good," Michael said.

While Michael checked out the glass works, Kate wandered over to some soft, pastel impressionistic pieces. She looked at the name plate and noticed Holla's name.

"I know what you're thinking," Holla said coming up behind Kate.

"Holla, these are incredible."

This got Michael's attention. Kate then noticed a painting of her house with pale green grass and yellow flowers surrounding it. There was the white house standing as the only testament to man's existence in the fullness of nature's splendor.

"Is this our house?" Kate asked. Michael looked over at it.

Holla answered, "Yeah, I painted that about a year ago when the house was vacant. It looked lonely so I went out and kept her company."

"Her?" Kate asked looking at Michael.

"Well, her as in her as the house," Holla explained.

"Did you go inside?" Kate asked.

"Nah, been up to it and peeked in but never inside. It was always a cute house. Sunny never wanted it because Gertie died in it. Thought maybe she would haunt it."

"You think it's haunted?" Michael asked.

"I have no idea. You tell me. You live there," Holla said with a smile.

Michael looked at the house in the painting. "This is pretty good."

"Thanks," Holla answered.

Kate looked closer at the painting and the house, at the front window in particular. The window was painted black but in the corner was a brush stroke that was slightly lighter than the rest of the black. The swab of paint looked like a tiny silhouette peeking out of the corner of the window. Kate leaned in for a better look.

She then asked, "What's this?"

"Don't look too close. You'll see the mistakes."

"No, what's this in the window?" Kate asked. Michael leaned in.

"What's what?" Holla came closer to see what Kate was pointing at.

Kate pointed with her finger making sure not to touch the painting. "What's this shadow?"

Holla gently pushed Kate back so she could get a better look. She looked at the window. "There's nothing there."

"No," Kate said. "That shadow in the window. You see it...in the corner there?"

Holla looked again. "Oh, that little blob...probably just a little of the white mixed with the black is all."

"It looks like the shadow of a head."

Holla looked at it again. "Nah, it's a poorly mixed portion of the window." Thinking about it, Holla added, "Hey, maybe it is haunted and I didn't know it." Holla laughed at her own joke.

Kate didn't laugh. She looked at the painting closely again and then backed away from it. The painting of the house and the green pasture and the way the trees framed it was perfect. Kate asked, "How much is it?"

"You want to buy it?" Holla asked.

"Yeah, it's our house. I think it would look great in the living room once it's done. Don't you think?" she said to Michael.

"I suppose so when it's done," he said.

"It matches perfectly with the green paint I have picked out for in there. How much is it?"

Holla answered, "Let's say it's a hundred bucks."

"No, it's worth more than a hundred dollars," Kate answered.

"You think so?" Holla asked.

"Oh yeah," Kate said. "Honestly, if I saw this in a gallery in LA, it would be like five hundred at least."

"Yeah, but that's LA. Here, tourists want cheap and fast mementos to take with them."

"I wouldn't call a painting a cheap and fast memento," Michael said.

Kate added, "It's a work of art. One of a kind. You should get top dollar for it. Back in LA, people would make a big deal about how much their art cost. They'd spend thousands of dollars on stuff just like yours."

"Seriously," Holla said.

"Oh yeah," Kate offered. "That's the thing about art collectors. It's not the piece, it's how much they paid for it. I really think you should raise your prices. These are works of art, aren't they?"

"Yeah, I guess so."

"You guess? They're in an art gallery aren't they?" Michael said.

Not waiting for an answer, Kate jumped in. "They're works of art. So what if you sell less pieces, you'll be making more for each piece."

Michael added, "They're not something you can replace quickly. This type of work takes time."

Holla said, "Funny you say that. My mom always tried to get me to stop fooling around with the paints and get focused on my studies. She thought I wasted too much time on painting. Time I should have been studying was spent getting a painting just right. My mom wanted me to be a doctor or something like that. But honestly, I wasn't ever really good at school. When I met Sunny, here was this easy-going, free-living artist who promoted a lifestyle I could support and it was all over. We moved in together and soon we were selling our stuff at art shows up and down the coast -- living out of his van. Crazy."

"Sounds interesting," Michael said.

"I guess," Holla continued. "Before I knew it Sunny's Pop died and Mason was on his way. It all happened so fast and here we are. I know most people look at me and Sunny and think we're strange. But the truth is we're just like most people. Trying to live our lives the best we know how, doing what we think is right for us, our son and the planet. While I may act different than most people, on the inside I'm this girl, this mom, just like every other mom, who wants nothing more than for my kid to have a good life."

Kate added, "You're a good artist too. And on top of that, you seem to be comfortable in your own skin – happy with who you are. That's a big deal."

"You wait, hanging around Harmony gets boring. You tend to fill in the silences with self-diagnosis."

"That's probably true," Michael said.

Kate looked back at the painting of the house. She then looked over at Michael. "We should check back at Juanita's and see if a table opened up."

"Yes, we should," he said.

Kate turned back to Holla. "Can you hold the painting for us? Can we pick it up once the house is done?"

"Sure. Of course the price will be three hundred dollars then." Holla smiled at her.

Kate smiled back. "It's worth it."

Michael added, "And you stick to your higher prices. Make these tourists pay for art."

Kate said, "You know, Michael could probably help you with the pricing. He used to do estimates for graphic art stuff all the time."

"Really? That would be great," Holla said.

Michael didn't know what to make of Kate's idea.

"Hey," Holla said. "Do you know anything about putting together websites?"

"Of course," he said.

"He did web work all the time," Kate assured Holla.

"Great, we could really use your help. We've been selling stuff online through some of those big corporate online auction sites and we've been wanting to do something on our own. But none of us knows too much about computers."

"Let me get the house in order," Michael said. "Then I could properly work with you on getting a site up and running."

"That'd be awesome. It's just what we need to boost our visibility. Wait 'til I tell Sunny and Stan."

Kate added, "Michael's really good at what he does. He really is. You know, he could probably do some promotional stuff for everyone here. Maybe even help Raye bring in more weddings for Ruth."

"That would be killer!" Holla was excited. "Something to get people interested in stopping here again. Back in its day, Harmony was a thriving colony. These days it seems no one wants to stop and see us. Everyone's in a hurry to get to someplace else."

Michael reminded her, "Just let me finish stuff on the house first."

"Oh, no problem," Holla said. "Bet that place is a money pit. Sunny would be relieved to hear that. He'd tell me that's exactly why he didn't want to buy the place."

Kate thought for a minute before speaking. "Let me ask you, did you ever see or hear anything odd around that house?"

Holla looked back at Kate puzzled. "Like what?"

"I don't know, like anything out of the ordinary...like I don't know, a child."

Michael squeezed Kate's elbow. "I think we should get going. You know Juanita's closes early."

Holla asked Kate, "Why? Did you see something? What was it?"

Michael nudged Kate toward the door.

"Wait! That shadow in the window, you thought it was someone. That's why you asked me about it? OMG! Is that place haunted?"

"No, no," Michael answered. "It's nothing like that."

Holla asked, "Then what is it?"

Kate answered, "We're not really sure. I'm not even sure it's anything. It may be all in our heads."

Holla approached them. "Well, tell me what it was. Sunny is going to be so glad we didn't buy that house. He hates all this ghost stuff around here. He thinks it's all a bunch of BS."

"There are other stories?" Kate asked.

"Oh yeah, all sorts of stories," Holla said. "Stories of people who seem real but aren't. All sorts of real trippy stuff like that. I love hearing about it. You saw something. How awesome is that?"

"Holla, don't say anything to anyone," Kate said. "It may be nothing."

Michael added, "Right. Who knows it may turn out to be paint fumes."

Kate looked over at Michael.

"Oh don't worry," Holla said. "You can trust me. I won't say anything to anyone."

Outside the Creamery, as they walked back around to the café, Kate said, "Some real interesting things in there. Didn't you think?"

"I was actually impressed. I didn't see one thing there made of hemp."

Kate nudged Michael in a playful way. "You know something did get me thinking."

"You want to join their cult?"

"Michael please! I'm serious."

"I'm sorry. What're you thinking?"

"When Holla asked about websites and how you could help them it all sounded so great. You are so lucky to have selected a career that you enjoyed. I wish I had done what you had. How stupid of me to get my degrees in poetry and work at a consolidated data company. What a waste."

"It wasn't a waste. You did what you had to do to pay for school," Michael said.

"I don't know. Maybe it wasn't all for the best. I doubt Mom was really proud of me for doing something she never quite understood."

Michael said, "Your mom was proud."

"I don't think so. I was nothing but a disappointment to her. She would have preferred I become an attorney or something. I know she didn't think getting my degree in poetry was a wise decision either. I'm not even sure I think it was. What did it get me? That nonsense cubical job."

"That helped pay the bills."

"Sure it did but at what price? It's just the people here are happier because they are doing what they love and it's not about the money for them. It's about the enjoyment of doing it."

Michael asked, "I hope you don't regret our life together."

"Absolutely not! I regret nothing with you, Michael. I'm lucky to have you in my life. Besides, had I not worked where I did, you and I would have never met."

Michael agreed.

"Back in LA I was so focused on my career and the house and Mom and becoming a mom, there wasn't that time to think. Now with that out of the way, it's given me a chance to realize that none of that was who I really am."

Michael said, "I get that."

"It's almost like all that we wanted for ourselves back then was nothing we were meant to be or do. Now, we get this chance to start over."

Michael said, "We're lucky I guess. It's not everyone who gets a chance like this."

CHAPTER 21

The following morning there was a knock at the door. For a second it startled Kate from the kitchen. A whole day had gone by without Ruby making any appearance. She called out, "Michael, there's someone at the door."

Michael came into the living room from the bedroom slipping a shirt on. He walked over to the door and opened it quickly.

"You ready Mike?" Beck asked, coming in.

"Yeah, let me just grab my wallet."

"Where you two off to this morning?" Kate asked.

"Oh, I thought I mentioned it," Michael said. "Beck's got a friend down in Morro Bay who is looking to get rid of some appliances. He's a contractor or something." Michael looked over at Beck for some additional details.

Beck explained, "He had a customer who didn't pay him for some high-end kitchen stuff. He's trying to unload it for his cost just to get rid of it."

"Some real nice stuff," Michael said. "Beck's taking me down to look at it. He's got a range, a double oven and a fridge."

"We don't need a fridge, do we?" Kate asked.

"Not really, but if it's all the same and matches, I thought it would be nicer."

Beck chimed in, "Besides we need a fridge."

"Oh yeah," Michael said more confidently. "Lucy and Beck need a fridge. I told him they could have ours if we got the new one."

"How long you think you'll be gone?" Kate asked.

"Oh, I bet two hours maybe," Beck answered. "Roy can be a talker. Likes to tell people how well he's doing. It can get annoying, but hey, aren't we all?"

Michael walked over to kiss Kate. "You okay?" he asked.

"Yeah, I'll be fine. Go on, you two. We need to finally put this mess to rest."

Beck turned and walked back out to the porch, saying as he stepped out, "See ya, Kate."

"Bye honey," Michael said and kissed her again. She kissed him back, her lips hanging on his for a moment. Michael smiled at her and kissed her one more time.

Beck called out, "Come on, lover boy!"

"Be safe," Kate said.

He laughed. "I will. We're just going down to Morro Bay."

"I know. I just want you to be safe."

Michael disappeared behind the open door. Kate walked over to see them off. Michael's truck started up and the two men were off up the gravel road kicking up dust. Kate closed the door to prevent the dust from getting in.

She turned around and looked at the continued disarray of the living room. "Living room," she said out loud. "This is living?" There was trash from all the projects they had going on scattered all over the living room. Plastic bags from stores filled with discarded trash of packaging from purchases. Empty boxes from the move and others from items purchased. There was a time she would have never let the house get like this, let alone let someone in the house when it was like this.

"What a mess," she said. Realizing she was talking to herself, she stopped for a minute wondering if she really was alone. She looked around. The vanilla living room walls were filled with shadowy reminders of their past life. Silhouettes of where pictures were hung, furniture was placed and living was done.

She walked over and flipped on the radio. She dialed it away from the classic rock station Michael had it on to KMOR once again. She tuned in the station from the static and Doris Day came on mid-song. It was "It's Magic." Kate remembered it being one of her mom's favorites. She turned it up.

Kate started cleaning up the discarded trash in the living room. It was a start. The song reminded Kate of her mom humming along to Doris Day around the house while doing housework. It was her happy hum. Kate could feel the tears starting to well up and the sniffles started. She reached for a tissue on the table.

"Why are you crying?"

Kate quickly gathered herself, wiping her eyes and nose. "What...me...crying?"

"Yeah, you seemed so happy then all of a sudden you started crying. How come?"

Kate looked around and didn't see anyone. She recognized the voice. She called out, "Ruby?"

"What?" the girl answered.

"Where are you?" she asked.

"I'm here, in the living room."

"I don't see you," Kate said.

"Ah, it's alright. I can see you fine. Why were you crying?"

"It's silly really. This song reminds me of my mom. It made me a little sad, I guess."

"How come?" the girl asked.

"Well, because my mom died and I miss her."

Ruby said, "Don't be sad. She's in a wonderful place."

"She is?"

"Uh huh."

A tear began to well in Kate's eye. "Where is she?"

"In heaven."

"She is?"

"Of course she is."

"And how do you know? You don't even know my mother."

"I know because, well, I've been there. I've seen her there."

"What?"

"I've seen her there," the girl said again.

"You've seen her?" Kate asked, feeling a little silly talking to someone she couldn't see. *This is crazy.*

"You're not crazy. I've really seen her there."

"In heaven?"

"Yes, in heaven."

"You've been to heaven?" Kate asked.

"Of course. Where did you think I came from?"

Ruby came from behind the couch and Kate could finally see her. The girl walked around the room. She looked over the boxes and the piles of trash. Kate studied her. Her golden blonde locks, the tiny dimple in her cheek and the cherries on her small dress.

"This place *is* a mess," Ruby said, covering her mouth to avoid laughing.

"I know. We're still getting it all together. It's a lot of work," Kate said.

"Yeah, I know." The girl continued to walk around. Kate studied her tiny dress of purest white and shoes, ones with buckles like the ones Kate had when she was a girl. Kate remembered herself looking down at the patent polished black shoes and being able to see her own reflection in them. They were by far the prettiest shoes she had ever seen. She was so proud to wear them.

"You don't have kids, do you?" Ruby said.

The question lingered. With little thought the reply flowed out of her. "No, I don't."

Ruby looked over at Kate from across the room and said, "It's okay. I just wondered if there'd be anyone to play with around here."

Ruby walked over to the stereo. She reached out to touch it...

"Honey, be careful," Kate said impulsively.

Ruby looked at her in shock. She didn't like being scolded. Without a word, she continued to walk around. There was silence between the two of them for a while.

Kate asked, "So how come you're here?"

"Don't you know? I told you I live here."

Kate thought about how well Ruby spoke for such a little girl. "How old are you?"

"That's hard to say. How old do I look?"

"I was going to say around five," Kate answered.

"You're probably right. You can see me so you probably know best."

Ruby walked right up to Kate. Kate was a little nervous. The child studied Kate. "Bend down here," the girl asked.

Kate did as she was told. She squatted down so that she was face to face with Ruby. Kate studied the girl's features as the two looked at each other. Ruby's face was pure. It appeared to be real. This was no ghostly image. It was solid. As Kate studied Ruby's face, their eyes locked. Ruby's eyes were deep blue and Kate felt like she should see a thousand miles into them.

"You're very pretty," the girl said.

"Why thank you. You're very pretty too."

"I can see what Michael sees in you. You're prettier up close. I hope I'm as pretty as you someday."

Kate was embarrassed. She wasn't even wearing any makeup. She stood back up.

Ruby said, "Don't get sad. Okay?"

Kate answered the girl's concern. "I'll be fine."

"Good." And with those words, the girl walked toward the doorway to the kitchen. She turned around, her hair falling into her face, and asked, "I'm here if you need me. You don't mind me being here right?"

"Oh no."

Ruby turned back and walked away. Kate shouted, "Ruby!"

Turning back again, the girl said, "Yeah?"

"Who are you? What are you?"

"I'm just a little girl. Someone like you." Ruby smiled at Kate. She had a beautiful smile.

Without any further interaction, Kate heard Ruby walk out the door of the screened porch, the screen door slamming behind her. Kate ran to the back porch and looked out toward the grassy fields behind the house. No sign of anyone. Not even a path of crushed grass.

Kate played the entire conversation over in her head. She focused on what the girl had said about her mom. It thrilled her. Her mom's cancer had spread undetected to the bladder and throughout the cervix. It was a painful death for her mom and for her. There was solace in knowing her mom was okay. Kate then thought about the girl. Ruby was adorable.

CHAPTER 22

Kate finished going through all the remaining boxes in the living room. Her pace was quick and before she knew it the living room was starting to at least look orderly. She thought about Holla's painting of the house and how nice a pale green color would look on the walls. All the room needed was some paint and then they could get the hardwoods stained. The room would be complete. *A real living room.*

Inspired by her efforts in the living room, Kate spent the rest of the afternoon getting stuff put away in the kitchen. Michael and Beck returned and had the kitchen appliances installed that same day. The kitchen was complete. That night at dinner, for the first time, Michael and Kate were able to eat in the kitchen at the small table – one Kate picked out that was just like her mother's.

At dinner, Kate told Michael about her visit with Ruby. He hung on her every word. Kate couldn't stop thinking about her. While they sat there eating, Kate said, "I think I'll go with you into the city and get some material for curtains."

"You're going to make curtains?"

"Sure. Why not? I'm sure Lucy has a machine. I was thinking some white cottony curtains for in here with maybe tiny cherries on them."

Michael smiled. "Cherries?"

"Why not?"

"No reason."

Kate was proud. "It does look good. Homey. Just like I always pictured a small country kitchen to be." *Mom would like it.*

Michael scooped up what was left on his plate with his spoon and shoveled it in his mouth. "Whatever you say. You want cherries. I'm fine with that."

"You know what else?" Kate said. "When we're in the city, I want to get the paint for the living room. I think I'll stop by the gallery and pick up the painting. I want to make sure the color I get matches. I want everything to be perfect."

"Sounds good."

"Can we go first thing in the morning?"

"I shouldn't see why not."

Kate looked at her watch. It was just after 5:30. "I think I'll run down to the gallery and get the painting before they close up. Then we can get an early start."

"You go on and do that," Michael said. "I've got some things here to finish up."

As Kate made her way to the door, Michael stopped her. "Kate, the place looks really great. You did good today."

"Thank you."

Kate, still in her LA ways, grabbed the truck keys and drove down to the gallery. She would have normally walked and left the truck for Michael but she wanted to make sure she didn't get there after Holla locked up. When she arrived at the gallery, there was a note on the door. It read, "For assistance, come next door." The writing was accompanied by an arrow that pointed to Ruth's shop.

As Kate entered Gifts from the Sea, there behind the counter was Holla.

"Hiya Kate," Holla said.

"Where's Ruth?"

"I think she said she had to go see her doctor. She asked me to keep an eye on the shop for her."

"Is she alright?" Kate asked.

"Oh sure, Ruth is Ruth. I think she had an appointment to keep."

"Does she drive?"

Holla thought about that. "To tell you the truth I'm not sure. But I wouldn't be surprised if Hijo took her. He's always running Ruth or his mom down to Cayucos or SLO."

Kate wondered why Ruth hadn't asked her to drive her. Her eyes wandered around the shop as she thought more about Ruth not asking her to take her to the doctor.

Holla noticing Kate's eyes surveying the store said, "Kinda creepy in here, huh?"

Kate looked surprised.

Holla explained, "I mean it's, you know, not really what most people are looking for."

"I suppose you're right."

"I've always wondered how she makes it, you know, selling this stuff."

Kate answered, "Well, she does have the chapel."

"That's true. Weddings help a lot of us pay the bills. It's been a long time since we've had a wedding here." Holla then asked, "Is this stuff your sort of thing? You seem to come in here a lot and I thought maybe I put my foot in my mouth when I said this stuff was creepy. Sorry if I offended you."

"It's okay. I'm not offended," Kate replied. "I wouldn't say religion is my thing but I guess maybe a little bit of me wonders about it sometimes. I wonder about my mom and what is out there for us when we die."

"I know what you mean. It's so confusing. Sunny is pretty set that there is no God. I think that's his dad talking. I'm not really sure what I think. I go back and forth. I do wonder about my own dad and where he is now. He died. He was out drinking one night and rammed his car into a pole. Sometimes I think about him and about Mason and what we're going to tell him about God." Standing up straight and authoritative, Holla continued, "I'm sure Sunny has his whole speech planned out. He's always got something to say. That's his dad in him. You know, sometimes you just want to enjoy people's company, even the tourists, without having a lecture. They don't come here for a lecture."

"Does Sunny lecture them?"

"Oh, all the time...about their lifestyles and clothes. Don't get me wrong I'm a vegan heart and soul, but I don't think it's smart to lecture your customers about the leather they're wearing. You know what I mean? In the end, we gotta make a buck just the same from them as anyone else."

"I could see that."

"Of course, you can. See that's my point. Sometimes you need to be practical about things. That's what I like about Ruth. She sits in this shop with all this religion around her and yet she doesn't lecture. She's practical. She's just this sweet grandma type. There's comfort in what she's selling. Does that make sense?"

Kate said, "Absolutely."

"See, you know what I'm saying. I think we all need to take a little of what the world has to offer and create this melting pot of peace. Religion is like a recipe. You know a little bit of Karma, add in some Kabala and finish it off with some of the Koran. Take the best of what the world has to offer and make it your own."

"I guess I never thought about it that way."

"I like to say 'God is good and Mother Nature nurtures.' Sunny thinks I should put that on a bumper sticker and sell it. I don't know. It's just something I like to say I believe."

"Holla let me ask you, do you believe we can see things that aren't really there?"

Holla quickly answered, "Oh yeah, I've seen things. In fact, Sunny says I probably have glaucoma. He always tells me I see things that aren't there and that I should go get a prescription for weed. He thinks that's a good excuse for us to grow our own – that way we know it's organic."

"Aren't you concerned about pot smoking in front of your son?"

"Oh don't worry. I don't let Sunny smoke when Mason's around. I know the effects marijuana has on people – first hand. My kid isn't going to do any of it. Just look at Sunny, I love him and all, but he's sometimes a little too laid back. I'm not kidding. Sometimes it takes an army to get him to take out the trash. I don't want Mason to be like that. I want Mason to be energetic. I want him to strive to fulfill his own goals. Not just be content with what his father can give him."

Kate wasn't sure whether Holla knew exactly what she was asked. She asked again, "So do you see things or people who aren't really there?"

Holla thought about it. "I don't know. Kate, there are so many voices in my head. Honestly, I'm not sure I even know which one is mine." Holla laughed at her own statement.

Kate politely joined her.

"I'm serious. It's why I don't want Mason experimenting. I feel kind of guilty for being a hypocrite to my own son but hey I want him to learn from my mistakes."

"I'm sure you're a good mom," Kate told her.

"Ah, thanks Kate. I try. I know people don't think I'm the smartest person around town. But I'm smart. Sometimes I'm just not sure with everything going on in my head whether I come across as smart."

Kate replied, "I think you do fine. You seem smart enough to me."

Holla smiled.

Kate paused the conversation for a minute with her own silence. She hoped her own silence would encourage Holla to think more about what

Kate was asking. The tactic didn't seem to be working. Holla lost interest and focused on braiding her hair in a nearby mirror.

"So, these voices in your head, are they adult voices or kid voices?"

Still fussing with her braids, Holla answered, "Both. All sorts actually."

"And you never see anyone?"

"Well, there's Pete an artist who comes into town. Some people see him and some don't. Sunny thinks it's all a fluke. Sunny says the reason some people don't see him is due solely to coincidence. Pete's like this homeless guy who comes into town from time to time. It's funny. He's got a thing for Della. Della gets so mad because Juanita feeds him when he comes to town. She says he's just like the cats in town. They only stick around because people feed them."

Kate said, "So do you think this Pete's a real person?"

"Well, he has some of his artwork in the gallery. That's proof he's real to me. I know some around here don't trust that. They need to be more open-minded. See beyond their own reality. Sunny's never seen him or so he says. I just don't think he wants to admit it."

"Why not?" Kate asked.

"Juanita feeds Pete because he's God's soldier," Holla said rolling her eyes. "I'm not so sure about that. He never really says anything to any of us. I honestly think he's nothing more than a homeless guy that hides out as much as he can and that's more or less why some don't see him."

"Interesting. I almost forgot," Kate said. "I came in to pick up the painting from the gallery. The note said come over here…"

"Yeah, I put up the note here when I came over here. Anyway, let me get the key and we'll go over there and get the painting. The house must really be coming along."

"Oh absolutely! When we get everything in order we'll have you over. Still plenty to do though."

"Yeah, I figured."

Holla and Kate walked out of Ruth's shop. Holla looked up and down the road and saw no one around. "We'll just be a minute," Holla said and she simply closed the door without locking it. They then walked quickly over to the entrance to the Creamery. As Holla reached for her keys, Danny was coming out of the post office next door.

"Hey, what're you two up to?" Danny asked.

Holla said, "Nothing much. Ruth went to see her doctor and I'm watching both shops this afternoon."

"Well, Holla-day! You should have asked me to watch the gallery for ya. It's my day in the post office."

"I just figured you'd be busy and all," Holla answered.

"Honey, you oughta know I'd be okay with it."

"I know. I just didn't want to trouble…"

"Don't you say it! Don't you say it! I'm here to help. No need to be bashful."

Holla just nodded.

Danny moved on to Kate. "And you! You never stop in and say hello anymore. I see ya all the time in Ruth's shop and you never think to pop your head in to say hello. Lucy was just asking me if I've seen you in town. And I said, 'Oh, I see her. She's seems pretty cozy over in Ruth's shop.'"

"Oh, I'm sorry," Kate said. "I just never seem to think of stopping in the post office."

Danny added, "I know, no one does. The only thing we get in there is invitations to go out with the Harmony postmark. Raye's supposed to be the postmaster and she's never even there."

"I know how that is," Holla said. "Sunny's always over at Stan's and leaves me alone in the shop all the time. And I have Mason!"

"It's kinda funny," Danny said. "Those two guys with those kids. You know, I'd love to go over and watch them for Stan but Lucy doesn't want me to have anything to do with him. I think she's afraid I'd end up falling in love with the kids and walk down the aisle at the chapel with Stan just to be near them. She's probably right they are cute kids. Holla, you ever hear from Tess?"

"No, I haven't heard from her since before she left."

"That's too bad. You two were so close."

"I know. I think she feels too guilty to call. Sunny told me she's up in Oakland. She's got a boyfriend I think. Well, at least, that is what Stan thinks."

Danny asked, "She ever coming back to get her kids?"

"I don't think so. Seems she just walked away from them all. Didn't like being tied down I guess."

"That really is too bad," Danny said.

"It is," Holla added. "But she always was a bit flighty."

Holla then looked over at Kate. "You stay here. I'll run in and get the painting for you."

Kate agreed.

Danny turned back toward the post office. "Come on in, you can help me catch up on the postmarks."

The post office was small – not much more than a counter and a stool. Danny ducked under the counter to get behind it. Kate noticed the huge stack of white envelopes in a tray. She asked, "Do you usually have this much mail in here?"

Danny laughed. "Only when we have wedding invitations to get out. People come from all over to drop their invitations off so we can stamp them with the Harmony postmark. People think it's clever to have their postmark read "Harmony, CA." for their wedding invitations. So we postmark all of 'em -- generally right over a love or heart stamp. It's pretty unoriginal by now. I've seen more than my share of wedding invitations come through here. Sometimes we even get calls from brides who want to know if her invites have gone out yet. It's crazy. But you know how brides can be – it's all about them and their day."

"I guess we both do." Kate replied.

"Yeah, suppose you're right. Except Ben and me's wedding was pretty small – only a justice of the peace and his parents. I wore a simple white dress and Ben wore his uniform. He bought me the most beautiful flowers – gardenias. I love gardenias. Love the way they smell and their pretty white petals. How about you and Michael? What was your wedding like?"

Kate said, "Well, our wedding was simple compared to most. We got married right on the beach. Both our moms were there. It was small just some friends and family. We had a nice reception down at a hotel that overlooked the ocean. The day went by so fast. I seem to only remember certain details. Other memories are just those I've seen in pictures."

"I know how that is. It's like Ben's funeral. It was all a daze. There were so many people there. Guys from his unit and their wives, a bunch of locals and our friends near the base. It was much more overwhelming than the wedding. I honestly didn't want to even be there."

Danny stopped stamping envelopes and just stared out the small window to the empty road outside. "His momma and daddy were so torn up. I felt like I needed to be there for them. We all did our best that day to put on the bravest faces we could. Ben would be proud. I'm certain of it."

"It must have been hard losing him."

"It was. I came here to Harmony right away with Lucy and Beck. Getting out of South Carolina was a good thing. Looking back, I had no idea then just how great it would be. How much closer to Ben I would be here."

Danny picked right back up with her work. The door to the post office opened and Holla came in with the painting. "Sorry I won't have time to wrap it."

Kate said, "It's no trouble. I just need to take it up the road."

Holla handed Kate the painting and Kate took a look at it. Danny looked over Kate's shoulder and said, "I've loved that one for a while. It is beautiful."

Kate agreed. "It's going to look perfect in our living room."

Holla, embarrassed, said, "I should get down and close up Ruthie's shop. It's nearly six o'clock."

Danny looked back at Kate's painting and said, "It seems perfect doesn't it? Holla's got a real eye. Doesn't she?"

Kate still looking at it said, "She does. Funny thing about it is the house reminded me instantly of the one my mom and I lived in when I was young. It just called to me."

"I know exactly what you mean," Danny said. "When I first came to Harmony there was something about the inn. Like a moth to a flame I was drawn to it."

Kate asked, "What was it like when you got here? Did you experience anything unusual?"

Danny smiled. She picked up her pace stamping the envelopes with the postmarks. She asked, "What do you want to know?"

Kate asked, "Well, have you...I don't know...you know... they say that people here have seen things. Have you ever...um...heard that or ever experienced that yourself?"

"I thought that was what you were asking. I heard the same thing when I came to town. I'll admit I wasn't too optimistic back then. I did have Lucy and Beck but that didn't bring me Ben. In some ways, it made me miss him more. Seeing the house he grew up in and seeing his photos all over the house – it was kinda tough."

As she listened, Kate began to help box the invitations Danny had already stamped.

Danny continued, "But then Lucy told me the story of how she and Beck came to Harmony. Her sister had just died. She and her sister had been close. While they were at the funeral, they met a woman who heard about Beck being out of work. This woman, assumingly some friend of someone at the funeral, offered to let Beck and Lucy live in the house she had in Harmony for free! All Beck had to do was repair it. I guess it had been in real bad shape. With Beck being out of work and Lucy pregnant with Ben, they really didn't have any other options. So they jumped at it. Some years later the woman died and willed the house to them."

"No!" Kate said.

"Oh yeah. Here was this woman they had never met before and barely ever heard from and she wills them her house."

"That's unbelievable. Who was she?"

"Lucy told me she still had no real idea who she was. She knew her name but didn't even know much more than that. Lucy only met her the one time and imagined that she had dreamt up the image of the woman over the years. Other than the day they met, they only talked on the phone with her and wrote letters back and forth. This woman came into their life without warning and disappeared soon after. Leaving their lives forever changed."

Kate said, "I've never heard anything like that before. What an incredible story."

Danny agreed. "Isn't it? Then when I came to Harmony, I felt like I was all alone. I missed Ben so much. I would try and hide my crying from Lucy and Beck. I didn't think it was fair for me to fall apart on them since they were grieving too. So I would confine my crying to when I was in bed. One night there was a full moon out. I had my window open and I heard this voice."

Kate froze.

"It was a man's voice. It sounded familiar but I didn't recognize it right away. The voice told me that I was going to be okay. That everything was fine. That I had no reason to still be sad."

A stunned Kate dropped some of the envelopes on the floor. Danny came around and helped her gather them up and then continued her stamping.

"Well," Danny continued, "when that happened I was totally freaked out by it. Then it happened again, as I slept. I heard the voice again and it spoke to me. I was in a deep sleep but I recognized it instantly this time. It was Ben's voice. This time I could see him with his red hair and broad shoulders. He was in his uniform. He always looked so handsome in his uniform. He told me that I needed to take care of his momma and daddy for him and he would see to it that they would take care of me. I know it sounds strange but I swear that night I could actually feel him put his arms around me. I could feel the warmth of his hug. I woke up that next morning with a new confidence.

I knew I would never leave this place. It had this special connection to Ben and now I had it as well."

"That's amazing. You actually heard and felt his presence?"

"Something truly extraordinary," Danny said. "I told Lucy about it and she said she wasn't surprised. That's when she told me the story of how she and Beck came to Harmony and about the woman who changed their lives. Kate, things happened here to people like I've never experienced before. Something most people here take for granted."

Kate said, "What do you mean?"

"Well, take Della. She's lived here for such a long time. Lucy told me Della had confided in her after Dobb died that he came to her on the beach. That they walked hand-in-hand and he shared with her how much he loved her. Della would never admit it to this day. She insists Lucy made it all up. I guess she's embarrassed about it. Grief is hard on everyone who experiences it. Della is just one of those who refuse to accept how lucky she was and is."

Kate said, "I wonder if she sees him still."

"I doubt she'd be the way she is if he still came around."

Kate was silent as she gathered up more envelopes for the box.

Danny asked, "Has something like that happened to you? Has someone come to you?"

Kate didn't answer. She wasn't sure she wanted to admit it.

"You don't have to say a word about it," Danny answered. "I see it in your face. I know it's hard to talk about. Some people here will tell you it's all in your head. I shrug that off. I don't care if it is all in my head. It's real to me and it means more than almost anything else. Hold on to it though. It won't likely last forever."

CHAPTER 23

The house was progressing nicely. Kate spent more and more time at home. The more she did, the more she saw Ruby. There was no longer the pretense that the voice she heard was not the child. It no longer surprised her.

"Kate?"

"Hi Ruby," Kate said.

"Hi," Ruby answered as Kate hung the linens outside on the clothes line behind the house.

Kate asked her, "Where are you?"

There was a tug on Kate's dress. "Right here."

Kate looked down and there she stood in utter perfection. Her face and figure as visible as if human. She met Kate's eyes with a smile that revealed that dimple on her lower left cheek that Kate had grown fond of.

"You hang your clothes on a wire?"

"A clothes line."

"Why?" Ruby asked.

"Well, the back porch doesn't have enough room for both a washer and dryer and there really wasn't anywhere else to put it so we use this. Plus, this is more environmentally friendly."

"Huh?"

"When you use a clothes dryer it uses electricity, and that isn't necessary. Hanging your clothes on a line like this uses only the sun – no other energy is needed. At least not any you have to buy."

"What about wind? Is that energy?"

Kate said, "It is in a way. But it's not manu-factured energy like electricity."

Ruby watched Kate hang their clothes out to dry in the sun. She then looked up at the sky and the nearly white sun. Finally she asked, "What if it rains?"

Kate laughed. "Well, then we don't hang them out to dry. We have to wait until the sun comes out again."

"I thought so," Ruby said.

"You're a pretty sharp little girl."

"I sure am and I'm curious too."

"Curious?" Kate asked.

"Yep. About everything. I'm even curious about you."

"Me?" Kate asked.

"Yeah, you and Michael. I find you both fascinating. He loves you, doesn't he?"

Kate said, continuing to hang the linens out, "Yes, he does."

"And you love him?"

Without hesitation, Kate answered, "I love him more than anything."

"I could tell. You both have fun together and you're kind of mushy over each other. Kissing on the lips and all over and stuff like that."

Kate embarrassed said, "That's what people do when they're in love. They want to be so close to that person so they feel like they are one. Closer than they've been with anyone else."

"Like a mommy and daddy."

"Yes, but you don't have to be a mommy or daddy to show love."

"I know that. You're not a mommy and you show love."

"That's true."

"Do you ever think that someday you'll have kids?"

"Truthfully, some people can't ever have children."

"Oh, everyone has kids. That is what you do. Fall in love, get married and have kids."

"Except not everyone can have kids. Sometimes it's just not possible. And I happen to be one of those people who can't."

Ruby said, "Really? I thought everyone had kids."

Kate shook her head. "No, the doctors told me I would never have kids of my own. It's just the way it is."

"That's okay," Ruby said, "because you have me. I can be your kid."

Kate stopped hanging clothes. She looked down at Ruby who was smiling at her. Ruby asked, "You wanna play?"

"Play with you?" Kate asked. She was having a hard enough time adjusting to whether this child was real or not. This entire conversation was making it even harder for her to distinguish.

"Yeah, let's play chase or hide-and-seek. Those are my favorites."

Kate looked over at Ruby and then at all the grassland around the house. Not a single person for miles. Ruby touched Kate's leg and said, "You're it." And she ran away, squealing with laughter.

Kate felt her touch. She could hear her laugh and watched as she brushed through the grass like an out of control rake.

Ruby stopped running. She called out, "Kate! You need to chase me and try and get me."

Kate looked around again and decided to let her guard down. She took off chasing after the girl. Ruby screamed and ran farther away. Kate chased her all over the yard until Ruby fell. Kate ran up to her. The girl was about to get up again and run when she shrilled. Kate was standing over her and stopped just short of tagging the girl. Without warning Ruby jumped up and with her arms out fell into Kate. Kate lifted her up as a natural instinct to having a child in her arms. "I've got you. I've got you," Kate said as Ruby howled with laughter.

The girl felt real. Her weight solid, likely around thirty pounds.

"Okay, put me down," Ruby said. "It's my turn to get you."

Kate didn't want to put her down. She held onto her for what she hoped would be forever but was only a minute. The girl wiggled in Kate's arms. Not wanting to drop her, Kate put her down and Ruby shouted, "Ready or not, here I come!"

Kate yelled, "Wait! You've got to give me a head start." Kate took off with Ruby right behind her. Kate picked up the pace and pulled away from the small girl, running and laughing as she ran freely. The sun at her back and breeze in her face, Kate ran around until she couldn't continue.

Ruby tagged her. "Got ya! Now, you're it." And again Ruby was off running and laughing. Kate stood there watching the girl as she caught her breath. She was terribly winded.

"Come on, Kate. Come get me!"

Kate played with Ruby that entire afternoon. Only when Kate went inside to use the bathroom did Ruby disappear again. Kate called for her but she didn't return. Left with her solitude again, she questioned the events of the day but there was no mistaking this. It was all real.

Michael returned a few hours later from Beck's. Kate was in the kitchen preparing dinner when Michael approached her from behind. "Hi honey," Michael said as he greeted Kate with a kiss.

"Hi, dinner's going to be a little late. I lost track of time. Ruby was here a good part of the day."

"Was she?"

Kate stopped chopping and turned toward Michael. "Yeah, she was here all afternoon. We played tag outside. Michael, it was unbelievable. I was able to touch her. And she touched me. I even picked her up in my arms." Kate demonstrated to Michael how she had picked up the girl.

"You're kidding?" he said.

"I'm not. It was like she was real. Amazing as it sounds, it was real."

"Where is she now?"

"I don't know. I came in to use the bathroom and when I came back out she was gone. She has the most adorable laugh. She's gorgeous."

When Kate spoke about the girl there was pleasure in her tone. Michael was proud. It was what he wanted more than anything to bring out in her.

"Kate, look at you."

"What?" she said.

"I can't tell you how long I have waited to see you happy like this."

Kate thought about her happiness. How the afternoon with Ruby had made her feel. "It was so special – this afternoon. Like nothing I had ever felt."

"I know it," Michael said. "I can see it in you – in your smile." Michael approached Kate and wrapped his arms around her. Her body was warm. He kissed her softly on the neck and moved his hands down her backside.

"Michael! Wait!" Kate pulled back from him.

"What?" he said.

"We can't. Not here."

"Why not?"

"Because we don't know where she is. She could be right here next to us. She's seen us kissing. She told me so this afternoon."

"What did you say?"

"I was embarrassed. She obviously saw us that night on the bed."

"Well, what can we do about it?"

"I don't know. I don't want her to see us like that. I don't want to have to explain it to her."

Michael said, "So what are we going to do? I've waited for you."

"I know. I know. It's just I'm not sure I can. Not with her here."

"Kate, I've been patient. And now after all this time, I can tell you're ready and I've been ready. But now you're saying that because this girl might be able to see us we can't. Why don't we try it in the shower? With the door locked and shower door closed. She couldn't get inside the shower with us. It would be private."

Kate thought about it. Michael came back over to her and rubbed against her while he kissed her neck again. "Come on, let's try it."

"Michael, no. I'm not ready." She pushed him off.

"Well, I guess I'll just go and take my shower myself."

He started to walk away only to turn back toward her. "Kate, this can't continue this way. I need to be with you. We need to be together."

"I know," she said. "Give me some time to think this through."

"You've had nothing but time." He turned and walked over to the bathroom and slammed the door, locking it behind him.

Kate understood his frustration. She didn't know how to do things any differently. She went back to chopping vegetables and worried that having a child around was going to change their relationship. It was not exactly what she was expecting when they came here.

CHAPTER 24

The sunny kitchen with its white and cherry curtains, newly tiled white and cobalt blue trim counter and all new appliances was everything Kate hoped it would be.

The living room had also come to life. The sage colored walls were the cozy addition to living that only an overstuffed coffee colored sofa and high back chair could anchor. Holla's painting was the perfect opposing complement to the large picture window. The tranquil house in the painting enjoyed the same view as the home that held it. The forest green and chocolate accent pillows along with the restful color of the walls echoed the serenity of the view that the bay window held. The breathful existence outside transcended to the inside of the house.

The refinished pastel bathroom with modern touches of a glass enclosed tub and shower, new pedestal sink and marble tile floors was nothing like the afterthought of the previous room's condition. "High fashion and highly functional," was the way Kate described it to Ruth.

Their bedroom, a distinguished blue, hadn't turned out to be the color Kate wanted it to be. Michael didn't much care for it either, but stated, "It's our bedroom. No one's really going to see it. The color is fine." So that's how it stayed. The bed was adorned with a chenille comforter and about a dozen mix-matched frilly pillows. The pale walls of the room were bare of any embellishments. It was a project Kate would tackle later.

The pressure to entertain was all about Kate. Every time she went into town, someone, if not everyone, would ask when the house would be ready. Raye insisted they needed to have a housewarming. Michael wanted to give it some more time. He saw more, than Kate did, still needing to be done. Details he hadn't had time to get to. The reality was he wasn't the one going into town all the time. He never felt the pressure to be hospitable.

As they put the back bedroom office together, with its fiery brick-colored walls and countless shelves, Kate started in. "Michael, I had no choice. People want to see the house. Everyone's been asking. I just figured we'd get it over with all in one night."

"Oh, Kate. Come on!"

"Well, Beck and Lucy will be here."

"And?" Michael asked.

"And Danny. Raye, Holla, Sunny and Ruth. It will be fine. They're all so laid back I'd doubt they'd notice those things that bother you that are still out of place."

"You know I hate having people over."

"I know, but again, what was I to do? They want to come see the house. It's a small town. It's not like we can hide away."

Michael asked, "What about Ruby?"

"What about her?"

"I don't know. How do we explain her?" Michael asked.

"Who says we have to? She may not even show up." Kate looked up from her box of books and said loudly, "Right Ruby? You won't visit when our guests are here. No, I know you. I can trust you."

Michael rolled his eyes. "Let's just feed them and get them out," Michael said. "We'll leave the girl out of it."

"Michael, are you embarrassed about Ruby being here?"

"No, it's not that. It's that I'm not sure how we explain her. I'm not even sure I can explain her to myself."

"I understand but this isn't necessarily new to them. There've been others."

"I'm not comfortable explaining how we live to them. I know Beck would want nothing to do with it."

"How can you be so sure?"

Michael answered, "He's the one who told me not to read too much into what the others say about Pete. I could just imagine what he would say about Ruby."

Kate didn't feel the same way but nonetheless, she agreed to keep Ruby a secret.

With their dinner party just days away, Michael and Kate worked day and night on the small details of the house that bothered Michael. Kate wanted him to feel as comfortable as possible. Ruby was with them the entire time. While Michael and Kate worked, Ruby sat and watched.

Kate explained to Ruby, "It's an adult party. No kids."

"What about Mason?" Ruby said.

"I think Stan's going to look after him. He didn't want to come. So you understand that you can't stay or interrupt the party."

"I guess so," Ruby said.

"Good. Don't worry we'll make it up to you somehow," Kate told the girl.

The night of the party, time was working against them. Kate was busy getting dinner prepared and Michael was touching up some paint in the bathroom. With an endless list of things they wanted to get done going undone, what the house looked like was as good as it was going to get for their dinner party.

"Knock, knock," came from the front screen door. Without waiting, the screen door opened and Kate panicked.

"Kate, it's just us," Lucy said. "We thought maybe you could use some help."

Kate came into the living room to greet Lucy, Beck and Danny. She was both anxious and relieved to see them. "So glad you could come," she said.

"Uh, where's Mike?" Beck asked looking around.

"He's in the bathroom touching up the paint."

"Well, I better go see if he needs me to check anything. Plumbing holding up?" Beck asked.

"So far," Kate said.

"Beck, leave her alone," Lucy nagged. "Go find out what Michael needs. Can't you see she's stressin' the party?"

Beck just waved a hand at his wife, grumbled something and went to find Michael.

"What do you want us to do?" Lucy asked.

"Well," Kate said looking around. Noticing Danny holding a dish, she pointed to Danny's dish with a frazzled look.

"Sugar, it's just some muffins. They're for you and Michael. You know, for the morning. It wouldn't be very Southern if I showed up empty-handed." As Danny went to hand off the muffins to Kate, Lucy pushed past them both and went into the kitchen.

"Danny, come with me, let's take a look at what we might help her with."

Danny followed and mouthed "I'm sorry" to Kate as she went to see what she could do to help keep Lucy at bay.

Kate stood there alone in the living room for a minute. She didn't know what to do. When she heard the oven door opening, she rushed to the kitchen.

"What do we have here? Some sort of fish?" Lucy asked.

"It's salmon. I found this recipe for it. Thought I'd give it a try," Kate said rushing into the kitchen.

Taking a whiff, Lucy said, "Smells pretty good. What are you serving with it?"

"With it?" Kate answered.

Empathizing with Kate's nervousness, Danny spoke up. "I'm sure Kate doesn't need us poking our heads in her oven."

Lucy closed the oven door and shrugged her shoulders.

Danny suggested, "Would you like us to set the table for you, Kate?"

"The table?" Kate said. "Sure, set the table. The dishes..."

"Don't worry, we'll manage," Lucy interrupted. "You just attend to what you need to in the kitchen. And if you need us for anything just say the word."

Lucy quickly pushed past both Kate and Danny en route to the living room. Danny followed closely behind. Kate stayed in the kitchen where she heard Lucy say, "I wonder where she..." and "Where'd you suppose she has..." to Danny who quickly resolved all her mother-in-law's issues so Kate could focus on what she had going on in the kitchen.

Only a few minutes later, there was another knock at the door. Kate froze. *What hippies show up early? That's not laid back.*

Michael came in from the bathroom and threw a paint brush along with some trash in the drawer of the desk in the living room. He greeted his guests at the door. "Hey, come on in. Wow, you made it." Sunny and Holla came in. As they did, Beck came out from the hallway. "Hey Mike, that shower seems to still be leaking. I'll go get my wrench. It's in the truck."

Michael said, "Hey, don't worry about it."

"It's no worry. While you folks are getting things together I'll work on that shower."

Lucy answered up, "And what about when someone needs to use the toilet?"

"Lucy, they just need to tell me. I'll step out and when they're done, I can finish up. I'll be discreet."

"Discreet? Beck, you don't know discreet. How about you just leave the shower for another day? We're here for dinner and no one wants a bathroom monitor around."

"Lucy, you overreact," Beck insisted.

"No, I don't! Remember those guests we had stay with us from Austin? You insisted they let you know every time they flushed the toilet in their room. You were adamant about wanting to check the bulk load of that new low-flow toilet you put in. My goodness, that was embarrassing. Who wants to talk about the bulk load of a toilet to strangers?"

"I just wanted to ensure it was satisfactory to them. You and Danny are always talking about customer service, right?"

"Beck, it's a toilet! They were our guests! They don't want to talk about their bulk load in our toilet!"

Danny interrupting, "Okay, you two. Let's forget about the toilet and shower and have a good time."

Lucy went on, "Danny, you know how he is. Something had to be said. He's obsessed with plumbing.

"I know, I know. Dad, maybe you can give Michael a hand with the shower later and let tonight be about enjoying each other's company."

Michael had held the guests at the door while all this was going on. Pushing past Michael, Sunny interrupted, "Beck, anytime you want to ask me about my bulk load and our plumbing just let me know."

"SUNNY!" Holla shouted behind him.

"What? I was just saying," Sunny then handed off a six-pack of beer to Michael. "Hey man, I didn't know if this was BYOB but brought my own anyway. I suggest you get this on ice -- immediately. Seems pretty hot in here already."

Holla said to Michael, "I'm sorry but Sunny goes nowhere and I mean nowhere without his brew."

"Hey, it's good stuff," Sunny said. "I brew it myself. It's all organic."

Michael looked at the box of the homemade brew in his arms and walked it over to the kitchen. As he walked away he said, "Kate, why don't you show our guests around."

Kate with sweat running down her forehead wiped her brow and said, "Well, there's not much to see. This is the living room."

Holla said, "Before I forget. Raye and Ruth send their regrets."

"They're not coming?" Kate asked.

"No," Holla continued. "Seems Stan went down to Morro Bay to get something and hasn't come back yet. Stan was going to watch Mason but Raye ended up with all three kids at her house."

"And Ruth?" Kate asked.

"Raye reminded me that Ruth doesn't generally go out after dark. Raye probably could have convinced her but with Raye with the kids, Ruth stayed in town."

Kate looked disappointed. So Lucy interjected, "Let's not worry about who isn't here. Let's celebrate those who are. Shall we?"

Kate nodded.

Lucy, keeping the conversation rolling, said, "You did a wonderful job. The place looks great."

"Thank you."

Looking around, Sunny agreed. "It is. Way nicer than I expected."

"Sunny!" Holla said.

"What? It is," he said.

Danny noticed Holla's painting on the wall. "Holla, your painting looks great in here."

This got Sunny's attention. He looked over at Holla's painting. "Looks great, babe. Let me go check on Mike and see how that beer's coming along."

"I think I'll go with ya," Beck said. And with that both men disappeared into the kitchen. Kate worried about them peeking in on any of her dishes. "I'll be in shortly to check on the dinner."

Lucy said, "Oh never mind them. With those two out of here, we can all talk girl talk. Let's see the bedroom."

"Sure," Kate said. "It's still a work in progress. Keep that in mind."

Holla still looking at her painting said, "Well, you were right. The painting looks like it was meant to be here."

"I told you it was perfect," Kate said.

Lucy agreed. "It does look nice in here but I don't see any family pictures."

"I know," Kate said. "I still haven't found everything. I am hoping they are in some of the boxes we still haven't gone through. I know where our wedding album is but I still haven't found a bunch of our pictures. There are ones of me and my mom that I know I packed and I still can't find them. I'll be heartbroken if they don't turn up."

"Oh, I'm sure they will," Danny assured her. "Things like that always turn up."

The three guys emerged from the kitchen at the same time the ladies were back from their short tour. Sunny sauntered in with a tall glass of beer in his hand that had ice floating in it.

Holla noticing said, "Sunny, you couldn't wait?"

Taking a swig, "No, I couldn't. I worked hard today."

Michael consoled Holla. "No worries. It was a little too warm for the rest of us."

From the kitchen a timer went off.

"Oh, let me check on the salmon. It might be ready. Excuse me," Kate said and walked passed her guests in the tight quarters of the living room.

Holla said, "Not that it is any big deal but you know Sunny and I are vegan, right?"

Kate answered, "Yeah, I knew that. I made plenty of roasted vegetables."

Holla happily replied, "Hope it was no trouble. It's just Sunny and I feel like…"

Beck interrupted, "Oh brother, Holla. Man was made to eat meat. You vegans are what these low flow toilets were made for."

Lucy shrieked, "Beck! Again with the toilet talk?"

"I'm just saying any man who eats his weight in meat can't..."

"Not another word about it, Beck!" Lucy shot him a glare he was all too familiar with.

The new potatoes took a little longer than Kate had anticipated. Their quick dinner party was being prolonged by the delay of the potatoes. Everyone sat around the table in the living room waiting and enjoyed both the beer and wine. By the time Kate finally brought out the food everyone was already well into their drinks.

With the food flowing, everyone ate, laughed and joked, mostly telling funny and embarrassing stories about their partner. With things at the party rolling along, a crash came from the kitchen.

Sunny hollered, "What the hell."

Beck stood up immediately to go and see what happened.

Kate and Michael looked at each other. Michael stood up and said, "I'm sure it's nothing, probably just the wind knocking something over."

Kate stood up to go with him. She looked concerned. Michael motioned for her to sit down.

Lucy eyed the couple's exchange of body language. Kate sat back down as did Beck, and Michael went into the kitchen to check it out. With all eyes on her, Kate said, "Michael's right. It's probably nothing."

Beck asked, "You want me to..."

"No, no. It'll be fine," Kate said. "Michael will be back in no time."

Holla asked, "Kate is that what you were talking about in the gallery?"

"Talking about what?" Lucy asked.

Holla said, "Kate was hearing things."

Sunny said, "So you're hearing things in the house? Oh no, you're one of those then?"

Danny to Sunny, "What's that supposed to mean?"

"You know very well. Right Beck?" Sunny said.

Lucy shot Beck another look and he knew better than to answer.

So Danny posed the question. "No, I think he should answer. What does it mean?"

Sunny answered, "You gonna take this one, Beck, or should I?"

Beck grabbed his beer and washed down the rest of it.

"No problem," Sunny said. "Some of you around here make more out of things than should be. You're always looking for meaning in the meaningless. Making things out of some "guy" like Pete and things you think you see."

Lucy wasn't having it. She looked right at Sunny. "Maybe it's some of us have more clarity than others."

"Clarity? Holla's always hearing things. You think she has clarity?"

"Shut up, Sunny," Holla said.

"Kate, you know this place is haunted don't you?" Sunny asked.

"No, it's not haunted as it turns out." Kate answered, fumbling for words.

Sunny asked, "So Kate what is it you think you have been seeing?"

"Miracles," Danny answered.

Sunny said, "Oh no. Kate don't tell me you are buying into this. People and their stories of messengers and miracles and seeing things that aren't really there. It's all bull."

Danny said, "It's not bull."

"My old man had a story of his own. I always thought it was his habit." Sunny brought his hand up to his mouth as if holding a joint to his lips.

"Like father, like son," Holla added.

"Oh and you're so innocent?" Sunny responded.

Holla turned red. "Hey I don't do that... anymore."

"Not any more my butt," Sunny said.

Lucy to both of them, "Alright you two, none of us is perfect and we all know it."

Kate asked Sunny, "What about these stories? What stories?"

Sunny answered, "People seeing things that aren't really there."

Holla added, "Like I mentioned to you about Pete."

Sunny added, "Not the Pete story again. My god, Holla, it's all a coincidence."

Holla to Sunny, "Oh yeah, how come you've never seen him?"

"Well, I'm not looking for him, I guess."

Kate then asked Sunny, "But you saw him that day in town when Della was chasing him didn't you?"

"All I saw was crazy old Della chasing after nothin'. I wouldn't put too much into that Kate. Della's a crazy old witch anyway."

"SUNNY!" Holla said.

"That's not nice," Danny added.

"Oh and she is?" he answered back.

Kate interrupted, "So besides seeing Pete, who else has seen something?"

"Danny and I have," Lucy said.

Beck remained silent.

Holla said, "And Raye."

"Everyone's seen Pete. Everyone except Sunny here," Danny answered.

Sunny said, "That don't mean a thing. These things or people or whatever you all think there are, aren't miracles."

"Then what are they?" Danny asked.

"They're just people trippin' out on some bad acid probably," Sunny explained.

Lucy asked, "You saying I dropped acid, Sunny?"

Sunny blushed. "I don't know. Did you?"

"Absolutely not!" Lucy answered.

Holla to Sunny, "If anyone was trippin' it would be you. You've dropped more acid than even your father."

"Again, I wasn't flying solo most of the time, my dear Holla."

Danny attempting to change the direction of the conversation asked, "What about you, Kate?"

Afraid to say, Kate looked out for Michael. She couldn't figure what was taking him so long.

Holla answered, "Kate saw someone."

"Someone?" Danny asked.

"Who was it?" Lucy asked.

Everyone waited for her response. Kate struggled to admit it. "It's...It's a...a little girl."

Danny yelled out, "No way!"

"You see, Michael and I can never have children. Then we came here and this little girl appeared to us. It's a sign."

Holla replied, "That's a trip."

Michael finally coming back into the living room said, "Nothing to worry about. Just the wind knocked over a plant. I got it all cleaned up. So what're we talking about?"

Sunny said, "Kate's just telling us about the little girl you guys have here."

Michael looked over at Kate. Kate ignored him. She turned toward the ladies. "She's adorable, around five years old."

Danny asked, "And you can see her?"

"As plain as day. Right here in this house and all around it."

"Incredible," Holla said.

"It is," Kate agreed. "It really is."

Lucy said, "You know, Juanita has a very similar story."

Kate said, "Does she?"

Danny added, "Juanita says she met this man once on the beach. He reminded her of her late husband but wasn't exactly him. He had a more angelic presence as if surrounded by pure light. She said it was like in those pictures of saints and the Virgin Mary where a gold orb surrounds them."

"I wonder why this little girl would visit us then," Kate said. "We never had a little girl."

Danny said, "I'm sure you'll find out."

"You know Kate," Holla said, "Juanita's very old school when it comes to religion. None of this may mean anything."

"Whether you're religious or not has nothing to do with it. I was never raised religiously," Danny explained. "And I believe."

Kate added, "And Ruth says..."

Sunny interrupted, "You can't always believe what Ruth has to say. She's set in her old ways too."

Kate was offended. "What I was going to say was that Ruth says we're all here in Harmony for a reason. Some find out those reasons right away while others wait. I really believe these visitors we're talking about are messengers. I'm waiting to find out why ours is here."

Sunny rolled his eyes.

"We all have the right to believe what we do," Holla said. "If you want to believe they're miracles, do so."

Kate turned to Danny and Lucy and affirmed, "Well, I have seen with my own eyes this girl and I know her appearance is real. I've talked to her and touched her and she's touched me." Kate looked over at Michael for his support.

He didn't say anything.

Holla then asked Michael, "So, out there in the kitchen. Was it the little girl?"

Everyone turned to hear Michael's answer. "No, it was the open window. The breeze knocked over that fern." Michael looked over at Kate. "The pot's broken."

The room fell silent.

Sunny said, "Well, no worries. I can certainly replace the pot for you."

Again, no one said a thing.

So Sunny added, "You know, I meant the ceramic kind."

No one laughed.

"Tough room." Sunny got up from the table and went to the bathroom and patted Michael on the shoulder.

Kate knew Sunny's gesture meant he thought Michael supported him. Kate looked over at Beck and asked, "Beck, you've been quiet. What do you think?"

Beck was slow to answer. "My dear, I love my wife and I love my daughter." He put his hand on Lucy's at the table. "If they believe they have seen someone and that someone has helped them with their grief then I am happy to support them."

Danny and Lucy smiled at him.

Holla couldn't help but ask, "What about you, Beck? Have you seen anything like they have?"

Beck was quiet again then said, "Truthfully, I'm not sure what to say I've seen. If it were up to me," his voice began to quiver, "I would love to see my boy again. To hear him laugh again or say 'Hiya Pop' or even just smile – that's what I long for." A tear welled up in Beck's eye and he quickly wiped it away. The room stayed quiet. Lucy put her arm around him, hugged on him and kissed him.

Before anyone else could say a thing, Lucy summoned, "Danny, help me clear the dishes." Both women got up and started for the kitchen with armloads of dishes in their hand.

Without missing a beat, Kate said, "No, no. You're our guests." She followed them into the kitchen.

Michael, Beck and Holla were left alone in the silent room for a moment. Then Holla said, "I'm with you, Beck. I'd love to see my daddy again. I don't really know what to make of any of it. I've been here awhile now and can't figure any of it out." She looked up at Michael. "It's hard to believe when you don't know what you are seeing."

Sunny reentered the room from the bathroom and patted Beck on the back. "Well Beck, the bulk load on the toilet in there is working just fine."

Shortly after everyone left, Kate and Michael put the room back together in silence. Michael knew what was bothering Kate. But he chose not to say a thing. She wanted him to apologize. But Michael felt like he had done nothing wrong. So the two went to bed and said nothing to each other the rest of the night. Michael tossed and turned all night long wanting them to get on with it. He knew an argument was coming but Kate wasn't playing along. Kate was waiting for Michael to apologize. Facing their opposite ways on the bed, the distance between them now didn't seem too different from the way they were in LA.

CHAPTER 25

The next morning was a cool one. The coastal fog lay heavy on the bed of green hills around the house. Michael had gotten up early out of habit. He looked out the bedroom window and couldn't see a single thing around him. Just a pale gray haze surrounded them that morning.

Instead of working on the house, he turned his attention to a garden he had started. He and Kate had wanted a garden to grow some of their own food so they wouldn't have to go into the city to buy as much. Outside the house, Michael gathered up what he would need; a rake, a shovel and trowel. As he started his digging, the sun's faint golden rays seemed to only break at the plot for the garden with pure sunlight. Michael was bent over turning the soil with a shovel when he heard, "How did you sleep?"

He looked around toward the porch. Ruby sat on the porch rail behind the swing facing Michael at work. She had her left leg up on the railing and looked to be picking lint out from between her toes.

The way the sunlight hit her she looked like she glowed.

Michael stood up to get a better look at her and answered, "Alright, I guess." She was wearing a plain white cotton dress that was gathered under her as she sat. Her golden hair hung over one eye as she cocked her head to one side studying her toes as she worked. Michael hated himself looking at her in her wholesome light. Last night, he had been embarrassed by Kate's honesty. He couldn't be that honest. Looking at Ruby made him mad at himself. He realized he didn't want their guests to judge him like he had judged Kate.

He knew Kate was falling in love with Ruby as if she was her own child. With those feelings brewing, he grew concerned about their situation. The less people knew about Ruby the better. Michael stared at Ruby and couldn't imagine what she could be to them. Ruby looked up and saw him watching her. "Something wrong with you today?" she asked.

"Why?"

"Because you keep staring at me," she said almost exasperated.

"There's something different about you today."

"That's because I am getting older, silly."

"That must be it." He couldn't stop staring. He realized that they were living in this fantasy world. As real as she seemed, this child wasn't real.

"Is Kate still asleep?" she asked.

"Yeah, she's still asleep."

Michael listened but focused on her features; her cheeks, her nose, her throat as she spoke. She was really talking to him. The certainty of Ruby was more than he could object to.

"Hey, I almost forgot," she said. "Come on. I want to show you something." She swung around effortlessly on the rail and jumped down on the porch. As her weight hit the floorboards there was noticeable sound to the impact. She headed down the steps of the porch and ran around the gravel drive to the pasture on the east side of the house. As she ran along every few feet she skipped. Michael followed but didn't run. As he came around the corner of the house, the sun was so bright he could barely see her. All he could see was the silhouette of her in the field. The whole view was luminous light. He put his hand up to shield his eyes from the glare.

He was drawn toward her. The tall grasses felt dewy as they brushed against his leg and shoes. Whish-wash, whish-wash, went his damp pant legs. As he came close to her, the details of her features were undeniable. She was bending down looking at something in the grass. He bent down next to her.

She put her hand on his knee. "Do you see it?" she asked.

"Yeah. What is it?" He wasn't really sure he was looking at the right thing.

"It's a small sunflower," she said. "These're my favorite. So bright like summer. Doesn't it make you feel happy?"

The idea of a flower making anyone happy was absurd to him. He came in for a closer look. He noticed the tiny blonde hairs on her cheeks. The speckled details in her eyes with flecks of blue and green and black. Details that were unavoidably real. He finally answered her, "Yes, it does make me feel happy."

She looked up at him and said, "Isn't it special?"

"It is," he answered. "You know, I have never seen an actual sunflower grow before."

"Are you serious?" she asked.

He chuckled and admitted, "I am. I've bought them for Kate sometimes but I've never seen them growing from the ground."

"Wow," she said.

"Thanks for showing this to me, Ruby." He said her name for the first time.

She gazed up at him. She wasn't paying attention to him saying her name. That was totally missed by her. Instead, she studied his face. With a wrinkled brow, she looked him over.

"Is something bothering you?" he asked.

"It's nothing," she said turning away and looking out at the pasture. "I wondered how many other sunflowers were out there in that field. Growing, stretching to be seen. I know I won't ever see them all." Her happiness seemed to turn sad.

"Ruby, did I say something to upset you?" he asked her.

She turned back toward him. "It's sad to think that they'll die someday and it won't be happy then. I just wish happy things didn't have to end."

"Hey, don't you worry." He bent further down to her level to comfort her. It came natural to him. As he bent down, he could smell the faint scent of jasmine on her.

She looked down at the ground, avoiding his eyes when she said, "Everything comes to an end, Michael."

He felt his throat suddenly tighten. He worried she was right. He also knew she was waiting for him to say something to her. Something supportive. Nothing came. Michael could see her look off at the horizon as she waited for his words.

"I remember when you and Kate first came to visit. I saw you hug her and kiss her and it was funny. Then when you came back and moved in, I watched you every minute you were here. I watched you both and found it all kinds of fun to watch. Why can't it always be happy?"

"What?" he asked a little unsure what she meant.

"Why do things like sunflowers have to die? Why don't happy things just stay with us?"

"It's the way things are I guess."

"I just want you and Kate to stay happy."

Michael was quick to respond. "We are happy."

Ruby looked over at him. "You are?"

"Yes, of course."

"Sometimes I don't know. You can be in the same room together and it feels like you don't even know it. Then sometimes when you're fiddling with something in the house and she's off doing something else in another room and she'll start humming some song. And you'll start humming along with her."

"Wait, I don't hum," he said.

"Oh yes you do," she said. "I heard you. You'd hum and she'd hum and I thought these two seemed really happy. And that made me happy. The more I watched the happier I was. Until finally I couldn't take it anymore and I had to talk to Kate that day in the kitchen. I wanted her to know I was there."

"Why?" Michael asked. "Why did you come here?"

"That's funny. Back then you didn't even believe what Kate was telling you about me. But you do now, huh? You may not say it out loud but you believe it. It's why you study me like you do. You see me up close and it makes you believe."

He didn't know what to say. Here he was in the tall grasses next to his home talking with this adorable little girl who was winning his heart and she knew him better than she should.

"Well Michael?" she said.

He looked over at her and waited until she was looking at him when he said, "I do."

She smiled and said, "I knew it!"

It was her smile. He looked at her smile and it made him happy. He could no longer deny it to himself or her or anyone else that she made him happy.

Kate finally emerged from the bedroom. She looked out the kitchen window and saw Michael sitting and talking to Ruby. She didn't care what anyone else thought, she knew they were here to take care of her. The three of them together were a family.

CHAPTER 26

KMOR had been reporting on the red tide that had swept into the coast. News of a red tide had everyone in Harmony buzzing about the expected appearance of luminous lights in the surf later that night. It was a somewhat common occurrence during a red tide that the appearance of indigo lights would be seen in the crashing surf up around the beaches near the lighthouse. Explained as a biological event, the appearance of phosphorescent lights in the water was a true spectacle for the town's people.

Kate decided to go into town to check on Ruth. She hadn't been at the party and Kate had spent the entire next day at home. She wanted to make sure Ruth was doing alright. Walking down Old Creamery Road, Kate ran into Holla in front of the courtyard.

"Great party the other night," Holla said bringing out her daily variety of pots that sat there waiting to draw attention to her shop.

"You think so?" Kate asked.

"Oh yeah, even Sunny thought so. Of course, he's sure your house is haunted but don't let him bother you."

"I'm not really worried about it," Kate said.

"Good. Did you hear about the red tide?"

"Yeah, I heard about it on the radio this morning."

"We're all going up to the lighthouse tonight. If you really want to see something, you and Michael should come see the lights."

"The lights?" Kate asked.

"The lights of the souls will be out tonight or so the legend goes," Holla said in a spooky tone. "I bet you'll get a kick out of it. Whenever there's a red tide up here, the legend says the ocean swells stir up the spirits of those who have died and you can see their glowing spirits in the surf as they make their way to eternity. Of course, Sunny read up about it and says it's nothing more than the bloom of the red algae or something or other. It has to do with the decaying organic matter of the algae or something. I don't remember exactly. Anyway when you see them at night these particles glow blue-green lights that you can see in the surf. It's pretty cool. You and Michael should come and see it."

Kate said, thinking about it, "Sure, we just might do that."

"I'd be curious to see what you make of it," Holla said. "Is it science or spiritual? It should be interesting."

"Sounds like it. I'll have to check it out."

"Then let me know what you make of it."

"I will," Kate said. She wasn't sure what to make of how Holla phrased it. *Is she making fun of me? She's not that clever to be that facetious. Sunny maybe but not Holla.*

Kate walked on to Ruth's thinking about the lights. Ruth saw Kate first. Ruth was out sweeping the walkway in front of her door. "Your mind looks to be running wide this morning," Ruth said.

"What?" Kate asked.

"Your mind. You look like you have a lot on your mind this morning."

"I do but how are you?" Kate asked her.

"I'm well, honey," Ruth said guiding Kate to the door with her frail hand on Kate's back.

"We missed you the other night – at the party, you know, at our place."

"Honey, no need to worry about me. No one there likely missed an old lady like me. I'm sure everyone had a great time regardless." Ruth walked back inside and Kate followed her.

"I missed you," Kate said. "Why didn't you come? You know, I could have picked you up."

Ruth put her broom away behind the green curtain and headed straight for the tea pot. "Please, my dear, don't worry about me. I'm fine. I'm not really the party sort of person."

"Well, still I would have wanted you to see our place."

"I will. Don't worry about that." Ruth brought the tea service to the counter. Kate sat down on her usual perch. "Out there, it seemed something was on your mind. Was something else troubling you?"

Kate reached for a cup and added cream and sugar to it. She stirred it quickly and let the tea cool. "Let me ask you; what do you know about tonight's tide?"

"Pardon?" Ruth said stirring her tea more times than necessary.

"There's a red tide and everyone's talking about the light show tonight."

Ruth crinkled her brow, raised the hot tea to her mouth, lipped a small sip and said, "Well, what do you want to know? I'm sure people in town have their own opinions about it. I'm sure they've explained it to you already."

Kate said, "It's just everyone here has a different perspective about nearly everything. Have you ever seen these lights they are talking about?"

Ruth relented. "It can be a marvelous thing – the lights dancing on the waves. You know one might believe the lights lend credence to that legend of the lighthouse. They say a red tide is a mix of both new and old life. If you go and smell the ocean air during this tide you're sure to smell death. It's like the souls of those lost at sea being dredged up from their depths on their way to the heavens. The lighthouse beacons for old souls here. 'Lighthouse, lighthouse, keep us safe and sure, off the rock coast and into eternity evermore' or so it goes. These lights give me proof that Harmony is a special place. I often think about it in terms of the harmony between those who are living and those who are not. Like a red tide, where new life springs forth, there beneath the surface of that new life is the old."

"You're talking more than just biological terms. Are you talking about spiritual harmony?"

"I am. You once asked me about your mother and heaven. Well, I think tonight's events represent a poetic justification for what the legend of the Piedras Blancas Lighthouse says. While a lighthouse warns mariners of the coastal dangers with rhythmic light, during a tide like tonight the ocean surrounding the lighthouse will light up on its own. As the waves lap the shore, lights will be seen reaching out for the beach and the air as if they were souls reaching from the depths of one plane for the next."

"Like souls reaching out to heaven?"

Ruth smiled. "That's exactly it."

"What do you think it means for those of us watching it?"

"What does it mean? Why does it have to mean anything? Some things just are. Legends just are," Ruth said.

"Well, if everything happens for a reason, what does it mean for me? What should I expect?"

"Kate, my dear, sometimes you overthink things. Perhaps that's my fault. Maybe I've confused you."

"I'm not at all confused. I've experienced more than I expected here. Things I can't explain. All this talk about the tide and the bright lights from the sea gets me excited about knowing more."

"Well, as with anything special, you should take away from it what you will. People will see what they want to see in things that are out of the ordinary. Poetically, I like to think these luminescences are like a multitude of the heavenly hosts floating in and out of the ocean's plane. Of course, scientists explain even the most supernatural things in formal and quite nauseating terms. Attempting, I guess, to sterilize the super in the natural."

Ruth went on, "In life, you get out of it what your heart puts into it. It matters not what you see but what happens to you because of seeing. All God expects from us is a willingness to be open to his inspiration. So keep your mind open. Open minds change the world. Closed minds destroy it."

Kate asked, "Why is it there are so many ways of thinking in the world? Even here in Harmony, there are just eighteen of us and nearly eighteen different ways of looking at things."

"Kate, it's best if we just focus on what can unite us and forgive that which divides us. I'm sure even Sunny and Holla would agree with that. All of this is really beside the point. I get from you that you are looking for tonight to mean something more."

"I guess, maybe, I am," Kate said.

"I don't want you to put too much into it. Sure it may have a supernatural effect on you but what it really boils down to is that the tide means change and that in its most basic form is a good thing."

"Ruth, are you going to go out to see it?"

"Oh, I'm not sure I could make the trek out there by foot. The bluffs around the lighthouse are not easily navigated by a woman of my age. But no worries. I'll be fine. I'm sure I'll experience it in my own way. It's one of those things you just don't miss when you're me. You and Michael go and enjoy it together."

"I hope I can convince Michael to go and see it."

"He's not interested in going?" Ruth asked.

"I don't know. He and I don't seem to see eye to eye on things lately."

"And I think I know why," Ruth said. "If you spent as much time talking about these things with him as you do with me then maybe you and he would be connecting more."

"You're easier to talk to I guess."

"Maybe I am but I'm not who you committed your life too. My dear, I love my time with you, but why did you come to Harmony? Did you come here to spend all your time with me?"

Kate didn't say anything.

"From all I know about you, Katie, your mom was your rock. You want to know things happen for a reason and I know you believe coming here was for a reason. What do you think that reason really was? I'm not saying I haven't enjoyed our time together. It has meant more than you know. I just want to make sure you're committed to the right relationship."

Kate looked over at the window and sighed. "What if I made a mistake with Michael? Maybe that's the problem."

"You think that's it?"

Kate turned back toward Ruth. "I don't know. The problem is I don't know what my problem is."

"Why is it that people don't see what good is right in front of them? There's a ground swell that pulls the tides to Harmony's beach the way it does. It is also the reason the sea has been such a metaphor in poetry and writing for centuries. It's that supernatural effect that it has on those who witness it. Sometimes it's calm and tranquil. Other times, it's powerful and commanding. It's the balance between the two that demands our attention and respect. So whether it's sunny and warm or cloudy and violent, it captures our soul completely. It beckons us to see beyond the clouds in our lives to witness something special out of such darkness.

"Anne Lindbergh said of marriage and love that you don't love someone in the exact same way all your life. There is, like the tide, an ebb and flow in a relationship. We can't live in fear of the receding tide and welcome the flowing of a new tide without appreciating both. There is give and take and with each cycle there is balance. What goes in also needs to come out. You have to accept what your relationship with Michael is now and not look at it for what it was or what you think it should be. You won't always see eye to eye and that doesn't mean it isn't working. Have faith in what you have with him and soon enough a new tide will present itself with all the glow you long for. Then when it does you will likely be so caught up in the wave of love that you will wonder why it can't always be this way."

"Why can't it always be that way?"

"Because a constant rush no longer feels like a rush at all. It feels like an everyday thing. It's marvelous to think about how much our emotions are like the waves of the ocean. The constant changing – new directions, the ups and downs, the give and the take. You may feel like nothing is making things better for you and Michael but just like the sea works wave by wave to change the coastline eventually the change will become noticeable.

Kate didn't say anything.

Ruth continued, "Love isn't those fluttering feelings you have when you begin a relationship. Love is that commitment you make that no matter what comes you accept that person, their smells, their aging body, their emotional outbursts, even their differences and hold firm to them no matter what. All because you, like them, are on this journey of love that begins with the flutters of a heart and end when the heart stops beating. Go talk to Michael. Convince him to go with you to the lighthouse tonight. I think it will do both of you some good."

CHAPTER 27

Kate and Michael still hadn't discussed what was becoming a chasm between them since the party. Kate was silently resentful that Michael hadn't been more supportive of her. Hearing Kate going on and on about the luminous tide and how it meant something special was going to happen, quietly bothered Michael. For him, believing in Ruby was one thing but all this talk from Kate about spirituality was another. Michael worried about who Kate was becoming. The influences in town were to blame and he decided it was time to go and straighten it all out with Ruth directly.

He entered the shop with an obvious agenda. One that Ruth noticed upon him entering the vacant shop.

"Michael, I'm surprised to see you," she said. "To what do I owe this honor?"

"I want to talk to you about Kate."

"Kate?"

"Yes," his venom being quashed swiftly by Ruth's little old lady demeanor. He mustered up his courage for the sake of his marriage. "I'm sure you know Kate has been in a very vulnerable state for the past year."

"I understand that. With all you two have been through, it's understandable how difficult this last year has been for the both of you."

"Yes, it has. But here's the point I want to make. Kate's still vulnerable. She's not the hard-driven woman she once was."

"I would think not. Kate is a wonderful girl – so loving and kind."

"Yes, she is. And sometimes when someone is so loving and vulnerable they are susceptible to believe things that they wouldn't otherwise."

Ruth asked, "What are you saying Michael?"

"I'm saying that all these ideas you are filling Kate's head with may not help her. What happens when she finds out this stuff isn't real? Who will be there to pick up the pieces then?"

"Why are you so convinced that this 'stuff' isn't real?"

Michael couldn't think of an immediate response, so he stammered through it. "Ruth, here's the thing. From what I have seen this past year, I'm not too sure of anything anymore. I'm worried you have my wife hoping for something that will lead to her getting hurt again. I don't want to see that happen to her."

"Well, if you ask me, Kate seems very happy already. Much happier than when you both first stopped in my shop."

Michael said, "She is. I'm just afraid this is the high before another crash. This is how she was before the miscarriage. Then she was devastated when that happened. I can't see her go through that again."

"You can't see her go through it or you can't go through it?"

Michael acted insulted. Then he said, "I suppose it's a little of both."

"Michael, you are a good husband. It is admirable the way you want to protect Kate. But it's not sensible. Life is about both highs and lows. For you to expect Kate never to feel sadness again or get hurt is unrealistic."

"You're probably right but I'm asking you to stop pushing her towards that pain. Stop telling her she's seeing something that will change her. There's enough going on up at the house already."

"I'm not pushing her. She's asking for guidance and I have been giving it to her. I don't think you understand how hard it is for her not to have her mom in her life. You know they were very close."

"I know they were close. I was there."

"Perhaps you don't understand the significant influence her mom had on her. How much her mom's words meant to her. In keeping her on track; in keeping her sane; in keeping her moving forward. A parent's job most of the time is to reassure their child that they can do it and then ensure they stay on that right path. It's a lifelong relationship and frankly I think Kate misses and needs that. If I don't fill that role who will?"

Michael didn't say anything. So Ruth continued, "You and I know who should be filling that role for her. You are not her mother and not even her father but you are the one who she is bonded to."

Michael was exasperated. He didn't seem to be getting through to Ruth. "But what am I supposed to do? I can't carry her through everything all the time."

"Who is asking you to carry her? Why not just hold her hand and go through it with her together?"

"Ruth, with all due respect, it doesn't work that way."

"Why not?" she asked. "Is it because it doesn't work for you? You know, no one expects you to be the one to pick up all the pieces by yourself. It's not humanly possible anyway. Trust me I know that Kate doesn't expect that from you. She wants you to open up enough to be with her."

"I think I know my wife a little better than you do."

"I have no doubt about that. Is that what scares you? That someone else knows her this well?"

"No," he said abruptly. "I'm not that controlling. I just want to do all I can to protect her."

"And you have. I think you worry too much about what is going to happen to Kate instead of enjoying what is happening for the both of you. Michael, what is it that you think is going to happen? What is it that worries you? Is it me? Is it the girl? Or is it the harmony that you are experiencing? Is that what you are afraid will end?"

"I'm worried about Kate and her feelings. I'm not worried about anything else."

"What is it that you think is happening here?" she asked him again.

"You know, I'm not concerned about what it is. I'm concerned with what it isn't. And what you are filling her head with is what isn't."

"How can you be so sure?"

"I just am. You got Kate believing that Ruby is some holy messenger or something sent to us for some reason. When in fact, it's not likely the case at all."

"You don't honestly know that. Why can't it be the way Kate thinks it is?"

"Because it makes no sense. It's not logical."

"Michael, you yourself have seen Ruby, right?"

"Yes, but..."

Ruth interrupted him. "Then what is she? Is she demonic?"

"No – nothing like that."

"Is she real?"

"I don't know."

"Then what is she to you?"

It was a difficult question. One he had a hard time answering.

"Michael, what is it you are afraid of?"

He didn't answer.

"Michael, do you believe in God?"

Her frankness made him snap. "What?"

He heard her but she repeated it anyway. "Do you believe in God?"

His eyes filled with fear. Ruth could see him struggle for an answer. She came around and approached him. "There in your eyes is the pain that holds the answer," she told him.

"I don't know what to believe anymore," he said.

"Did you ever believe in God?"

"Yes, for most of my life. Not that I was overtly religious or anything. I mean, Kate and I never attended church. But I believed. I even prayed."

"So you believed?"

"I believed but don't anymore," he said to shut her down. "You see when I believed, I prayed and prayed for God's help with Kate and the baby. I prayed knowing that the *in vitro* was our last hope. I prayed for God to intervene. And I was left all alone. Where was God when I needed him?"

"I can see that with everything you have been through why you would think that God had left you. But I know God. I know he works in mysterious ways. You may have given up on him but he hasn't given up on you. Don't get me wrong, I understand how you feel. Can I share with you a story about myself?"

Michael nodded.

"You know I was a nun once. But did you know I was married?"

"No, Kate never mentioned that."

"That's because I don't think she and I ever talked about it. Anyway, while I was a nun I met a man at the parish and I fell in love with him. We were young and in love. So much so I left my position in the church in order to marry him. We were married a long time and remained actively involved in our parish. Then he got sick. I prayed that he would not leave me. Then when he did I was devastated. I even thought God was punishing me for giving up my vows to the church. I felt so much guilt. So much so that I devoted myself to becoming a nun again. Except this time the church wouldn't allow it. I was crushed. I felt like people were preventing me from doing God's work. I was convinced it was God's will for me to become a nun again. I felt betrayed by my own church.

"Then nearly a year after that, this woman whom I had known when I was living in the convent came and visited me unexpectedly. We talked and laughed about our time together all those years ago. I talked to her openly about the loss of my husband and how the church had turned its back on me. Looking back on that reunion, I realize now that I was able to get off my chest those things that were in my heart, things that were holding me back and preventing me from moving forward. Sometime after that I came to Harmony for what I thought was just a visit and have been here ever since. Had it not been for my old friend's counsel I would likely be a bitter old woman. Longing for my husband, hanging on to my anger and circling the past over and over again until I left this earth. I needed someone to listen to me and guide me through the rough patch in my life. And in looking back on my prayers for my husband and my desire to become a nun again, I realized something. I realized that I was praying not for my husband or for the church...I was really praying for myself. What I wanted was more important than what was God's will. I look back at that now and feel foolish. I see that had all those things not taken place – the death of my husband, the pain I felt when he was gone, the rejection of my church and then that visit from of all people a nun – I would not be the person I am today. I would not be living here. I would not be offering travelers to and fro gifts from the sea. I would not be a friend to the people of this town and a counsel to those in need, like I needed all those years ago. All that has happened in my life has served some purpose. And you know what? I believe that it was God who sent my old friend, the nun, to me. She appeared to me out of the blue and I never saw her again. You see God often uses supernatural ways to do his work on earth. There are some things that cannot be done without his divine intervention. Michael, there is nothing logical about it. And because there isn't anything logical about it – you have to admit that what Kate believes and what I believe is a possibility. Don't you?"

Michael didn't immediately respond.

Ruth continued, "Sometimes it's the illogical that makes the logical all the more meaningful."

Michael half-heartedly nodded his head. While he was not yet willing to fully believe what she was saying, he couldn't help but allow a sliver of possibility to sink in. After all, Ruby wasn't something that was logical but his own admission of her seemed logical.

He said, "So you're saying that seeing something makes it logical?"

Ruth smiled. "I'm saying if that is what you believe it is, then it probably is."

CHAPTER 28

As night approached, the fog moved into the valley once again. It swept both down and up the coast, seemingly breaking only around the lighthouse. There the lighthouse stood with a ring of fog around its slender north-right finger. Like an eye in the middle of a storm, it blinked its light at those who could see it.

By late afternoon that day, everything in Harmony had closed. Handwritten signs stating "Left early for the day. Come see us tomorrow." were the norm. With the low-lying fog, it wouldn't matter much. Tourists don't shop on such a gloomy day anyway. They just speed by on their way to where the sun is shining elsewhere, oblivious to the miracles that whip by them.

As dusk came, everyone in town loaded up in all the available cars for the short drive up the coast to the lighthouse. Everyone came with packed food, folding chairs and blankets – all prepared to wait until the moment when the lights would arrive.

Michael returned home from Ruth's and found Kate sitting on the couch in the living room facing the bay window.

"Where've you been?" she asked.

"Never mind that, it seems everyone else in town is heading up to the lighthouse tonight. It would be a shame if we missed it."

"Alright," she said, trying not to act too excited.

"How about packing us up something to eat, while I load some blankets and chairs in the truck? It's going to be a chilly one."

Kate got up from the couch and hugged him. He put his arms around her and gave her a quick kiss. "We better get moving," he said. "It's going to be dark soon."

Kate went directly into the kitchen and started to prepare some sandwiches for their picnic on the bluffs. As she did, Ruby came in and watched her like she often did.

"What're you doing?" Ruby asked.

"Making sandwiches for a picnic."

"A picnic? At night?"

Kate laughed. "We're going out to the bluffs by the lighthouse tonight. To see these lights come up from the water. It's something special," Kate said.

"Yeah, I know about those," Ruby answered.

"You do?" Kate asked as she spread some deli mustard on the bread.

"I do. Everyone knows about them."

"So you've seen them?" Kate asked.

"In my own way." Ruby stared at the tile of the kitchen floor. Kate recognized her sadness and it scared her. Kate grabbed the girl's face in her hands. "Ruby, what is it? What's bothering you?"

"I don't know," Ruby said.

"You can trust me," Kate said.

"It's just, well, I'll be going soon."

"Going where?" Kate said in horror. "Why would you leave?"

"Because."

"Ruby, no one wants you to leave. You can stay as long as you like. We love you. I'm telling you that you don't have to go."

Ruby pushed Kate back so she could look her in the eyes. "I wish I could stay. But it will be time for me to go soon."

Kate said in a panic, "What do you mean? I don't understand."

"I know you don't but it's okay," Ruby replied.

Kate thought for a moment then said, "No, it isn't. I don't understand what you're saying. Ruby, please don't go." Kate became frantic. She held the girl's arms tightly, not wanting to let her get away. She wrapped the girl up close to her body and listened as the child's heart raced inside her tiny chest. "Ruby," Kate cried. "You don't have to go. Michael and I couldn't get along without you."

"But you love each other. Right?"

"Yes, we do and we love you!"

"Then continue to love each other. Love each other and hopefully I'll be back but I have to get going soon."

"Why?" Kate asked her.

"I came to make sure you'd be happy."

Kate asked the girl, "Who are you really?"

"I'm you. I'm what you want to be and what you want me to be."

Kate didn't understand. It wasn't making any sense to her. "But Ruby, if you leave us, what will we do? You've become so much a part of our lives. You can't go. I won't allow it."

Ruby laughed. Then realizing it was somewhat rude put her hand over her mouth. Ruby could see the desperation in Kate grow. The girl reached out with her hands and pulled Kate's face to her own so she could look directly into Kate's eyes. "Don't worry. Just be happy. Okay?"

"Where will you go?" Kate asked in defiance.

"I'm going home."

"I thought this was your home. Where's home to you?"

"You really need an answer to that?"

"This doesn't feel right," Kate cried. "What hope is there to act like our little girl and then go away? You don't know how much pain Michael and I have been through already."

"I do and I was here to see you grow. You're strong, Kate."

Kate stated, now gritting her teeth in anger, "I...won't...let...you...go! I won't." She shook her head and continued, "I won't. I won't." Then Kate began to cry. She reached out for the girl and held her tight again. She stroked the girl's hair, the hair she combed as if Ruby were her own. Kate smelled Ruby's hair and just like Kate knew, it smelled like strawberries. She rocked the child in her arms. Ruby put her hand on Kate's back and rubbed it gently.

"I won't let you go," Kate said.

"You don't really have to," Ruby said.

"Promise me you won't leave right away," Kate said. "I can't do this now so please don't go until we get back."

"Don't worry," Ruby said. "It's going to all be okay."

Kate and Michael loaded up their truck much the same way they would for a night of fireworks on Fourth of July. Kate hoped Ruby would be there when they got back. More than that, she hoped for something special tonight. She didn't share with Michael what had happened with Ruby.

Michael tried to be open-minded, but was cautious enough in case he needed to pick up the pieces of disappointment around Kate.

With the sun beginning to set, Harmony's residents greeted the arriving darkness on the bluffs overlooking the Pacific with song, laughter and good cheer. It was a celebration.

Everyone was close enough to each other to see and talk but far enough away to allow each family to experience the events privately. Kate noticed how everyone was assembled: Sunny, Stan and Holla with all the kids; Lucy, Beck, Raye and Danny next to Hijo and Juanita. No Della. No Ruth. No Ruby.

Everyone watched as the sun slowly dipped into the sea, the fog dissipating in time so that when the last ray of light ducked behind the horizon, those gathered around applauded. Kate put her hand in Michael's lap. Michael grabbed onto her hand and prepared for the worst.

Out on the bluff, the older ones shushed the younger ones until it was nearly silent. Everyone watching and waiting, you could hear occasional murmurs between couples and friends alike. Kate whispered to Michael, "Will you tell me when you see something? I don't want to miss it."

Michael assured her he would.

Minutes passed and with only the sound of the rolling waves breaking on the shore below, nothing seemed to be happening. Kate's fears started to get the best of her. Michael could feel her growing anxiety. He called out to anyone who would listen, "You sure this is going to happen?" There was the slightest hint of frustration in his voice. Kate shushed him out of embarrassment. The voices in the crowd were muffled with the sound of the crashing shore.

Nothing happened for what seemed like hours but was really only minutes. Then Danny finally called out, "Look! There in the water." She pointed out to the flat surface of the sea beyond the waves. Those seated stood up. Michael and Kate turned toward the spot where Danny was pointing.

There under the water was the tiniest point of glowing phosphorescent light. As the waves curled, grabbing at the land, there in the tresses was the glowing sparkle of something deeper.

"There it is. There's the light!" Raye shouted.

"Where is it, Michael?" Kate asked quietly.

Michael strained his eyes to see it. Uncertain whether he was actually seeing it or not, he didn't know what to say.

"Can you see it, Michael?" Kate asked again, wanting confirmation.

A tiny light had emerged and then became two and then three and four and then more. The tiniest points of light multiplied until they reached the waves. Miraculously the points became like stars in the sky under the water, following their own path toward the shore.

"Michael, I see it. I see it!" Kate said squeezing his hand.

"Phosphorescence. That's all it is," he said.

Kate took a step closer to the edge of the bluff and watched as the tiny lights traveled within the waves until they crashed upon the rocky shore below. Before long, through the streams of foamy white waves, could be seen long flowing bluish ribbons of light like spirits dashing through the waves.

The harsh crash of the waves against the rock-strewn shore created a mist of water that with the ocean breeze floated up to the bluffs, its moisture being quickly carried away by the wind. There in this mist, the tiny lights continued on their destined path like illuminated beings. Rolling and spinning in the air and water all around the shore line, the points of light were too numerous to count. It was truly a spectacle. As if the lights were bubbling up from the depths of the dark sea, sparkling emeralds and sapphires lapped in the waves like lustrous hands reaching out to those on the shore.

"Michael, it's amazing," Kate said as she grabbed his hand tighter.

"It really is," he admitted. "I've never seen anything like it."

From the corner of her eye, Kate saw Juanita light a candle within a lantern. Hers was joined by

Hijo's, the candle flames hidden behind glass of red. Juanita began to sing out a song in Spanish, her voice and the song both lovely.

An intoxicating sensation came over Kate. There was a euphoric feeling as if she was floating, hovering over the ground below her. The entirety of her senses were completely overwhelmed. It felt like a dream.

Kate then heard a voice. It was a calm voice, one she recognized but couldn't place. "Peace I leave you." Kate heard it clear as day.

"Michael, did you hear it?" she asked.

"Hear what?" he said. "Juanita?"

She realized it was only meant for her. All her life someone was always leaving her. She feared it was happening again. "Oh Michael," she said.

"What is it, Kate?" he said.

"Don't leave me. Don't ever leave me."

"I won't." He grabbed her tight so she could feel his assurance. "I will never leave you," he said.

With the sparkling waves in the moonlight, Kate grabbed onto Michael's hand. She looked at him and he back at her. "You're beautiful," he said to her. He could see her vulnerability. Kate grabbed his face with both hands and kissed him deeply. The two continued to kiss, running their hands over the other's body. In the moment, Michael reached for the bottom of Kate's shirt and began to lift it up slightly, his hand following the smoothness of her stomach upward.

"Michael," Kate said stopping him.

His body tensed up.

"Not here," Kate continued. "Follow me."

She took him by the hand and led him to a spot where the bluffs tucked behind a roll of pasture. It was out of sight of everyone else but still in sight of the spectacle taking place below. Kate took Michael by both hands and knelt down with him. She then pulled at the bottom of Michael's shirt and lifted it over his head. He grabbed Kate around the waist and pulled her closer to him. He kissed her ardently.

She reached around in front of him and undid his belt and jeans, pulling them down to his bended knees. She pushed him backwards and he fell onto his back in the tall grass. She stayed on top of him. In a state of undress, they rolled over onto their crumpled up clothes so Michael was on top of her. Michael looked down at Kate. She smiled at him and told him she loved him.

"I love you, too," he told her.

There on the bluffs overlooking the lighthouse and the magic of the ocean's phosphorescent display the two united, with stars above them and waves crashing below them. Kate enjoyed her husband's body like she hadn't in years. And he enjoyed her as if it were the first time. The two as one finally connected on a level neither of them had experienced before.

When they had finished, they noticed the sparkle of the waves crashing below them. The two lay there holding each other. At first, the coolness of the night was absent. The heat between them was keeping them warm.

Michael looked at Kate laying her head on his chest. His hand rubbing the small of her back, her soft skin seemingly endless, he told her again he loved her.

She looked up at him, her hair falling in her eyes and told him she loved him too.

"That was incredible," he said.

"It was. And the sex wasn't bad either," she said playfully.

He grabbed her, laughing as he told her, "That is what I was talking about."

"I know," she agreed. "It was."

They lay there a while longer. Thinking not of the group of people just over the bluff, but about what they had in each other. Kate realized that even without a child, she could be happy as long as she had Michael.

Michael continued to stroke Kate's back until he felt her skin tense and goose bumps appear.

"Are you okay?" he asked.

"I am. I'm perfect," she told him and he agreed.

"I'm also getting a little cold," she said.

"Let's get you home."

The two dressed and walked hand-in-hand back to the truck without anyone else noticing.

Michael and Kate drove home and enjoyed being alone together in the house. They made love and watched the sun come up, finally falling asleep in each other's arms.

CHAPTER 29

Kate awoke first that next morning. She got up, went to the bathroom and returned to the bedroom where she stood watching Michael sleep. She couldn't remember another time she loved him more than right then. He turned over slightly and she tip-toed out of the room to let him sleep.

Kate walked into the living room, stood still and listened. The house was silent. She looked over at the wall clock and it was after nine. The morning was cool but not cold. The sun was shining but not bright. It was just an ordinary day. Nothing out of the norm.

Kate walked over to the kitchen and put on the coffee. Filling the carafe with water from the sink, she looked out at the yard and pasture where the clothes line was. A lone lark sat on the line singing its morning song. All of a sudden, it flew away out of sight.

After measuring the coffee into the brew basket, Kate poured the water into the back of the coffeemaker and turned it on. She thought about flipping the radio on but decided against it, choosing the silence as her companion instead.

Kate walked over to the back door and opened it into the screened porch. The room was filled with baskets of dirty laundry but that wasn't what Kate was looking for.

"She's gone," Kate said out loud to herself.

"Who's gone?" Kate heard behind her. She turned around to a still sleepy Michael. He was scratching the top of his head with one hand and the front of his boxers with the other.

"She is. Ruby."

"How do you know?" he asked her as he walked over to get a coffee cup from the cabinet.

"She told me she was going. I didn't want to believe it. But she's not here this morning."

Michael yawned as he replaced the carafe with his coffee cup under the stream of brewing coffee. He let the drips of hot coffee fill his cup. "Man, what a night," he said.

Kate agreed, "It was incredible." She walked toward him and wrapped her arms around him. He kissed her forehead. Then he asked, "What's this about Ruby?" as if he was just realizing what they had been talking about.

Kate stood back. "She's gone."

"You sure?"

"I am."

"For good?" Michael asked.

"I'm not sure. I think so."

"You okay?"

"I am. I really am," she said to him.

"You sure?"

Kate thought for a minute. "I actually am. I want to miss her but I feel like she is still here with me. Everything just feels different after last night. You were incredible." Kate came right up to him.

"What about you?" he said pulling her into his arms. "You were so bold."

Kate playfully pushed him. "I was not!"

He playfully pushed her back. "You were too. You were."

The two began to play fight. Kate grabbed at his shorts and Michael tried to grab hers. Kate screamed and ran into the living room keeping her pajama bottoms up. Michael chased her and threw her down on the couch. He tickled her and Kate begged him to stop but in a playful way. She grabbed his hands and held him back. They froze for a moment and then he leaned in to kiss her. They continued to kiss and things progressed from there.

The two fell asleep soon after, tangled together on the couch. This time Michael woke first. He looked over at the wall clock. "You gotta be kidding," he said.

Kate woke up. "What is it?"

"It's two o'clock," he said.

"Two o'clock?"

Michael sat up and grabbed for his boxers on the floor of the living room. Kate from under the throw blanket, reached over for her shirt on the floor. She quickly pulled it over her head.

"I can't believe we slept this long," she said.

"I know. I told Beck I'd help him move some stuff upstairs today. He's probably wondering what happened to me."

"You told him you'd go over there today?" Kate asked.

"I did. I'm going to jump in the shower and go."

"Michael! Wait!"

He stopped and turned around.

"Wait," she said again. "I love you."

"I love you, too."

"Come here," she called for him.

"Kate, I gotta go."

"Come here."

He approached her from behind the couch and asked, "What is it?"

"Kiss me," she said.

He leaned over the couch and kissed her softly. Kate held on and the kiss lingered.

Kate told him, "I love you, Michael. Thank you for everything. For last night and for everything. This is perfect."

"I know. Kate, I love you too." He sunk into her and kissed her again. They continued to kiss until Michael realized how late he was for Beck's. "Kate, I really do need to go. It's going to be hard enough already to explain what took me so long in getting over to the inn. I'm sorry but I really should go," he told her.

"I know. I wouldn't want everyone to know what was keeping you. Some things we should be able to keep to ourselves." She kissed him one last time and he took off for the bathroom.

Kate watched him as he walked away. She then shouted at him from the living room, "Don't be gone long. I want you home."

"Okay," he shouted back. "I won't." She then heard the bathroom door close and the shower go on. Kate finished dressing and fixed the disheveled couch. She started humming then caught herself and listened. It was just her humming. She looked at herself in the mirror and decided she needed a shower as well.

Waiting on Michael, she went into the bedroom and made the bed. As she was making it, Michael came out. "That was fast," she said.

"Clean enough, I guess." He dressed quickly. "I'll be back soon."

"Okay," she answered. "I think I'll go into town and check on Ruth. I didn't see her last night. Then again, I wasn't really looking for her."

Michael threw on his shoes. "Okay, gotta go." He came over to her and kissed her again. "I'll be back soon."

"Okay," she said smiling.

As he exited the room, he turned around and said, "I love you."

"I love you too."

And with that he was gone.

Kate then proceeded to get ready. She showered, then did her hair and makeup. It didn't seem to matter if Ruby was really gone. Kate felt renewed. She felt like a newlywed again.

CHAPTER 30

Kate walked down to Gifts from the Sea. The shop was dark. A handwritten closed sign was taped to the window. Kate cupped her hands over her eyes and peered into the shop. No one was there. She knocked on the glass door. "Ruth? It's Kate."

She looked in again and still nothing. So she knocked again. She figured Ruth was back at the chapel. As she turned to walk around the building to the back, she heard, "I wondered when you would come down."

She turned around hopefully. It was Raye.

"Oh hi," Kate said.

"Well, hi yourself," Raye answered.

"Have you seen Ruth?" Kate asked.

"Honey, let's go inside and talk." Raye then pulled out a key and opened the door to the shop. Kate panicked. "Did something happen to Ruth? Is she okay?"

Raye held the door for Kate to come in. "She's fine. Just come inside." As Kate came in Raye locked the door behind her.

Raye said, "Sit down over here at the counter."

"What is it, Raye? You're scaring me."

"Come and sit down."

Kate finally did. She sat at the counter on the same stool she sat on nearly every day since coming to Harmony.

"Okay, where's Ruth?" Kate asked.

"Boy, you and Michael disappeared last night. Where did you two run off to?"

Kate blushed.

"Oh, I knew it. I told Lucy that you two were probably enjoying the night." Raye shoved Kate lightheartedly. "Good for you! I mean it. Good for you."

"Please Raye. Tell me where's Ruth? I'm worried."

Raye's face turned from giddy to serious. "Oh, you shouldn't worry. Wasn't last night incredible? What a sight."

Kate answered, "It was. Raye, tell me what's going on."

"What did Ruth tell you about this place?"

"About Harmony?" Kate thought for a moment. "She told me it was special."

"Kate, it is a special place. Not just for us but for those among us who, let's say, are really a part of us."

"What? I don't get it. What does that have to do with...Ruth?"

"I'm telling you that Ruth is gone," Raye said.

"She died?"

"Oh no, not died. Kate, those of us who live here don't just live in a town or some spot along a busy highway. It is us living in harmony with the spirits of another place. We're not just here on this earthly plane but also in conjunction with a heavenly plane."

"Are you saying Ruth is in heaven?"

"That is exactly what I'm saying," Raye said.

"Then she did die," Kate insisted.

"No, no, not die. Ruth wasn't human, Kate. She was a messenger sent here. A messenger sent to you."

"What?" Kate was shocked. "But wait...I touched her. She was real. She was."

Raye smiled. "She is real. What do you expect one of heaven's messengers to look like? They stand in front of us like I stand in front of you now. They can take on any image they need to get their message across. They could be an old woman, a homeless man or even a child."

"What?"

"That's right, even a child. And like Ruby, Ruth was sent as a messenger to you and perhaps some of the rest of us here in Harmony. That may not be clear to any of us right away but who knows what mysteries will be unraveled by Ruth's residency here."

Kate thought about it then said, "But what's the message? I didn't get it."

"You didn't? Ruth didn't teach you or show you anything while she was here?"

"No, she did. I just thought she would always be here."

"She is, Kate. Just not in the physical form anymore. For that phase, she served her purpose and now she lives solely inside you. I bet if you really think about it, you can feel her."

Kate paused for a moment. "I can. I really can."

Raye went on, "Harmony is a miraculous place. That old lighthouse is our beacon to the heavens. That is the only way I can explain it. Those of us who live here are the chosen few who experience these miracles. It was likely always like this and will always be even when its current residents are long gone.

"I know it's a lot to digest. Believe me. But things happen for a reason. There was a reason you and Michael came up here when you did. There was a reason you stopped in this shop that first time. There was a reason you fell in love with that house. It was all meant to be. It was part of a great plan. One in which you are still fulfilling. One in which Ruth and Ruby and myself and everyone else here was a part of. We all live here together in Harmony with the past and the present and even the future."

Kate said, "I can't believe it. Are you're saying that all of this..."

"Brought you the peace you needed. It's been a healing process and a cleansing one. But you are a better person for it as is Michael. From this point on, you and Michael are ready to truly start a new life together. It is what was always meant to be."

Kate sat there and thought about all she and Ruth had discussed. And all she had with Ruby.

"Are you okay?" Raye asked.

"I think so. I just wasn't expecting this."

"I know. No one ever does. When there is loss there needs to be hope. That is what this has all been about. It's not just you, Kate. It's everyone.

Sometimes it takes supernatural events to get people back on track. The Creator will do everything he can to change the course if necessary."

Kate didn't say anything.

"Kate, you could spend your whole life trying to figure all of this out or you could just go with it. Go and enjoy your life the way it is. From where you came to where you are and where you are going."

"How do I do that? How do I…this sucks! It really sucks."

"It may suck right now but truth be told it will not suck forever. Soon enough you'll move beyond this and realize it was all for the good. You've found your true harmony here with Michael."

Kate was silent as she looked around at the empty shop.

"There's a letter here for you. Ruth wrote it." Raye reached into her pocket and pulled out a soft pink colored paper. It was folded over and written on the front was "For Kate."

Kate unfolded the note and read it.

Dearest Katie,

You'll know now that I am gone. Do not be sad. You have so much life in you yet. I want you to take possession of the shop. It is yours now. I have left it and all its contents to you. I know you have grown to appreciate it. You're a fine girl and I have faith that you will do with the shop what you are meant to.

My dear, I wish for you the peace I give you. Peace in yourself. Peace in your marriage. Peace for a life in harmony with the spirit of heaven. Beyond that, there is nothing else you need to be reminded of. The life you seek is the life you live. Prepared is a place for you that only the Creator knows. I leave you this as a testament to what is true.

Always,
Your Ruth

A tear rolled down Kate's face. She looked at the letter as if a prize. Finally she said, "I don't know what to say. She's left me the shop."

"I know," Raye responded. Raye reached into the pocket of her coat and presented Kate with the keys.

Kate's nose began to run. She wiped it with the back of her hand.

Raye reached into her pocket again and pulled out a much needed tissue.

"Thank you," Kate said as she blew her nose.

Raye touched her on the shoulder. "You okay?"

"I have to be. This means so much. I had no idea. I'm just worried that now that they are gone what I most treasured here in Harmony is also gone."

"I doubt that. What you came here for you have. Don't get so caught up in what you don't have again. Enjoy what you do."

Kate's eyes began to well with tears again. She looked around the shop she once laughed at. She shook her head in disbelief. She could hear the roar of the cars flying by in intervals that mimicked the waves.

The shop looked cold. Barren of anything Kate had come to see. Without another word, Raye turned and walked away. Kate didn't watch her go. She didn't care. She heard the bells chime just as they always had. Kate watched the dark green curtains from which Ruth always emerged. The curtains remained in place with no hint of movement. Kate wandered the shop like she had so many times before. So many details of things Kate had never noticed before.

"This isn't me," she said. "Why? Why? Why?" she asked. "Why this? Now?" Kate walked back to the counter and looked over at the stools sitting there, the ones she and Ruth had used as they exchanged so much life over tea.

All at once life like the shop was cold. Kate felt a hollowness inside her. Here she was again in the same state she had been in all those months ago. Kate laid her head on the counter and cried. Cried and cried with no one there to comfort her.

The bells chimed on the door and Kate looked up with hope.

"Kate?"

It was Michael.

"Oh Kate, I am so sorry." Michael approached his wife and held onto her. She cried.

"She's gone, Michael. They are both gone." She buried her head in his chest.

"I know. I know. When I went to the inn, Lucy told me. I came right down here. I'm here for you if you need me."

Kate looked up at him. He said it again. "I'm here. I'll always be here."

With a tear rolling down her cheek she looked in his eyes and saw in them the same things she saw in Ruby's. Kate said immediately, "It's like she had your eyes."

"What?"

"Your eyes...the colors in your eyes are the same as Ruby's. It's like she really is a part of us."

Michael pulled Kate toward him. She held him.

"Are you alright?" he asked.

"You know what?" She thought for a minute as she listened to his heart beating inside him. "I am. I am. They're gone and I'm alright."

She pulled back and looked up at him. He looked at her in her miserable state and saw her big puffy lips and runny nose and kissed her.

CHAPTER 31

Life in Harmony continued as normal as it could. Kate spent much time at Gifts from the Sea and Michael worked with Raye and Holla on building the websites for the gallery and for the tourist trade. Raye found a new resident to take over the chapel. He was a stout man. Father Tom was a former clergyman of the orthodox order. He was a shy man. Very standoffish and keeping mostly to himself, he wasn't anything like Ruth. He spent most of his days down by the beach. You'd find him at Juanita's every day for lunch but other than that he stayed out of town, only performing the necessary wedding ceremony that Raye would book for the chapel. Kate wondered, as she was sure everyone did, whether he too was a messenger.

Kate was surprised that no one in town really spent much time speculating about such things. Was it something that you came to get used to? She wondered how long before she'd be used to the comings and goings. Not knowing who was real and who wasn't, it forced you to be kind to everyone you came in contact with in Harmony. Kate and Michael started to understand how it all worked.

Nearly three months passed, and things really started to feel settled for Kate and Michael. Kate spent more and more time in the shop. She had refused to change a thing about it. She wanted it to stay the way she always knew it.

Michael worked on the websites at the house but would come into town nearly every day to talk with Raye about it. It was a good excuse to come into the shop and see Kate. Things appeared to be fine for some time and then Kate seemed to retreat.

Michael asked her what was going on and she continued to complain that she wasn't feeling herself. It had started with the flu and Kate never seemed to be able to shake it. Michael wanted her to go see the doctor down in Cayucos but Kate refused. "It's just a lingering cold," she said. "The damp weather is having its way with me. Let me rest and it will go away."

Out of concern, Michael had Lucy and Danny check on Kate whenever he was off helping Beck or tied up with Harmony's web work. His concerns for her became their concerns. Each would come in and sit with Kate in the shop on alternating days. Kate would share with them tea just as Ruth had with her.

The occasional tourist would stop in. Some would come in as she did and snicker at the odd collection of beach and religious artifacts. Michael encouraged Kate to begin to make the shop her own. He wanted her to add her own touches to it.

Michael insisted the shop not be a shrine. Ruth would not have wanted it that way, he'd tell her. He also reminded her that the income from the shop would be required for them to stay. The house was long done and the money they had was gone. Kate knew everything Michael was saying was true but she couldn't bring herself to change anything in the shop.

Then one day while Kate was sitting in the shop, Holla came by with Mason.

"Mason and I wanted to stop by and drop off this invitation to his birthday party." Holla handed the colorful invitation to Kate. Kate looked at Mason who had grown so much since the first time she met him. His blonde hair was getting long. Kate looked at him and the chubby little boy looked back and shyly smiled.

Kate lost it. She began to cry. As she reached for the box of tissue under the counter, Holla said, "Oh no, Kate. Are you alright?"

Kate couldn't speak. The old feelings of all the children's parties in LA she had been invited to came rushing back. Anger grew within her. The invite was only a reminder of what she did not have and the short time she had with Ruby that wasn't enough to satisfy that craving.

As Kate cried, Mason started in as well. "Kate," Holla said. "I'm sorry. Should I go get Michael?"

"Michael? Go get Michael? He doesn't want to see me like this. Just go," she said.

Holla didn't know what to do. Mason wouldn't stop his crying and that was only making it all worse.

"Just go!" Kate insisted.

"Kate, I'm so sorry." Holla turned to walk out. As she did, the chimes on the door rang and instantly Kate looked up to see who it was.

"Hiya Holla. Hiya Mason," Danny said with her now annoying smile. She then noticed Kate crying behind the counter. Danny looked over at Holla who whispered something. Holla held on to Mason and left. As they did, Danny approached Kate.

"What's going on? You alright, Sugar?" Danny asked.

"Your turn to come in and stay with me?" Kate said wiping her eyes.

Danny answered, "Wait...what? I don't understand."

"Sure, you do. You and Lucy come in every other day to check on me."

Danny replied, "I wouldn't say we only come by to check on you. We're friends aren't we?"

"Well, sure. I'm sure Michael put you up to it," Kate said.

"No. Not really. I think he's worried about you."

Kate answered, "There's been nothing to worry about. I'm fine. I just can't shake this flu and I'm only crying because I'm PMS'ing."

"Kate, it's alright. I understand. Sometimes I get the weepies and think about Ben. It's okay."

"I know it's alright. They're my feelings and I have a right to have them."

"You're right," Danny replied. "I understand."

"Danny, how it is you are able to stay so happy all the time? I mean you lost your husband. Your parents are dead and you have no children. Don't you feel all alone like something is missing in your life?"

"Well, at first that is exactly how I felt. But now I have Beck and Lucy and they are like the parents I never had. You know sometimes it's good to lean on those closest to us in times of loss."

"I'm sure," Kate answered even though she truly didn't appreciate it.

"Did I ever tell you there was this one time this young man, who sort of resembled Ben, stopped by when I was down at the creek near the inn? It was a place Lucy had told me Ben liked to play as a boy. I often go out there to collect my thoughts. I feel close to him there. Well, this one time I went down with Baby and out of nowhere this man appeared, walked up to me and talked to me about the day and how pretty it was there. It was the voice I recognized first. That same voice that spoke to me when I was alone in my room."

Kate asked, "What did he say to you?"

"Oh I don't know. He gave me words of encouragement. Told me that my being here meant something. I knew it did because of Beck and Lucy. I had been raised by my Gramma and so many times I prayed for my folks to come back and take me with them."

Kate said, "Where had they gone?"

"I'm not really sure. No one knew. They just left me with Gram and took off. Don't get me wrong she raised me as best she could and I will always love her for all she did for me. But Beck and Lucy gave me a life here that I'd never had growing up. And as it turned out, I was able to give them both a connection to Ben and to a daughter they'd never had."

Kate asked, "Who do you think the man was?"

"I really think it was a messenger that Ben sent to me. It had to be. It was the oddest thing. When this man approached me, Baby didn't even bark. He just stood by and wagged his tail. It was so unlike Baby when he meets someone new. It was like Baby knew this man. I don't know I probably made more out of it than I should have."

"Did you ever see the man again?" Kate asked.

"Oh no, it was just that once. It's funny. I went down to that spot almost every day after that. He never showed up again. It became my special place. Then one day I was down there with Baby and out of the blue I heard someone coming. I turned around quick to see who it was, you know, hoping and there was Hijo. I laughed. He was walking along the creek. He and his mom had gotten into it about something or other. It was nice, he stayed awhile and we talked. Every once in a while we go down there and meet."

Kate perked up. "Really?"

Danny became anxious. "But please don't tell anyone. If anyone knew we'd be the talk of the town. We're just friends is all. I'd hate for anyone to find out about it and ruin it for us. Our moms would think too much of it. More than it is right now."

"I understand," Kate said. "Your secret is safe with me."

"Don't get me wrong. Hijo's a great guy. I don't want to make too much of it."

Kate said she understood then asked, "Did you know about Ruth? About her being, you know, who she was?"

"Oh no, not at all. It was quite a shocker at first but then it made perfect sense. She'd been so good to me and Lucy – too good. I guess I should have known. You never really know about a person. You learn to treat everyone better because you never really know who they might actually be."

That made sense to Kate as well. She then asked, "What do you make of Father Tom?"

"That's a tough one. He's a hard one to read. If I had to guess I'd say he was sent here to experience some healing of his own. That hard shell probably has cracks in it somewhere. We'll have to wait and see what happens."

Kate then asked, "You ever think you'd get married again?"

"Oh I don't know. If not, I'm fine with who I am now. I was lucky to love Ben even for a short time."

The bells on the door chimed again and both girls looked up to see who it was.

This time it was Della.

"Well, hello Miss Della. Good to see you," Danny said cheerfully as usual.

Della sneered and said, "You seen that no good homeless guy around town lately?"

"You mean Pete?" Danny asked.

"Is that is name?" Della asked as if she didn't know.

"Yes and no I haven't seen him," Danny said.

Kate shook her head no as well, working to regain her composure.

"It's funny. I haven't seen him around for the longest time. I guess maybe he decided to move on," Della said.

Danny said, "Oh, you know, Pete comes and goes like the wind. You never know when he'll be back."

"Well, I hope he doesn't come back. We don't need that kind around here no more. Upsetting the balance of things here in town. Drives away the tourists."

"Oh Della, he's harmless," Danny said.

"Says you," Della said. "He's been after me long enough. I just want to make sure he stays away."

Danny smiled then said, "Oh you. You know Pete's got a thing for you."

"Oh no he doesn't!" Della said.

"He does," Danny said. "I bet when he comes back through town he'll be bringing you something back."

"Back from where?" Kate asked.

"Back from wherever he is and wherever he goes," Danny answered. "He'll be back. If for nothing else than to get you to like him."

Della barked back, "That will be the day. Huh! Over my dead body!"

Danny laughed. "Miss Della you shouldn't fight with old Pete. He's looking out for us is all."

"Well, it doesn't matter as long as he's out of town. I think we're better off without him."

Just then Della saw something out of the corner of her eye. She turned to the window. "Why that no good miserable degenerate of a dog is out there crapping up a storm. And crappin' that vegan

crap that smells worse than regular dog crap."
Della threw the door open and ran after the dog.
From inside the shop, the girls could hear her go
on, shouting, "That's it. I'm getting the sheriff. That
dog don't even have a license."

CHAPTER 32

Kate's health deteriorated. She worked to keep it from Michael. As she continued to worsen, one thing played over and over in her mind. She remembered the symptoms her mom had right before she was diagnosed with ovarian cancer. Her mom often complained about being bloated and nauseated. Kate's constant issues with periods and infertility were beginning to make sense. Her mom's own worries that heredity would pull Kate into cancer's web no longer seemed an impossibility.

It was Saturday morning. Michael was up and out early. He and Beck had gone into town for roofing materials for the inn. Kate had a difficult time getting ready but knew she had to go into the shop. She struggled to get dressed and took some Tylenol to dull the pain. This was no longer just the flu.

Down at the shop, she quickly made herself some tea and sat on the stool to watch pet traffic go by. Buddha was on the loose and as always the two cats owned the road. It was a typical day. She hoped it would stay that way.

A few hours later, the chimes rang on the door. Lucy came in. She looked for Kate but did not see her immediately. She called out, "Kate? You have company."

Lucy headed to the counter and as she came around one of the table displays her heart began to race. "Oh no. Kate!"

Kate was lying behind the counter. It looked like she had fallen off the stool. There was a pool of blood behind her head and Kate was unconscious. Lucy came up next to her and shook her.

"Kate, Kate, it's Lucy. Can you hear me?"

Kate didn't respond.

Lucy shouted again, "Kate. Oh Kate. Wake up."

Lucy got up and ran to the door, opened it and yelled down to Danny at the post office.

"Danny! Help! Come quick!"

This not only got Danny's attention but the attention of Stan across the street.

Stan came out and asked, "Lucy, what is it?"

"It's Kate. Dial 911. She's collapsed."

Stan went back inside to call.

Danny arrived.

Lucy told Danny, "Help me get her up. She's bleeding."

"Oh no. What happened?" Danny asked.

"I don't know. This is how I found her. It looks like she hit her head."

Stan came into the shop. "They're sending an ambulance now. What happened?"

Lucy responded, "I have no idea. I came in and she was just lying here."

Stan came up to Kate and pressed his ear against her chest. He said, "She's breathing."

Danny said, "Maybe she fainted?"

Lucy told Danny, "Go get Michael."

"He went into SLO with dad."

"Oh my gosh. Okay, they'll be at the contractors' warehouse. Go get your jeep and get Michael. They'll likely take Kate to a hospital in SLO anyway."

Danny didn't wait. She grabbed her keys and was off in her jeep down the highway for Michael.

Nothing Stan nor Lucy did made Kate wake up. Lucy had gathered some paper towels up and was dabbing her head to stop the bleeding.

"She's lost a lot of blood," Stan told Lucy. Lucy's heart raced.

They could hear the siren. The ambulance was on its way.

The paramedics arrived shortly thereafter as did Holla and Sunny.

"Oh no!" Holla cried out as they entered the shop.

With the medics over her, Kate began to wake up.

"Ouch," she said rubbing her head.

"Kate lie still," Lucy summoned her.

"What happened?" Kate asked.

The medic said, "You alright?"

"I think so," Kate said.

Lucy told the medics, "She looks like she fell and hit her head. I can't stop the bleeding."

"Ma'am, stay still. Can you tell me your name?"

"Kate."

"How old are you?" he asked.

"What... I'm thirty-six."

"Okay good," he said. "It looks like you may have fainted. Are you taking any medications?"

"Just some Tylenol."

"Have you been sick? Or are you being treated for anything?"

"No. But I haven't been feeling..."

She shut her eyes again.

"Ma'am, stay with me." The medic patted her cheek.

Kate fell back asleep. The other medic called in the incident. "Woman in her thirties unconscious with a likely concussion."

Raye arrived. "Oh no, what happened?" she asked.

Sunny explained, "It's Kate. She's passed out."

Raye looked down at Lucy hovering over Kate. Lucy told her, "She hit her head and she's unconscious."

The medics brought in a stretcher and put Kate on it. Raye asked, "Where are you taking her?"

"We're taking her to San Luis Obispo General."

Lucy said, "I'm going with her."

"Are you family?" one of the medics asked.

"Yes, we're all family here," Raye answered.

Lucy told Raye, "If Danny or Beck call make sure they know they're taking her to General. Tell them to get Michael there quickly."

Lucy jumped in back of the ambulance and they were off.

By this time, everyone was out in the street and even the tourists had pulled off the highway to see what all the commotion was all about. Raye and Stan shared what they did know.

Sunny told Juanita and Hijo, "It doesn't look good. Kate's lost a lot of blood."

"Oh dios mijo," Juanita said clutching her rosary beads.

Della commented, "There hasn't been this much fuss in town since Dobb's heart attack."

"I don't understand? Why did this happen?" Holla asked.

Raye put her arm around the girl. "Don't worry about it. It's going to be fine."

Father Tom had been standing there silently. Raye asked him, "Could you maybe pray with us?"

Father Tom obliged. He began to pray. Juanita prayed along silently. As Father Tom prayed, Raye bowed her head and without thinking so did Holla.

CHAPTER 33

Waiting at the hospital, Lucy filled in as much information on the admission forms as she could. She occasionally checked the door for Michael or Beck. She struggled staying focused on the task at hand. She knew Michael would have to fill in most of what was left. She feared the worst for Kate and Michael.

Lucy peeked in on Kate. Kate was hooked up to oxygen and all her vitals were being monitored by one of the nurses. Another nurse hooked up an IV to ensure she was getting enough fluids. Lucy watched as a doctor went to work on the couple of stitches she needed in her head. Lucy paced back and forth waiting on Michael.

Kate would wake up, watch the medical staff shuffle around her and then fall back asleep.

"Katie," she heard.

The voice called out again. "Katie, it's going to be okay. Can you hear me?"

"Mom, is that you?"

"Yes Katie. I just want you to know you're going to be okay."

Kate opened her eyes and saw her mom standing there in the hospital room. "Mom, how are you?"

"I'm great. I want you to listen to me."

"Oh Mom, I miss you. I do."

"Katie, concentrate. I have only a short time here with you. I have a message for you."

"What is it? Mommy, I need you."

"Katie, you don't need your mommy. I don't want you to worry. You're going to be fine. You're strong. Much stronger than I was. You still have a lot of life in you to live. Katie, are you listening to me?"

Kate was quiet. She was so sleepy.

"Katie, listen to me. Remember this day. Cherish it. Do you hear me? You will not experience anything like today again. It will be like nothing before and nothing after it. You need to wake up and pay attention. Katie, are you listening?"

"Yes Mommy. I am. I will remember it. All of it."

"Good. I need to leave you now. There will be a light and you will see it soon. I want you to remember the light and this day and all that it is meant to be."

"I will, Mommy. I will."

"Here take this," the voice said. And then it was gone. Kate nodded and then fell back asleep both calm and unafraid.

Michael arrived, unsure of what to even expect, and approached the nurse's station. He cleared his throat as a precaution.

"I'm here for my wife. Katherine Fisher. She was brought in by ambulance from Harmony."

The nurse at the desk didn't even look up at him. She continued staring at her computer monitor and said, "Just a second, sir. I'll be right with you." She then proceeded to type in something that seemingly took minutes not seconds by his estimation. She scribbled something in a file, closed it up and threw it on a stack. She then looked over at the wall clock. All before turning her attention back to Michael who was standing there waiting to find out what had happened to his wife.

Looking over the top of her glasses, she asked him, "What can I help you with?"

He took a calming breath. "My wife, Katherine Fisher, was brought in by ambulance. Maybe like thirty minutes ago."

The nurse clicked through a screen on her computer and said, "Yes, she's in Bed 14. Just go right and down the hall, you'll see her."

He was flustered and unsure whether he heard her correctly or not. Everything at that moment seemed a complete blur.

He walked down the hall at a quick pace, looking at all the rooms with beds, and the countless sick people. Some old, some his age, some young; all faceless people to him. There was only one face he wanted to see.

"Michael!"

It was Lucy.

"Michael, I am so glad you're here," she hugged him.

"What happened?" he questioned looking behind Lucy for Kate.

"She collapsed at the shop. She hit her head and was bleeding."

"Oh no," he said.

"Michael, she was unconscious when they brought her in."

"Where is she?" he asked.

"She's in there," she said and pointed to the room where Kate was. "They brought her in through the ER and told me they transferred her over here. They won't tell me anything more than that."

Michael thanked Lucy and went toward the door where Kate was. Lucy gave him some space and backed away. Michael saw Kate lying there. A doctor was talking to her. Michael paused for the moment – happy to see that she was alive. But she didn't look alright. She had on an oxygen mask and was connected to a bunch of monitors. He then noticed Kate was awake but crying. The doctor removed her oxygen mask then put his hand on her arm and handed her a box of tissue.

Kate noticed Michael standing there. She reached for a tissue and wiped her eyes. The doctor turned around and saw Michael but said nothing to him. Kate cleaned herself up from the tears. She didn't want Michael to see her crying yet again.

"Michael, come in," she said blowing her nose.

"I'll give you two a minute," the doctor said. "The nurse will be in to follow up."

Michael smiled at the doctor as he went out. He wasn't sure why. The doctor never said a word to him. Michael approached Kate in the bed.

"Are you okay?" Michael asked. He grabbed her hand and Kate squeezed it. She took a breath. "I'm fine. I really am."

"Are you sure?"

"Michael, I'm fine. I am."

"Are you sure? Lucy said you were unconscious."

"I was. I'm fine now. Please don't worry."

Michael then noticed a small envelope on the table next to her bed but didn't think anything of it.

Kate noticed Michael looking at something so she turned her head to see it. "What's this?" she asked.

"Probably a bill," Michael said. "You sure you are okay?"

"I'm fine," she said. She reached over for the envelope and opened it. "It's a couple of photographs." She looked through them and began to cry uncontrollably. It upset Michael.

"Kate, what is it?"

"Hold on, give me a minute." Kate looked through them. There was a photo of her with her mom. It had been taken right before her mother had died. The next one was a photo of her mom when she was younger. "They're photos of me and my mom. Where did they come from?" She looked at the photo of her younger mother. There standing next to her mom was another woman. Inscribed at the bottom, in her mom's handwriting, was, "Me and Mom." Kate looked at the photo in shock.

"Oh my gosh." She became hysterical. "Oh my gosh!"

"Kate, what is it?" Michael demanded.

Kate turned the photo around so that Michael could see it. He looked at the photo. Kate pointed to the photo with tears rolling down her face. "That's my mom and there with my mom is Gram. The one I never knew growing up."

Michael looked at it unsure of what he was looking for.

"I thought I never met her. She died when I was young and I thought I never met her. But look..."

Michael looked at the photo again. The woman was a younger Ruth. "No! How could that be?"

"My mom came to me here in the hospital. I thought it was a dream. I did. It wasn't a dream. There was this light that washed over me just like she said it would. But it was no dream. She was here like Ruby was here and Ruth and all the others. She was right here with me. I saw her again. This is proof. She brought these to me. She came to me to tell me everything was going to be alright. It was a messenger. A messenger that looked like my mom so I would feel safe. She told me not to worry, that I was strong and had life in me to live."

Michael didn't understand.

Kate continued, "All this time here in Harmony it was just like Raye said. Ruby and Ruth and Mom, they were here to help me. I know I'm strong enough now because of them. I really have nothing to fear."

Kate was smiling. Michael still unsure what was going on asked, "Kate, but what did the doctor say? Are you sick?"

Kate started to cry again.

Michael interrupted, "I'm sorry."

"No," she said. "You don't need to be sorry." She then started to laugh. "I'm not sick, Michael. I'm pregnant."

"What? How? Wait…how could that be?" Now Michael began to cry. "All the doctors they said you would never."

"I know but I am. I am. I'm pregnant. The doctor said he thinks I am about three months along already. That's what's been going on with me. The moodiness and nausea and bloated stomach. It isn't cancer. It's our miracle, Michael. Just like my mom said when she was here. She told me there was life in me yet and here it is – a baby."

"I don't believe it. I don't!" Michael was beside himself. He wiped the tears from his eyes.

"It's a miracle, Michael. It's a blessing."

Michael leaned over and hugged Kate and kissed her on her forehead. Then realizing his weight was on her said, "Oh I'm sorry. Are you okay?"

"I'm more than okay. I'm great," Kate answered.

Just then the nurse came in. "Hello, congratulations mom and dad. The doctor wants me to check the baby's heart rate. I assume you both want to hear the heartbeat."

Michael asked, stunned, "You mean we can hear the heartbeat already?"

"Yes, of course. The doctor estimates you're about 12 weeks along." The nurse approached the other side of the bed. "Mom, you mind lifting up your shirt?" Kate did as she was told with a smile.

The nurse then switched on the heart monitor and glided the wand over Kate's belly. And there it was. Wom...wom...wom...wom...wom....wom.

"There it is," the nurse said. "Your baby's heart. Seems strong too."

Michael asked, "It seems fast. Does it seem fast?"

The nurse smiled and said, "All fetal heart rates are fast. It's normal."

Kate and Michael looked at each other believing in the miracle that was taking place in their lives. All the miracles they had witnessed since moving to Harmony were finally culminating at this moment in their life. Nothing would ever be the same.

The nurse then noticed the photos. "Oh, look at you. Already gathering photos up for an album?" The nurse put down the heart monitor and reached for the photos. "Do you mind if I take a look?" Kate nodded. As the nurse grabbed the photos one slipped out and fell to the floor. "Clumsy me," the nurse said. She bent down to pick up the photo she dropped. As she did, she said, "Oh, so is this your second child?"

"No, it's our first," Kate said.

"Is this adorable girl your niece?" the nurse asked. The nurse handed Kate the photo. Kate looked at it. Michael looked over Kate's shoulder. And sure enough there was a photo of Kate with Ruby. The inscription on the photo said, "Mommy and Ruby." Kate couldn't believe her eyes. She looked at Michael in shock. The nurse looked at both of them unknowingly.

"Why don't you get dressed? The doctor is going to discharge you here shortly. I'll have some instructions for you when you are ready and a prescription for some pre-natal vitamins. Again, congratulations mom and dad! It's always so exciting when a couple finds out they're having a baby."

The nurse left the couple alone.

"Our baby?" Kate questioned Michael.

"I suppose just about anything's possible," he answered.

"You're right. I love you, Michael."

"I love you." He reached in to kiss her and the warmth of that kiss was everything it was meant to be. Kate would remember it always.

As they shared the beginning of their new life together, Kate recalled the passage from *Gift from the Sea* that Ruth had inscribed behind the counter at the store.

"When we start at the center of ourselves, we find again some of the joy in the now, some of the peace of the here, some of the love in me and you which go to make up the kingdom of heaven on earth."

In that moment, Kate could see just how clear the journey was that led up to their life in harmony.

THE END

THANK YOU

I'd like to personally thank you for buying and reading my book. *Life in Harmony* has been a labor of love from its first inception to its completion. Much like Kate and Michael, my wife and I were told having children was an impossibility. We struggled for nine years with infertility and just when all hope was lost our miracle arrived in the form of a little boy. It was only after we pushed past our grief of not having children that we were rewarded with our sons.

I'd like to invite you to please stop by my website, bkbergman.com, and share your thoughts on the book. So much of myself and beliefs went into this book that I would love to hear from those of you who have read it. Discussing the book and debating spiritual issues are my life blood. Please stop by and say hello!

If you liked the book, I'd be honored if you'd share a review on Amazon, Good Reads or on the website you purchased the book from. Please also share with me that you have posted a review. I'd love to read it and respond.

Thanks again for your taking the time to read *Life in Harmony.*

B.K. Bergman

ABOUT B.K. BERGMAN

B.K. Bergman lives in Southern California with his wife, two sons, English Bulldog and California Desert Tortoise. He is currently working on his second book.

We invite you to visit his webpage, bkbergman.com, to find out more about what he is working on. He remains active with his readers through his website. Go there now to:

- *Communicate with B.K. directly*
- *Read & Subscribe to B.K.'s blog*
- *Request an author appearance for your group*

You can also find B.K. through the following:

Website: bkbergman.com
Facebook: facebook.com/bkbergman
Twitter: twitter.com/BKBergman
About Me: about.me/bkbergman

Welcome to Harmony!

*We invite you to continue your experience with "***Life in Harmony***" at our website:*

www.harmonynovel.com

Visit the harmonynovel.com website for a unique experience where you can "interact" with some of the residents of Harmony from the book. The webpage is full of surprises that blur the line between fiction and reality. We guarantee there is nothing else like it!

- *Share your insights and discuss the book with others in the Discussion Forum*
- *View a map of Harmony with book locations called out*
- *Read posts and comments from some of Harmony's characters*
- *Discover Harmony's History as told by Della*
- *Buy Harmony products*

ACKNOWLEDGMENTS

Like life, there is an ebb and flow to getting a book to publication with many contributors along the way. I'd like to thank my wife for her love and support during this long journey. I'd also like to acknowledge my writing classmates at both National University and UCLA for your feedback, suggestions and edits through the various rewrites of this novel. I want to also thank my test market Beta Readers for their time, survey answers and purposeful feedback. Specifically I'd like to thank Martha Carl, LaVette Webb, Nadine Walsh and Matthew Hefti for your contributions to this book as Beta Readers.

To Ken, thank you for your tireless efforts in editing this story chapter by chapter, page by page, sentence by sentence. You made this book all the better. I am eternally grateful for your encouragement and belief in the story and in helping to keep the journey alive. Without your efforts none of this would have been possible.

Finally to my sons, may God always bless you and let the road to your dreams not be made difficult by me. Always be true to the light inside you and never let the unbelievers tell you what you can't do or be or believe. After all, "life is but a dream."

FIND AN ERROR?

As a new publisher, Pangloss Sea Books works on a tight budget. While we have made every attempt for perfection, we are sure our imperfect abilities may have resulted in a typographical error or two. Through dozens of rewrites, revisions and various printings, our eyes may have lost focus here or there.

If you find an error, please let us know. You can submit errors by calling out the page number, paragraph number and sentence in an email and send to errors@vervetide.com.

If a change is made because of your submission, we will include your name in future editions of the book. We will also consider adding you to our voluntary review board which could include you receiving future advance copies of books we are publishing.

Together we make books better for everyone.